ANYTHING YOU SAY
CAN AND WILL BE
USED AGAINST YOU

ANYTHING YOU SAY CAN AND WILL BE USED AGAINST YOU

Happy Holidays Momster!

Stories

Laurie Lynn Drummond

Laurie Lynn Drummond

HarperCollins*Publishers*

This is a work of fiction. The characters, incidents, and dialogues are products of the author's imagination and are not to be construed as real.

Excerpt from *Making Contact* by Kenneth Robinson. Copyright © 2003 by Kenneth Robinson. Reprinted by permission of Kenneth Robinson.

Excerpt from *A Cold Case of Fear* by Philip Gourevitch. Copyright © 2001 by Philip Gourevitch. Reprinted by permission of Farrar, Straus and Giroux, LLC.

Excerpt from *Fifth Business* by Robertson Davies. Copyright © 1970 by Robertson Davies. Used by permission of Viking Penguin, a division of Penguin Group (USA) Inc.

Excerpt from *What Do We Know: Poems and Prose Poems* by Mary Oliver. Copyright © 2002. Reprinted by permission of Da Capo Press, a member of the Perseus Books Group, LLC.

HarperCollins books may be purchased for educational, business, or sales promotional use. For information, please write: Special Markets Department, HarperCollins Publishers Inc., 10 East 53rd Street, New York, NY 10022.

FIRST EDITION

Designed by Phil Mazzone

Library of Congress Cataloging-in-Publication Data

Drummond, Laurie Lynn
    Anything you say can and will be used against you / Laurie Lynn
  Drummond.—1st ed.
     p. cm.
    ISBN 0-06-056162-9 (acid-free paper)
    1. Woman—fiction. 2. Firearms—Fiction. I. Title.
PS3604.R86A84 2004
813'.6—dc21   2003051133

04 05 06 07 08 ❖/RRD 10 9 8 7 6 5 4 3 2

The following stories appeared previously, some in a very different form: "Finding a Place" in *New Delta Review* (1989); "Under Control" in *Story* (1991); "Taste, Touch, Sight, Sound, Smell" as "Learning to Live" in *Southern Review* (1992); "Cleaning Your Gun" in *Fiction* (1993); and "Absolutes" in *New Virginia Review* (1994).

As promised so long ago, this first book is for my family:

my mother, Marion Deane Drummond
my father, Kenneth H. Drummond
and my beloved brothers, Finlay and Carter

ACKNOWLEDGMENTS

This book has been twelve years in the writing, so there are many people who deserve my thanks.

It started a long time ago in a far-off galaxy called Flint Hill Prep where Colonel Alan Ferguson Warren and Lucy Gard Redfield fed the flame my Mother had ignited and nurtured: the power of stories and the beauty of language. My debt to these three people can never be repaid.

In more recent times, James Gordon Bennett pushed me to "just write"; I'm grateful for his persistence, guidance, and witty charm. David Bradley generously provided extensive analysis on several stories and taught me a great deal about writing in the process. Rodger Kaminetz showed me the importance of word choice and line editing. My thanks also to Tim O'Brien, Marianne Gingher, Rosellen Brown, Margot Livesey, Tom Gavin, and Lois Rosenthal for their feedback and encouragement.

Deep bows of thanks and a pitcher of Library beer to the LSU MFAers of 1988–1991. A tip of the hat and a wink to The Bobs. And cyberhugs to the Online Women Writers' Group who made teaching more joy than work.

Support in the form of coffee, wine, meals, and much more was provided in the early stages of writing this book by Helen and Stanley Miller, Leila Levinson, Jean Rohloff, Erin Johnson, Robin Roberts, Sigrid King, Betsy Williams, Bill and Monica Moen, Ralph LaPrairie, and John McLain. My thanks and love.

The Writers' League of Texas deserves a nod of gratitude for their many kindnesses, especially the amazing Sally Baker. My thanks also to the Sewanee Writers' Conference, particularly Cheri Peters. And I'm indebted to the entire staff of the Virginia Center for the Creative Arts for providing a true haven (and a puppy!) while I finished the final revisions on this book.

I am blessed to be a part of the St. Edward's University community. My students, past and present, have enriched my life more than they'll ever know. The administration has generously supported my endeavors through a variety of grants, full-time employment, and a sabbatical leave. Many of my colleagues made the juggle of teaching and writing much smoother and definitely more fun, especially Anna Skinner, Mary Rist, Lisa Martinez, Catherine Rainwater, Alan Altimont, Br. John Perron, Bill Quinn, Father Lou Brusatti, and Sandra Pacheco. Bill Kennedy took fabulous photographs. Brett Westbrook provided information on Victim Services. My former student and now colleague, Elizabeth Sibrian, provided the Spanish translations for "Where I Come From." Eric Trimble, Janet Kazmirski, Pam McGrew, and Anita Sing solved computer, postal, and photocopying challenges with aplomb. *Muchas gracias* one and all.

Portions of this book were written at the homes of Bob and Margy Ayers in Tennessee, Nancy Napier and Tony Olbrich in Idaho, and Barbara Duke in New Mexico—your generosity was huge, the luxury of time and solitude invaluable.

I'm immensely grateful to "Marjorie LaSalle," a true warrior of the heart, who trusted me to honor her truth while taking her experience off into fictional realms.

For over thirteen years Dinty W. Moore has provided the feedback I trust the most: honest, kind, thoughtful, thorough. *Namaste*, my friend.

My always sister Lynn has been an enthusiastic reader and is one of the great blessings of my life, as are my nephews Chase and Cole. Oodles of kisses to you all.

Those whose gestures, both large and small, often made the difference, whether they realized it or not: Paige Elizabeth Pozzi, Sherry Scott and Michelle Burns, Catherine MacDermott, Sanchi Reta Lawler, Patrick Ricard, Judy Kahn, Jack and Carolyn Hall, Casey

Miller and Pat Jackson, Kathy Brown, Pamela Cromwell, Bonnie Jean Dickson Winsler, Mary Janecek-Friedman, Katrina Dittemore, Lynda Shannon and James Vance, and Ted Rader. Abundant gratitude for your presence in my life.

I am humbled by the love and support I've received from my Alayans: Annie Province, Kimmie Jo-Jo Atkins, Beverly Alexander and Eldon Bryan, Molly and Russ and Tommy Fleming, Joan Raskin, Leebob Edwards, Steve Milan, Jerry-bear Rutledge, Bev Davis, Pete Erickson, Wendy Vermeulen, johnsmith, Tom Kimmel, and Abu Ali Abdur 'Rahman. Your beauty and courage fill my heart.

Special thanks to Anniebelle for finding the Robertson Davies quote and being willing to go the hard way with me, again and again.

Marjorie Braman has been passionate from day one; thank you for saying yes and for your keen eye and fierce commitment to this book. Thank you, Kelly Bare, for your always cheerful support and bottomless supply of answers.

Jandy Nelson, my angel of an agent, you're a peach! Your enthusiasm was boundless, your patience endless, your expertise invaluable, your faith my great good fortune. That we could talk food and books for hours on end was simply icing on the cake. Thanks as well to Dru, Stephanie, Mark, and Lucy.

I have been overwhelmed by the outpouring of help from so many of my former colleagues with the Baton Rouge Police Department: former chief Greg Phares and Chief Pat Englade for allowing me access and Lieutenant Mike Gough for facilitating that access; Lieutenant Ricky Cochran for tracking down the original crime scene photos of "Jeannette Durham" that I saw so long ago; Sergeant Roger Tully and Barbara Spears for finding, in a box, in a storeroom, the traffic reports I wrote some eighteen years ago; Sergeant David Worley and Sergeant James Kurts for stories, great debates, and always the coffee; Sergeant Brenda Miceli for her expertise in latent fingerprints; Lieutenant Sam Miceli and Detective John Colter for stories and answers; Captain Mike Colter for Ed's coat and for patiently reminding me these many years later what I'd forgotten; Sergeant Marian McLin for always being there and still making me laugh at the most inappropriate times; and Sergeant Ike Vavasseur for his friendship, trust, insight into working homicides, letting me ride along, lending me books, opening doors, and answering my bazillion questions with grace and good humor. Ray Jackson, whatever heavenly universe you inhabit, I have never forgotten the values you instilled and the example you set. To all the men and women I rode with, both at LSU Police and BRPD, thank you for the backup.

Finally, this book would never have been finished, let alone started, without the guardian angels of my heart: Linda Lue Kelly Woodruff, Linda Gayle Manning, and Kenneth Robinson. Thank you for helping me find my voice, my truth, my center.

CONTENTS

KATHERINE

One always learns one's mystery at the price of one's innocence.
—Robertson Davies

ABSOLUTES

This really happened, this story. I've never told anyone, not the whole story. When civilians ask, I say, "No, never killed anybody." Almost apologetically because I know they want me to say yes. Because then they can ask more. Because then their minds can twist the various elements of a-woman-with-a-gun-killing-a-man into their own vicarious masturbation of fact.

This will be just the facts: I killed a man. I shot him at 1:33 A.M. He died at 1:57 A.M. That's when I couldn't get a pulse, a heartbeat. That's when the EMS boys got there and took over CPR. When they said, "Shit, sister. You fucking flatlined him." I didn't have to look at the fist-sized hole in his chest where my own hands had just been, massaging his heart, swearing at the goddamn sonofabitch to come back to life goddamnit. I knew he was dead.

This really happened; it's the absolute truth. He was twenty years old. His name was Jeffery Lewis Moore. He had a gun, and I shot him. My job is to enforce the law and protect citizens. Our departmental handbook stipulates: A police officer may use deadly

force when her own life or the lives of others are in mortal danger.
So it must be true.

Every night when I go home after shift, I run my hands lightly over my
body as I undress. The tips of my fingers catch the new scratches on my
hands and arms, tiny red vines, an unreadable map. The burn from the
teeth of the cuffs, I remember it catching my skin only now; the new
welt on my side, unexplainable; the constant, steady bruise on the hipbone where my gun caresses the skin a deeper purple day after day; the
red mark, raised and uneven and mysterious on the back of my knee.
The knot on my arm from the night before is smaller, less painful; the
flesh is stained a darker green, a more vivid yellow. My breasts are sore
and tender from the bulletproof vest. I unbraid my hair and shake it
loose. One of my fingernails is torn and bleeding; my tongue glides
quickly over the rusty sweetness. I taste others' sweat.

I stand under the shower. I place both hands on the wall and lean
into the water, stretching out the muscles, pulling them long the
length of my body.

Okay, I tell myself. Every night I tell myself, *okay*.

In the newspapers, they don't refer to us by name. Not at first. I am
"the uniformed police officer"; he is "the alleged suspect." The official forms list us as Officer Joubert and Perpetrator Moore. Only in
his obituary do they print the full name of Jeffery Lewis Moore. He is
survived by his mother, two brothers and a sister, many aunts, uncles,
and cousins. He graduated from Roosevelt High, liked to skateboard,
sang in his school choir. Both of his brothers will serve as pallbearers.
No cause of death is mentioned.

In the newspapers, there are editorials about rising crime: armed
robberies, burglaries, carjackings, murders. Reporters call the
precinct. They call my home. "Do you believe your actions were
justified?" they ask. "How did it feel to shoot someone? Was there
anything else you could have done?" One reporter wants to write a
profile on female police officers; she says it's a chance for me to tell
my story. "Which story?" I ask her.

In the newspapers, they print statistics about the use of deadly force: how many civilians have been killed by police officers in Baton Rouge in the last year, the last twenty years. How many were "clean" shootings, how many weren't. They compile a series of articles, *In the Line of Duty—When Cops Kill*, and linger over the details of my shooting. They print my age, twenty-two, and my time on the job, fifteen months. My boyfriend, Johnny, says, "Notice they don't say how many police officers have been killed or almost killed, Katie." I point out that I'm still alive. "Exactly," he says.

In the newspapers, they say I was in the right. "Officer Katherine Joubert handled the situation correctly, absolutely within departmental procedure," the chief of police says. "An unfortunate incident," he calls it. In private he tells me about a man he killed. "The guy was crazy," he says. "The impact of the bullets flipped him over backward. Amazing. Never seen anything like it." He tells me counseling is available if I want it.

The woman across the street from my house is sweeping her porch. She sweeps all the time—the porch, the walkway, the driveway, the sidewalk. Sometimes even the street. I've lived here over a year, and every day, except when it's raining, Miss Mary sweeps. She's almost seventy and as black and shiny as a plum. "You jist a baby, be doin' this kinda thing," she's always telling me. I laugh when she says this. She's told me I remind her of her daughter, the one in California; she says we have the same toothy smile. I help Miss Mary pick the figs she can't reach from her tree out back, and she always lets me carry some home, warm and sweet from the sun.

After the shooting, I sit out on my front steps, like I do most every day after shift, drinking a rum and coke, fingering the small St. Michael's medallion that Johnny gave me, and watch her sweep. She won't meet my gaze those first days after. She sweeps fiercely—short, sharp strokes.

I like this neighborhood, my street in particular. The live oaks are old and heavy with ball moss, the crape myrtles fighting with them for room and light. When the wind comes through here, you know it; the trees sing to you. Most of the houses are shotgun style, built during the WPA. The yards are clean, and something is always blooming furiously in every one. We're all mostly blue collar here on the inside fringes of the Garden District. Two blocks west and you're in the projects—Magnolia Hills is the name on the map, but everyone calls it The Bottoms.

Cops tell me I'm crazy to live in this neighborhood, that it was foolish to buy a house here. "Dogs don't sleep in their shit," Johnny says. "You shouldn't be livin' where you're bustin' ass."

I think about words, how definitions can be stories in themselves. I pull out an old battered dictionary and flip through pages and find *Incident*: an event that disrupts normal procedure or causes a crisis. *Kill*: to cause the death of, or to pass the time in aimless activity; to delete. *Absolute*: not limited by restrictions or exceptions: unconditional or positive: certain <*absolute*> truth; pertaining to measurements derived from basic relationships of space, mass, and time.

I stare at these words, let them swim into a blur of gray. I run my fingers over the fine, icy lines, but they are stories without life, these definitions—no pores, no bones, no unguarded pain. No answers. Not really absolute.

I keep coming at what happened from different angles, like a tongue probing a sore tooth, testing memory against reality until the two blur. I never play what-ifs; they don't pertain.

I go to work. I take long walks, clean the house, water my plants. I avoid the meat aisle at the supermarket. I cook meals for Johnny and me that require long preparation and we sit down to eat with a freshly laundered tablecloth and two candles just so on the diagonal; the flames bend and rise in the tepid evening air. I pour wine and chew each bite of food slowly.

I sleep well, except when he starts breathing and I am jolted out of sleep. Jeffery Lewis Moore is breathing in my ear, the same desperate rasp as before.

*   *   *

What you want, what any cop wants, is an unconditional response. An immediate, reflexive response—absolute.

"Freeze," I yell. "Police." My voice is deep and strong and sure. And they are supposed to stop. They are supposed to raise their hands into the air.

"Hands behind your head," I say. You yell now only if there's a chance they'll run. You yell now only if you're afraid. You don't want them to think: if they think, they may fight.

The training films and the instructors at the academy, they tell you when you are sitting safe and cool in the classroom that you should say, "Do it NOW!" after each command. But there is never time for this: they respond or they don't. If they don't, I yell, "NOW MOTHERFUCKER!" You want to convince them you're mean, that you'll take them out in a second. You want to convince them not to do anything you'll have to shoot them for.

"On your knees," I say. "Drop." I have tried this dropping to the knees with hands clasped behind my head. It is hard to do. It hurts. You feel it all the way up into the jaw.

When they are on their knees, you must make a decision. Do you move in close and cuff them, or do you order them all the way down, face first into the concrete, dirt, gravel, grass, mud?

When I go in close, I step on their calf, hard with my heel on the right one, unless I know for sure they are left-handed. I holster my gun, but don't snap the safety strap, pull out my handcuffs and reach up for the left hand, bring it down, cuff it; then I bring down the right. Usually I throw them a bit of advice in a low, tight whisper: "You fucking move I'll blow your fucking head off, motherfucker."

I give them their Miranda rights, "Mirandize'em," it's called. If they don't respond, you shake them, yell—anything until you get some sound. Without a verbal response, it won't fly in court.

If they've responded quickly to my commands, I assist them to their feet by supporting their elbows. "On your feet," I tell them, sometimes nicely, sometimes not. It all depends on their body language and facial expression. If they haven't responded quickly, if they've been giving me lip, if they've made me nervous, I grab the happy chain—the thin links that connect the two cuffs—and yank up hard. I say, "Get up," as I yank again, bringing them up, their feet scrambling to find leverage.

Sometimes you hear the muscle tear in their shoulder when you do this. Just a slight sound, like a sheet being ripped.

"There must have been something else you could have done," people who don't wear guns for a living say to cops who have killed.

If I could, I'd give them a story they might understand, one that doesn't involve guns of course. Except I can't, no matter how hard I try. There is nothing to compare it to.

"Don't try," Johnny says, "it's futile. Soldiers understand. Maybe firefighters, medical personnel. But their work is about saving lives, not taking them."

"We save lives too," I say. "All the time."

He shakes his head, brushes a strand of hair back off my face, and tucks it behind my ear. "That's not the way they see it, Katie, when a cop shoots someone."

I change the topic. He doesn't understand either, not really. He may be fourteen years older than me and have eleven years more experience, but Johnny Cippoine has never killed anyone, never even fired his gun on a call. Not once. He takes great pride in this fact.

I tread carefully through my house. Pieces of that night come back to me suddenly, unexpectedly. His smell. The weight of his body against mine. It's like turning the corner on the roof of a high building and feeling a warm, nauseous rush of vertigo. I'll be washing the dishes, look down, and my hands will have become his hands, even the cut between his knuckles on his right hand is the same. The texture of the air shifts, and all the molecules in my body separate from skin, tendon, bone, fluid, and dance out into the room, rearrange themselves, weaving between then and now before they return, reshape into me as I stand here drying my hands.

"Mine," I whisper. "Not yours."

The first time this happens, I shut off the air conditioner and lie shivering under blankets, not sure whether I have stepped into his world or he into mine.

*   *   *

"You killed my boy," is the only thing that Jeffery Lewis Moore's mother said to me. Her voice was low, steady, weary. I don't know where she came from, but when I turned away from the detectives on the scene, she was there. Her skin was the color of just-brewed coffee; a dusting of freckles covered her nose and cheeks. She wore black stretch pants, a pink T-shirt, and no shoes. Her toes were freshly painted, deep fuchsia. She looked right at me, over the police unit throwing patches of red and blue light across our faces, and said, "You killed my boy." I nodded. I never saw her again.

"Better him than you," my mother says when I tell her about the shooting. She is patting me like a newborn, all over, pat, pat, pat, pat, pat. Ten fingers, ten toes, all the parts are there.

Watching Miss Mary sweep becomes a meditation, a way not to think. There is something hopeful about the process despite the results. The wind blows it all back, the trees keep dropping leaves, the crape myrtle blooms make red splotches on the ground.

Several weeks after the shooting, I come out my door and Miss Mary is just bending down to put something on my welcome mat. I fumble with the latch on the screen as she straightens up slowly, a covered casserole dish in her hands.

"Brought you sumpthin," she says softly.

I get the door open, and she backs up a step.

"Food?" I say.

She nods and holds it out to me. Her hands look as soft as homespun cotton; tiny folds of skin ripple like a sandy creek bed along the back of her arms.

"Food?" I say again.

Her eyes are the same familiar pools of deep, dark light. "Food." She pulls her hands away, leaving the casserole dish in mine.

"Thank you," I say, bewildered.

She nods again, hesitates, then turns around, starts back down the stairs, one hand resting on the rail to steady herself.

"Miss Mary," I say. When she turns to look at me, I raise the dish slightly up and toward her.

I swear we stand like that for hours, though it's probably only four seconds at the most before she gives me a slight smile and says, "It's the polite thing to do at wakes."

The next day, there's another dish at my door.

The crime scene detectives snapped on clear plastic gloves before they touched Jeffery Lewis Moore. They huddled over his body, rolling his limp fingers across the ink pad, then onto the paper. They took pictures of the entrance and exit wounds, my bullet cartridges on the ground, the body. They brought out tape measures and evidence bags. One of them looked at me, standing nearby watching, and said, "More blood on you than him."

I shrugged, said, "Tried to save him."

He snorted. "Save him? What were you thinking of, Joubert, sticking your hands up in this man's chest? These people have diseases. Better get tested."

Just before I shot Jeffery Lewis Moore, two quick shots, time stopped. We were there on the patchy grass, some ugly advancing dance with hot, ragged breath, and my mind was in my finger on the trigger. Then time stopped, and we were only sweaty bodies and breath and tiny pinpoints of light in each other's eyes. The air pressed in around us. No sound, absolutely nothing except our breathing: scratchy, heavy, exhale inhale exhale inhale. And then he said something and took another step and I shot. Twice.

They like to ask me, people when they meet me and find out I'm a cop, "Did you ever use your gun? You ever kill anybody?" I shake my head. "No," I always lie, "never killed anybody."

Jeffery Lewis Moore robbed an open-all-night restaurant near the Mississippi River Bridge, and I chased him on foot, tearing through narrow yards littered with toys, rusty metal objects, overgrown weeds. Weaving in and out between houses I began to regret the additional fifteen pounds of gunbelt around my hips. Everything flapped and banged as I ran: the holster and gun, the portable radio in its black half-case, the four-cell flashlight that doubled as a nightstick, a key ring too big and too noisy; even the bottom edge of my badge flip-flopped against my chest. And the bulletproof vest rode up, pushed higher by my gunbelt so that the top edge of the vest rubbed across my neck, cut in with each pounding step.

It was dog shift, around 1:00 A.M., and Jeffery Lewis Moore had a gun, although I didn't know that was his name at the time; he was just a B/M, 5'9", 17–25 yrs old, light-complexion, medium build, wearing T-shirt, jeans, and tennis shoes. And, of course, carrying a gun. A BIG gun, the hysterical counterman said, LOTS of bullets. It turned out to be a five-round, two-inch .38 Chief's Special with the grips removed. But any gun looks big when it's pointed at you.

I had no way to alert other units that I'd found the suspect; my portable radio was breaking up. But still I chased him. He stayed about twenty yards ahead of me, and my breath came in short heavy gasps. We ran past the point where time ceases to be measured in minutes or seconds. The noises of the neighborhood receded. Occasionally I caught glimpses of red lights revolving against the white backdrop of a house; other units were looking for Jeffery Lewis Moore, too.

When I rounded the front corner of a house and he was halfway under the porch, his feet digging the dirt for traction, his breathing as loud and desperate as mine, I wasn't surprised. In this neighborhood they all crawled under houses; it was merely a matter of staying close enough behind them so you knew which house when they did it.

What I didn't expect was Jeffery Lewis Moore backing out and coming up with the gun in his hand. And it wasn't the gun that scared me so much—I was wearing my vest, and only 17 percent of shots fired at less than ten feet in a crisis situation ever hit their target—it was the knife in his other hand. It was a BIG knife. But even a pocket knife would have terrified me.

Guns put holes in you, but you can live from a gunshot wound. Knives hurt; they open you up. They slice, slice you open and cut deep. Cut things off. Knives bring a long pain, lots of blood. Johnny knew this cop in New Orleans who was convinced he'd die if he ever got shot. When it happened, a gunshot wound just where arm meets shoulder, the cop died. "Not lethal, Katie, understand?" Johnny said. "He died because he *believed* he would."

I know it's a weakness, but that's how I feel about knives.

So here's Jeffery Lewis Moore with a gun and a knife, and me with no way to call for help. You might say this is stacking the story against him, but you can't go against absolutes, and this is the way it happened.

"You fucking move I'll blow you away," I screamed in a voice that probably carried more shrillness than authority.

He didn't listen. They'd always listened before, believed what I said. The cursed command, the gun, the badge, the woman on the other end of the gun always stopped them. He didn't stop. He grinned, that's what he did. He grinned a shaky grin and raised that knife. He took a half-step forward.

"Stop!" I yelled, several times. I quivered like a hummingbird; all the air going in and out of my body traveled through my mouth. But he kept coming with that funny little grin, the one I see in my dreams, and I was screaming my voice hoarse—my voice has never been the same—screaming at him to stop or I'll shoot, and then it was time. It was him or me, and the gun had become as scary as the knife. And when he was near enough, when he took the step that brought him into lunging distance, when I could smell his fear, when his eyes changed from brown stones to deep pools of reflected light, when he whispered low, "Come on," a coarse sugar whisper, I shot.

I shot twice like they taught us at the range: quick and tight, arms extended, left hand supporting the right. Aimed for the chest, the kill zone, saw him take the bullets, jolt several steps back from the impact, saw the ragged rose petals of blood bloom and spread. And his eyes, those deep brown pools went even wider, and the light rushed in. He stumbled forward, dropping gun and knife; he stumbled forward into me, his blood soaking my hands and uniform. I caught him in my arms and dropped with him to the ground.

One time a bird hit my car. I was driving back from the country, windows all rolled down. The bird came from nowhere; I had no time to avoid its flight. There was a thud on my windshield, then a smear of blood and yellow fluid, a rush of feathers. And something moved through me—a warm sweeping light of energy moved through my body. Then it was gone, and I was left light-headed and dizzy but with something new inside.

The same thing happened when Jeffrey Lewis Moore died. The gurgles of blood and air stopped, his arms, chest, legs ceased convulsing, and what was left swept through my body in a warm shuddering rush and came to rest in my lungs.

That's where he's been ever since. Internal Affairs cleared me. Everyone agreed I'd shot in self-defense. It wasn't my fault, no other choice; that's what the Weapons Review Board said. I gave them the absolute facts: The suspect was armed with a gun and knife, and I was in fear for my life. It comes with the badge, this possibility of killing. And I'm fine about it. Really, I am. I'm back out on the streets, not in the neighborhood I live in, but I'm working.

Still, sometimes when I sit alone in the hallway of my house, Jeffery Lewis Moore shimmers to the surface and sweeps through my body. His presence is here, in the back of my skull, tucked inside my brain. There is a piece of him inside now, and I can't deny him his right. Sitting in the long carpetless hall, the lights off, just the two of us, Jeffery Lewis Moore whispers low into my ear. "Come on," he says, "come on." And I lean into myself, waiting for him to say more, but there is just silence, and I am left wondering how dead we ever really are.

TASTE, TOUCH, SIGHT,
SOUND, SMELL

I tell the rookies, when I train them, that the biggest mistake they can make is to think they know it all. "You never will," I say, "trust me. I've been working this job six years, and I still learn something new every day—a technique, an insight into human behavior, the way the law works, even the limitations of my own body."

They always nod quickly, their bodies tense with anticipation and often just a touch of fear. I've learned to read the topography of their fears: some have none and they scare me; some have a panicky fear and they scare me too; but most rookies have a controlled fear, a minuscule flutter just under their cheekbone or along the smooth column of their neck that acknowledges their own mortality. I'm glad to see that fear. I tell them to honor it but don't let it stop them from doing what needs to be done. Without that finger of fear, you make mistakes. Without fear, you can die quickly in this job. There's a fine line between courage and stupidity.

I watch their faces and think how impossibly young and unweathered they are, how much the job will change them. Sometimes I want to say, "No, don't do this." But it wouldn't do any good. I know. They remind me of myself, many of them, when I was fresh out of the academy and thought I knew everything.

And so for the few months they ride with me, I teach them the way my training officer taught me: the practical skills, the necessary skills, the investigative skills, the life-saving skills.

The academy can do only so much.

For instance, they try at the police academy to prepare you for the sight and smell of death. They distribute autopsy and crime scene photos, selecting the worst of the worst for our careful perusal: dead children, brutalized men and women, swollen corpses, shattered body parts. It is like nothing else you've ever smelled, they tell us; it will cling to your uniform, stay in your hair. They offer us countermeasures: cigar smoke, a washcloth doused in cologne, coffee grounds, an oxygen mask.

We wrote it all down carefully. We had to; they checked our notes every week.

When I graduated from the Baton Rouge Police Training Academy on a humid August day, one of two women in a class of thirty-nine cadets, I was assigned to uniform patrol on the day shift out of Broadmoor Precinct. Johnny Cippoine, my training officer, laughed hard from the belly when I slid into the passenger seat of his unit and said, "I'm ready!"

"Let's take it slow, Joubert. Ever written a traffic ticket?"

Within two weeks I was standing at the back of a trailer off Airline Highway with Johnny, staring at a day-old dead body slumped headfirst into a toilet. The tentative morning light was dirty and gray, and the smell of rancid meat, rotten bananas, and the bitter tang of weeks-old oranges thickened the air. The rooms we had passed through were crammed with musty, stained furniture. The body's ninety-two-year-old senile husband sobbed beside me, holding my hand in a bone-crunching grip. When was I supposed to scoop coffee grounds, wet a washcloth, strap on an oxygen mask?

I didn't gag, I didn't throw up, I didn't even grimace, although it took all my willpower not to react to the smell. I studied my cuticles for a long while after we drove away, pushing each smile of skin firmly back down from the nail with my thumb.

"Be careful with your heart on this job," Johnny said. "And get used to the stink of death, there's nothing you can do about it."

He was right. I've seen only one cop, a detective on the bomb squad, haul an oxygen mask out of his unit to work a body. The department doesn't issue oxygen masks to uniform patrol. Coffee grounds, which they told us should be stuffed up our nostrils, aren't used by any police officer I've ever met. Vicks VapoRub, smeared liberally around the nostrils, is often passed around at autopsies, but then autopsies allow that luxury of preparation. And, truth be told, it cuts the odor only somewhat.

Because a dead body does smell. And it *is* unlike anything else. It is not enough for me to tell acquaintances and strangers who push for more that this smell is beyond words. So for those who push, for those who need to slow to ten miles per hour to see the bloody, mangled body parts on the interstate, I say: Imagine the smell of rancid hamburger. Now multiply that one pound of meat into 150 or 220 pounds of rancid meat. Then increase the smell by fifty for every twenty-four-hour period that passes—unless it's the dead of summer, then triple or quadruple that sum. This is rancid meat with maggots and rotting, seeping body fluids. It is a dead body. And it is unlike anything else.

I quickly became a semiexpert on dead body smells; I could often determine how long someone had been dead simply by the stench. I worked with one cop who'd bet me, as we entered a hallway or room and caught the first unmistakable whiff of death, how long the body had been a body.

A body newly dead has a sweet thin smell to it, a gentle sigh of a smell if the death wasn't gruesome, although some suicides have that same sweetness. Sometimes there is the acrid cutting edge of gunpowder that bites the eyes, the nostrils, the throat. Violence has a heavy smell that lingers for days—a taste as well—and a presence, thick and gray and swirling. A burned body is the most nauseating: bitter and permeating; not much remains to deal with, though flakes of skin come off and attach to your arms, clothing, face, hair. With most bodies, there is the smell of urine and feces; what they don't tell you, what the movies and TV never show, is that at death, bladder and bowel control ends, the muscles relax, and any waste matter left in the body comes out.

As a body settles, fluids build up and are released. The optimum time to work with a body is before these fluids seep out. As rigor mortis sets in, the body swells into large dark blisters (much more quickly in the relentless Louisiana heat), and eventually the skin pops. Then smell becomes a taste. I wasn't prepared for the taste of death, how it would coat my tongue and throat and lungs. Smoking cigarettes didn't help; neither did scalding coffee or the most corrosive alcohol I could think of, straight gin. I would taste death for days after contact with a body.

The only consistent concession I see cops make, at least the plainclothes detectives, is removing their suit jackets around the really noxious bodies. My first encounter with this was in the middle of an aggressive, sweltering Louisiana summer afternoon. I smelled the body as I walked up the outside stairwell of a run-down apartment complex off Flannery Road. Three days, I figured. Turns out I was short by a day.

"Something died in there," the manager told me.

"Yes it did."

"Maybe an animal? A dog or something?" His voice had more hope than I'd expect from someone his age.

"Maybe."

The body lay in the back room, sitting up in bed. No signs of violence or forced entry. The body was so deteriorated I couldn't tell if he was originally black or white; actually, it was tough to figure out if "he" was a he or a she from the bloating and disfiguration.

I notified the dispatcher, requested a Homicide detective, an ambulance, the coroner, an assistant DA. Detective Ray Robileaux, a short, intense man I'd worked a few calls with before, arrived first, took off his coat, and handed it to me.

"Hold this," he said, then went inside.

I'm standing there holding this man's coat, and I don't know why. I thought, *What the fuck, I look like his wife?* and followed him in. He was puffing away on a cigarette asking me questions about the scene, and I was responding, my voice funny-sounding because I'd shut off my nose and closed my throat to a slender cocktail-straw opening to cope with the smell.

Suddenly Robileaux noticed his coat in my hand. He started this high-pitched scream of words: now he'd have to get it dry-cleaned and why the fuck did I think he'd asked me to hold it?

"Uniform isn't around to hold coats for fucking detectives," I snapped back.

He paused in midstep, tucked his tongue between his teeth, then laughed. "You got some *cojones*, Katie Joubert."

But uniform patrol doesn't have the option of removing at least some of our clothing to work a body. On those days, at the end of shift, I make a beeline for my house, strip, and let the shower—as hot as I can stand it—and a pitted bar of rosemary soap rinse away the exterior vestiges of death. I lather my hair twice, massage in conditioner, slather vanilla lotion over my whole body afterward, apply perfume to all my pulse points. I put on a dress and let my hair fall down the middle of my back.

"Whoo boy, what the hell you been doing?" Johnny asked the first time I worked a body after we got married. "You smell like the whole goddamn perfume counter at Goudchaux's."

"I don't shop at Goudchaux's," I said, and then I told him about the body, an elementary teacher two days dead, strangled, laid out on her bed as though she was taking a nap, still wearing her bra but no underwear. We suspect the boyfriend.

The next week, he came home with a gift basket full of perfumed oils, lotions, and soaps. "All natural," he pointed out shyly, "just like you like." It took me three years, but I finished off every item in that basket.

I don't use the washer and dryer at home for uniforms that are drenched in the smell of death; I worry that some lingering residue might attach itself to my other clothes. Some officers claim that digging a hole and putting the clothes in the ground for several days cuts the odor. I've never tried this; the thought of burying my uniform is too painfully absurd. Kean's Dry Cleaning has a special deal for uniforms that have done the death beat: two washings, a steaming, and a buck-fifty off the regular price. So I take my uniforms, tied up in a white plastic bag, to Nancy at the Kean's on Government Street, and she returns them three days later starched and hanging in clear plastic.

But I imagine I still smell it, that the fibers have absorbed something holy and horrible that no amount of washing can erase. It's only recently that I've realized I have absorbed it. This smell, death, it is a part of me, as pure and real and present as any memory of the child I once was.

Almost every morning of my childhood I awoke, reluctantly coming to consciousness, soothed by the warm, drowsy smell of yeast and flour and sometimes cinnamon. I would lie there in bed and hold an image of my mother downstairs, still in curlers perhaps, up since 5:00, now reading the *Boston Globe* and drinking her coffee while the morning's bread rose and turned golden behind her. And from the bathroom that adjoined my room came the squeak of flesh on porcelain, the lazy lap of water as my father, dozing, dreaming of his boyhood, shifted in the bathtub.

My mother baking for her family in the quiet of their slumber; my father distant in his memories, immersed in water: this is how I woke nearly every morning in my parents' house.

Fall in Massachusetts: burning leaves, roasted chestnuts, Indian summers, baked beans simmered slow and long, the salty bite of distant ocean in the air, and a crispness I've never found in the Deep South. That brilliant splash before the winter retreat when the world was swirling, crackling leaves waiting in some pile to embrace me. The wet, hungry earth; the sharp, sweet grass and mulch. In the winter, the world out my window had no smell but cold. It was a glittering fairyland of black and white—sparkles and snowflake patterns and frost and fluffy waist-high snow draped on trees, fences, my mother's garden.

During the spring and summer, our house stayed fragrant, full of flowers and cuttings: pine, wisteria, pansies, forsythia, violets— always something from outside, from one of my mother's greatest loves, the garden. She would often pinch loose the petals of a rose or peony, snap a twig of French lavender or basil and crush it in her hand, and say, "There, smell." And we did, my brother and I; we smelled the dirt and warmth of her hand. Years later I would yearn for this tenderness at times of terror: inching through a dark building, talking down a suicide, alone in a house with a burglar twice my size.

Suddenly, irrationally, I wanted her hand there, cupping my chin, the feel of her roughened moist flesh, the gritty soil full of mystery and promise.

As I grew older, into the double digits, I sought time alone in the house, without brother or parents. I prowled from room to room, standing in each doorway for a minute or so, taking it into me—the sight, smell, feel of each room, as though this absorption could somehow help me read and correct the increasingly strange and distant interactions between my mother and father, between my parents and myself.

I would stand in the semidarkness of my parents' two-room closet. First my father's side, carefully leaning into the sleeve of a coat: scratchy deep wool, anonymous cleaning fluid, and a hint of the lemony sting of 4711 cologne that he wore. I'd finger through his ties, inspect the rows of shoes gleaming with polish, brush my hand along the line of belts, count the change scattered out across a shelf.

Then my mother's side. Burying my face in her clothing, pulling it close around me, I inhaled the lingering trail of Chanel and her own sweet musky scent mixed with the undertone of tears that always nestled in the dip between her collarbone and neck. I stood here the longest, as though by fragrance alone I could understand her better.

Up until high school, when we moved to Louisiana "following the economy," as my father called it, my best friends were Mary and Emma Long who lived across the street. Mary was my age, Emma two years older. I adored Emma: her laugh, her white-blond hair, jungle-green eyes, a tummy that didn't have ripples of extra flesh when she bent over. Mary was chunky, earnest, average. I was gawky, clumsy, emotional. According to my parents on an application to day school they filled out when I was six, I had a "sensitive nature which responds quickly and at length to joy or sorrow. Once familiar with an individual or situation," the form reads, "Katherine tends to attempt to manage it."

As far as I can tell nothing has changed, except Mary has disappeared—untraceable—and Emma is dead: drugs, prostitution, suicide.

This is how I remember us at play: A rich, late-afternoon light ribbons through my mother's wood-paneled kitchen. We have closed all the doors and shutters to keep the adults out. The tang of soy sauce and heavy promise of honey are in the air. Mary and Emma sit blindfolded at a table, an old cherry table with deeply etched *e*'s and *c*'s, a result of my brother's and my early attempts at writing. The table is laden with my mother's tan dishes full of carefully chosen food. This is the tasting game.

Mary has taken her thick, black glasses off and has a grin on her face, braces poking forth, while Emma sits quietly, hair pulled into a ponytail, face smooth and still, waiting. Her cheekbones catch the light, and in this memory, she could be Michelangelo's model for the *Pietà*. I stand across the table, trying to decide what to test them with first.

This image hovers in my mind: them blindfolded, me standing nearby, watching, in control of what happens next. I could never decide which role I liked best: tester or tested. I liked being in charge, that power over outcome, but I also liked the thrill of detection, of getting it right. We would play for hours, rotating turns as game hostess, challenging our powers of smell and taste. We wanted to be able to tell, even with our eyes closed, what was going on.

I tell the rookies that their hands are more important than they realize. Their jaw and cheek muscles go slack, and they stare at me: either they are bewildered or they think I'm an idiot.

And so I continue to teach them, patiently, all I have learned.

One evening, not long after I'd graduated from the academy and was still riding with Johnny, he drove our unit into a deserted, little-used park off Harrells Ferry Road.

"Get out," he said, "and show me how you unload and load your gun."

I stood there in the warm fall breeze, dumped my rounds and reloaded, two bullets at a time, proud of how quickly and efficiently I moved.

"No," he said, the wind kicking his dark hair into errant tufts. "First, this isn't the firing range. Always eject rounds into your hand. You get in the habit of dumping them on the ground and what if they hit cement? Roll and hit something metal? Whoever's firing at you hears that and knows your gun is empty."

I blinked at this obvious lesson and nodded.

"Second, learn to reload by touch alone," he said. "You'll need your eyes for other things."

So I practiced, sometimes at night before I placed the gun on my nightstand and went to sleep, sometimes in the early morning on dog shift, between four and five o'clock when the city held its breath and was quiet. Over and over I thumbed the ejection pin and caught the bullets in my hand. My eyes closed, I quickly fed six bullets into the chamber, thumbing the cylinder round, using the groove by each chamber as a guide for the hand feeding the bullets. When we went to speed loaders, wondrous contraptions resembling a black Ferris wheel turned on its side that dropped bullets into the chamber with a twist of a knob, I continued to practice both methods of loading.

Touch, I slowly learned, was an important tool. My hands could feel the car hood and discover how recently it had been used; my hands could test the car trunk to see if it was indeed closed; my hands could gently twist the doorknob, tap the screen, tug at the window; my hands could probe the entry marks from the bullet or knife; my hands could check the tension in a person's body—would he or she come willingly or was I in for a fight?

"And the reason for training your hands," I tell the rookies, "is because observation, a close, instantaneous cataloguing of details, is essential."

Often there are so many details to process that survival depends on honing this sense to an exquisite intensity. When I respond to a call—whether an armed robbery, or traffic stop, or suspicious person, or family fight—I focus first on the hands, then on the eyes. "The hands will kill you," Johnny would say over and over again, "the eyes will tell you."

Late last year, Sarah Jeffries and I went 10-7 on a family disturbance. Although we are different in personality and background, and she's more rookie than seasoned cop, we both believe in intuition, in paying attention to the feel of a scene or a person. Sarah calls it "reading the vibes." We'd been working the same shift together for over a year, and we'd learned to read each other—and a situation—in an instant, without words. Sarah's young, but she's got potential. And she learns quickly.

The apartment complex we were dispatched to was a decrepit building on Nicholson Drive just off the LSU campus, mostly occupied by married or international students. A long narrow hallway and even longer, more narrow inside stairway led up to a landing that had just enough room for one of us. Lighting was poor. Raised voices and the thump of furniture—or a body—against walls came from the apartment.

"This feels bad," Sarah said.

"Yep."

I stood on the edge of the landing and knocked on the door, hard, said "POLICE" in a loud voice, deep from the belly. Sarah stood a few steps down. Our hands rested on the butt of our guns, the leather guard strap unsnapped. I was acutely aware that I had nowhere to go, had no available cover.

The door opened about seven inches and a white male in his late twenties, over six feet tall and well built, stared at me without expression. I could see only one hand, and it was empty. His dirty-blond hair was shoulder-length, his eyes flat. Behind him, against the far wall, a woman with long, black hair paced back and forth. Her face was puffy and bleeding, her expression crimped with fear.

I don't remember what I said to him. What I always said, I suppose: We got a call, neighbors are concerned, can we come in and talk, we're just here to help.

His face didn't even twitch. He just looked at me with those eyes, his inner eyebrows raised slightly, and my dread deepened.

"Could you step away from the door, sir. Let me see your hands."

No response.

I was vaguely aware of Sarah speaking into the portable radio, asking for backup in a low but urgent whisper. I wasn't sure how we'd all fit or where, but more officers seemed like a good idea.

I continued to talk, using a soothing but firm tone, words cascading out of my mouth, anything to keep him focused on me, anything to get through and resolve this without force, without injury. I kept one hand, my left hand, out in front of me moving slightly. I wanted him to stay focused on my hand, its reassuring movement. Whatever I said was my usual family fight spiel: people sometimes have problems, we're here to help, let us in the apartment so we can help sort this out, I'm sure this can be settled. Is your wife all right? Are you all right? Are there any weapons in the house?

With my last question, the wife halted behind her husband and nodded vigorously.

Dread turned to icy fear.

And then it turned to near panic as Sarah backed down the stairs. *Where the fuck is she going? Can't she see this is about to go way wrong real quick?*

But I kept talking, kept my eyes on his eyes, on the muscles in his face, on the one hand in sight, on the lines of his body, looking for any sign he was about to move, that the hand I couldn't see might be holding a weapon. I didn't draw my own weapon, not yet; I didn't want to give him a reason to escalate.

Briefly, I thought about leaving, about joining Sarah down-stairs—*where the FUCK is she?*—regrouping with backup and trying again. But returning here a second time could be uglier, more danger-ous. He might hurt his wife, or worse, in the intervening time. He'd be ready for us, and those eyes had already told me he was debating whether he should attack.

Attack with what, was the question. If he had a gun in that other hand hidden by the door, I had little chance. Bullets clear doors with ease. For all I knew, one was already pointed at my chest. Despite my bulletproof vest, I worried about a head shot, a leg shot, a shoulder shot, about clearing my own gun from the holster and not falling back down the stairs in the process.

If he had a knife, I had a chance, although I hate knives. He'd have to open the door farther to come at me. If I didn't fall, if panic and fear didn't override clearheaded reaction, I could draw my gun and shoot him before he reached me.

If. If. If.

I kept talking. He kept staring. His wife continued crying and pacing behind him.

Suddenly Sarah was beside me again, her gun drawn, held down the length of her leg so he couldn't see it. "Portable was breaking up, but backup's on the way," she whispered. I nodded.

"Sir," I said, "there are other officers coming and I'd like to settle this quietly, as I'm sure you would. We aren't here to cause any prob-lems. Now, step away from the door and let us in."

He and I stared at each other until something shifted in his eyes, a barely perceptible flicker of minute muscle movements rippled over his face, his lips compressed slightly. Sarah's gun came up as my own hand tightened on the butt of my gun, pulling it up out of the holster, my knees bent. He took one step back, flung the door open.

I rushed in, fists clenched and arms perpendicular to my body, as though I were a fullback moving in for a tackle, which was exactly my intent. I hit him full force against the chest, Sarah behind me, one hand hard against my back, and I drove him clear across the room and up against the wall. I never said a word, and neither did he. He was strong, and it took all our combined strength to get him flipped around, spread-eagle against the wall. As our backup arrived, three officers pounding up the metal stairs, I yanked the automatic out of his jeans where he'd placed it against the small of his back. Loaded. Safety off.

To this day I remember the look in his eyes. I've seen that look only a handful of times in my career, and each time I've survived. Somehow. Sometimes I see that look in my dreams and wake, the dread just as fresh as that moment on the landing outside his door. Why he didn't shoot is a mystery. But then so much of what happens to us—or doesn't—on the job is a mystery.

And luck.

Here's another story I tell the rookies: Four o'clock one morning, in the poorer, more industrial north section of town, four of us went 10-7 with a silent burglar alarm on a big warehouse off Acadian Thruway, an alarm that went off frequently and was always false. Joe, Beth, Jerry, and me. No security lighting, interior or exterior. The area was black; the humidity enhanced the velvety feel of the night.

As we were getting out of our units, laughing softly—we'd been handling calls all night together and were feeling good—something made me focus on a dimple in the texture of the darkness of the cavernous entrance.

You don't look directly at objects in the dark. For one thing, staring too hard produces imaginary spots of movement. To locate and evaluate danger you can't look at it. As I shifted my eyes slightly right, the shotgun pointed at my chest came into full focus. Or at least full enough focus for me to rack one into my own shotgun and yell at the others. There was a tangled rush for cover, and the anonymous gunman fled around the corner, disappeared, blending back into the blanket of night. We were left with thundering heartbeats in our throats and the exquisite, painful rush of adrenaline.

It was the slight clink of metal that registered as wrong, as an alert. Whether it was the burglar's keys or gun whispering against the side of the building, or belt buckle meeting the button on his sleeve, we never knew because we never caught him. But we did find the loaded shotgun in a lot behind the building.

It's one of those calls we still talk about. Small and insignificant in proportion to so many other, more serious calls, yet huge because in that moment, we were acutely aware of luck's hand brushing past our faces, aware of the gift of our lives handed back to us—intact, breathing—simply because I heard a sound and the gunman chose not to shoot.

Like sight and touch, I tell the rookies, hearing is also essential to survival. Sound is often our first clue of something gone wrong. It is an undeveloped attribute, and though I had been a ferocious listener as a child, trying to discern the patterns in my parents' voices, Johnny taught me to listen below and beyond the obvious. I developed headaches from the strain of intently looking and listening, trying to peel back layers of the air. Sound—whether the tone of voice, the whisper of metal against metal, the squeal of tires, or even the absence of sound itself—reveals so many secrets.

My sense of hearing has become so acute that I can differentiate among sirens. Fire department, rescue van, Emergency Medical Service, Acadian Ambulance, Gilberts Ambulance, police unit: each has a slightly different tone. Ambulances have a lower whooping sound; fire trucks a slight bellow; EMS has a sharp *dee-doo-dee-doo*, which stops and starts as they usually punch the siren button only at intersections. Police cars howl.

Those screaming-banshee sirens. Inside my police unit, the siren blaring, filling every pore, I am the siren—*Get out of the way, help is coming, gonna get you, hurry, hurry, hurry.*

Even now, I stop momentarily when I hear a siren to catalogue the source. Johnny teases me about it, but, like Pavlov's dog, I just respond at some chemical level. And if it's a police car, I imagine myself there beside the unknown officer: *Careful,* I always think; *please be careful.*

Before I cut each rookie loose to ride on his or her own, I tell the story of my shooting, about Jeffery Lewis Moore. Just the facts, nothing more. It is quiet in our patrol car after I finish talking. For a long time. They don't ask questions.

Idle chatter and random, silly questions at some choir practice out on the Mississippi River levee one night with Johnny and Joe and a bunch of other off-duty cops: "What is *the* sound of your childhood?" The proverbial brick wall appears. No answer, no sound.

I want a sound. Johnny's is the idle of his pa-pa's bass-boat engine; Joe's is the burps of his family after a meal. Beth Sanderson says hers is the sound of the screen door slamming on the back kitchen door; her daddy was always threatening to run off with another woman. One by one they relate sound stories, guffaw over the funny ones, clink beer bottles over the sad ones.

But I can't hear anything.

Frustrated, I search and search through sounds, trying to detect which one defines my childhood, as though with this sound I will understand the cop I've become, the child I once was.

"Ah Katie, don't scowl and mess up that pretty little face," Joe says. Joe Boudreaux is Johnny's best friend. He secretly has a crush on me, though it's not all that secret. "It's no big deal, girl. Give me a smile."

And so I smile, but I direct it at Johnny and he smiles back, all those wrinkles that I love to touch running like precious fault lines across his face, and we kiss, and the others hoot, and for a while, I forget about searching for my sound.

But it's there, the question, in the back of my head, and I keep listening.

In the spring and fall, windows and doors to the houses on the cul-de-sac where we lived outside Boston were thrown wide open. Our short lollipop of a street was filled with children playing hard: olly olly oxen free, kick the can, murder ball, sardines.

Intertwined with our sounds of play was music—a piano being played passionately, furiously. Mrs. Long, Mary and Emma's mother, was a part-time piano teacher and frustrated concert pianist.

Beethoven and Chopin would storm over our heads, and I often pictured the keyboard cracking with the next chord under her large, freckled hands.

I admired yet feared her passion and control of the keys. I was grateful I took my lessons from Mrs. Carruthers next door. Mrs. Carruthers had a Chihuahua named Prissy that nipped at your heels if you moved too suddenly or too fast. Prissy was the only obvious danger in the Carruthers household. Not so the Longs'. Noises other than sonatas and études came far more frequently from their house. On late-summer evenings and early-spring mornings, screaming and the sound of flesh hitting flesh would drift across and around the circle.

"Don't listen and don't mention it," Emma told me.

It was hard to avoid, hard not to think about my best friends being beaten and slapped by their parents. I had seen this abuse in person, seen them dragged by their hair, thrown against walls, backhanded repeatedly, so in some ways the sounds were worse played through my imagination.

But I didn't mention it. I didn't stop and stare at the house. None of us did. Not the adults, not the children.

Still, screaming isn't the sound of my childhood, though it is part of the answer as to why I chose police work.

Another sound: My brother beating his head against his pillow. Lifting and dropping his head over and over again while a low-pitched O sound comes from the back of his throat. This is a strong, fierce memory that even now binds me to him. Almost every night for four or five years I drifted off to sleep with the sound of my brother inches away on the other side of the wall, pounding, pounding, pounding.

Some nights I joined him, dropping my head down, submitting to that blissful, seductive state, that quiet, painless oblivion, as our voices rose and wove. Some nights we talked, lying head to head with only the wall between us, saying each other's name every five minutes or so. In the den below us, our parents talked in indistinct murmurs, out of reach, indecipherable.

Yet this is not the sound either, although Johnny tells me I hum sometimes in my sleep.

Finally I have come to recognize one sound as emblematic of my childhood. And it is a sound that cannot be disconnected from touch or smell or sight. I am standing barefoot in my room on the second floor, tucked in the back of the house I grew up in. Books are scattered about. Daylight: sun rushes in through the windows, patterns of light two-step across the hazelnut rug, dust motes float lazily, the sweet smell of grass and earth cocoons me.

There is no sound, for the sound is the absence of sound. A deep, waiting silence. Everyone is outside, somewhere else. Perhaps my mother is in the garden, standing near the wisteria or picking cucumbers under the living Christmas tree we planted when I was seven; my father is raking leaves in his khaki pants and white V-necked T-shirt; my brother is not yet born, or he's in my mother's womb waiting for the world, or perhaps he has arrived and toddles near my father, mimicking the sweep of the rake through the summer, winter, fall, spring leaves.

Everything pauses in the quiet. It is the last heartbeat before death; it is the next heartbeat of life. I am in the house all by myself. I am alone. Waiting. Waiting on the edge of my life, and it's as though the whole world holds its breath on the lip of the canyon of the universe. Anything is possible, and the child, the cop, the woman come together in this memory. And the feeling is power.

KATHERINE'S ELEGY

We heard about Katherine long before we ever saw her. Every cadet who attended the Baton Rouge Police Training Academy learned about Johnny Cippoine and his widow, Katherine, sooner or later. Officers who visited our academy class in the former city court building off North Boulevard all mentioned, at some point, the story of how Johnny Cippoine had died, tragically, three years earlier. Although it's been twenty years now since we graduated, they're probably still telling the story.

We heard lots of stories about a lot of cops, but this one was different. Each officer relayed the event in the same manner: briefly and with a clipped, matter-of-fact tone, yet with a touch of lingering regret, the way one might refer to an old lover let slip away. At least that's the way it seemed to us. Such emotion was rare, still is, and this made Johnny and Katherine even more intriguing.

So when Johnny Cippoine's name was evoked, we all paid attention a little closer. It's a simple story, really, told to illustrate how even a good cop can get killed. But Katherine's part in it made the story compelling.

Johnny Cippoine had been a seventeen-year veteran known for his strict adherence to procedure, superb instincts, and passion for bass fishing. His wife, Katherine, was much younger and worked uniform out of what was called Highland Precinct in those days. They'd been married five years, two years after she joined the force. That's a good love story, how Johnny and Katherine met, but we didn't hear about it until much later, when it was unsettling instead of satisfying.

The day Johnny died, he and Katherine were about to meet for lunch. Johnny stopped two teenagers in a neighborhood off Monterrey that had been plagued recently with a rash of daytime break-ins. He did it all by the book, Johnny did; he was never one to take unnecessary risks.

He put those two teenagers on the ground right away, patted the first one down, found a gun, secured it, called for backup, then moved to pat the second teen down.

It was cool that day, early in December, with probably the first hint of winter in the air and the crape myrtles finally dropping their leaves. Katherine had just pulled into the Shoney's parking lot nine blocks away when she heard Johnny go 10-7 with two white males loitering in a driveway. She drove over to back him up, something we had drilled into our heads like a mantra: If you're available, always back up the closest unit out on call, no matter how small or insignificant the call appears to be.

When Katherine and another unit arrived on the scene only seconds after Johnny's call for backup, two white males were running up the street, away from Johnny sprawled out on the ground beside his unit.

"Officer down," Katherine barked into her radio mike. "Ambulance 10-18."

Witnesses said later that when Johnny moved to pat the second kid down, the first one pulled out another gun, one buried deep in his groin that Johnny had missed, and shot him three times, real quick: twice in the chest, neither of which penetrated his bulletproof vest but was enough to put him on the ground; it was the third shot that did it, point-blank in the head.

This all happened in less than a minute.

Many of the officers who told us the tale would snap their fingers at this point in the story. "It can happen like that," they'd say. "Boom, you're dead. Reflexes. You've got to react before the act," and they'd snap their fingers again. "Think like the perps. Suspect everyone."

And we would nod, all of us cadets, visualizing the scene, already thinking that we would never ever let our guard slip the way Johnny had.

According to the story—and everyone told it the same way, memorized as carefully and faithfully as the Miranda warning—Katherine ran to Johnny, checked for a pulse, removed his sunglasses, kissed his face (some said his eyes, some said his cheek, but they all mentioned she had his blood on her when she arrived at the hospital later), then took off running in the direction of the two suspects.

"Don't move him," she yelled.

Even as the ambulance was taking Johnny to the hospital, Katherine was searching the neighborhood alongside fellow officers, looking for the two white males, questioning residents, peering in sheds and under houses, climbing down into the concrete drainage ditch three blocks over.

"They're here," she kept telling the others. "They can't have gone far."

But, as the academy staff continually reminded us, you've got to think like a criminal and remember fear can make feet fly and desperation can create cunning just as easily as stupidity and blunders. The officers were angry, a savage anger provoked by their own sudden awareness of vulnerability and mortality. Units gunned down streets, tires squealed, brakes screeched: by God, they'd flush out the sonsofbitches who'd dared shoot one of their own.

We thrilled to the adrenaline that surged inside us with this story, felt the fury in our blood, our bodies tense and breathless from imagining ourselves there on the streets, looking. And we hated at that moment, more than ever, being confined to the white, overly bright classroom.

And Katherine, we knew, was thinking of Johnny even as she was doing her job; of course she must have been frantic, though she didn't show it. But she was right: those boys hadn't gone far, at least one of them hadn't. She and another officer found him hiding in a drainpipe nearly a half-mile from the scene.

"And let me tell you, she was PROFESSIONAL about it," the

academy staff told us. She handcuffed the boy—he was only fifteen—while the other officer read him his rights. She even protected the boy's head, one hand pushing down on his crown, as she put him in the back of a unit.

"She did what had to be done, and she did it right," the training officers said. Of course she did, we thought, it was in her nature. You could tell just from the way she'd reacted when she saw Johnny on the ground.

But the other suspect eluded capture. Finally, after more than an hour, with Johnny's blood turning black on the cement, the Crime Scene officers collecting samples and combing the ground for evidence, the Homicide detectives beginning a house-by-house investigation, and every officer not on the scene calling every CI they had a number on (and those who had neglected the nurturing of confidential informants beginning their own aggressive shakedown on every corner within a five-mile radius), Katherine's captain physically placed her in his unit and drove her to Earl K. Long Charity Hospital.

Yes, we thought. Of course it would be Earl K. We already knew that Earl K, the dilapidated hulk out on Airline Highway that passed for a hospital, was the place to go if you were shot or stabbed. They'd wheel your gurney in right past the fifty or so drunks and drug addicts, scumbags, poor white trash, bafus, prostitutes, and low-down good-for-nothings who'd been waiting, some of them, over five hours to see a nurse, and the best doctors in the business—the ones without name tags or fancy surgical garb who treated more stab and gunshot wounds in a week than the Lake or BRG treated in six months—would save your ass.

Katherine sat beside Johnny for nearly two days, watching his brain swell larger and larger from the bullet lodged inside until two faint pencil lines were all that remained of his eyes, and his nose sank as the flesh around his face bloomed with fluid. She listened to the slow *blip blip* of the heart monitor and watched the downward path of numbers that signified brain activity. When the numbers hit the thirties, she had them disconnect the air tube and the IVs and held his hand until he stopped breathing.

Whoever was telling the story would pause for a moment, and for the first time not make eye contact, but would look out over the class, above our heads, to some spot on the far wall and pronounce softly yet emphatically, the words varying slightly, but the judgment the same:

Strong woman.

Damn fine officer.

One tough lady.

Handled it like a man.

Never broke, not once.

Did the uniform proud.

Oh, we could all see her, tall and straight in her charcoal gray and black uniform at the funeral, brass polished, the black band over the badge perfectly centered, her shoes buffed to such a shine you could see your reflection in them. Hat pulled firmly down on her head, the brim just even with her eyebrows. She would have worn dark glasses, and everything about her would have screamed restraint and professionalism. Perhaps tears fell, but quietly, without any distortion to her features. And she would have saluted her husband at the casket, not kissed him, her wrist snap as sharp and accurate as any honor guard.

And every one of us males in that class, just like the academy classes before and after ours, fell a little in love with Katherine, and every female wanted to be just like her.

We itched, how we itched to hit the streets and show what we were made of.

Richard Marcus was born to be a cop, we could all see that right off, which is why we made him our academy class captain. He wasn't very tall, maybe 5' 9" or so; some might even call him stocky, but his build was compact and muscular. He'd grown up in one of the Carolinas and had the drawl particular to that area. His fingernails were always trimmed and clean, his cadet khakis pressed, his strawberry-blond hair razor-shaved. He was top of our class in all areas: academic, out on the pistol range, the physical agility tests—he made it to the top of the rope and touched the gym rafter first, the only one who didn't even grimace initially when Sergeant Jackson walked across our stomachs as we did leg lifts. He had a peculiar combination of relaxation and intensity about him that was engaging yet kept you at a distance. He and his fiancée, Ellen, who was just as clean-cut and sweet as you'd expect, didn't drink at our after-hours parties, kept themselves slightly apart as though theirs was a world no other could truly enter. But no one held this against them; it was just the way they were, and we envied them their calm assuredness, the steady glances they gave us, the way they moved on the dance floor as though they belonged there.

And Richard was a kind man, still is even today from all we can tell, those of us left on the force.

Back then, the academy lasted twenty-three weeks, and just over halfway through, our thirteenth week, we went out on the streets before returning to another ten weeks in the classroom. That's all changed now. No thirteenth week patrol—you get assigned to an FTO, field training officer, when you graduate and spend four months under careful supervision by someone who's learned how to train new officers. But in the early 1980s, they threw us to any cop with at least three years' service who was willing to ride with a raw, eager cadet without a gun—or they'd put you with whomever the Sergeant or Lieutenant was pissed at that week. Some of us ended up with old farts who'd never passed the sergeant's test and were just working out their time in between stops at relatives' houses and coffee shops. But most of us ended up with the hot dogs, the cops who liked to shake things up and believed that the more trouble you were in, the better you were doing your job.

Richard was assigned along with five of us other guys to what cops called the dog shift, 11:00 P.M. to 7:00 A.M., out at the old Winbourne Precinct, the high-crime, high-poverty area of town. We were nervous that first night, coming into roll call, and it's only now, years later, that we know how obvious our nervousness really was. We stood out: shoes too spit-shined, hair too neat and short, faces too blank and smooth, gestures too jerky. Most of us had spent a good two hours getting ready: polishing our name plates, PD pins, and belt buckles with Brasso; rubbing saddlesoap into our shoes; clipping all the loose threads—Sergeant Jackson called them ropes, and if he found one during academy roll call, it was worth at least ten push-ups.

The first few minutes in the precinct are still a blur: crammed with uniforms, sweaty bodies, shotguns being checked out, portable radios being tested and clipped to gun belts, telephones ringing, radios chattering, keys rattling, loud voices and laughter, shoving and jostling, swearing and stories, men and women who knew what they were doing and looked like they belonged in the three small beige tile rooms that made up the bulk of the precinct.

We hung back against a wall, awkward in our uneasiness, wanting to fit in, knowing we didn't, unsure what to do with our hands as roll call started. Only Richard seemed certain of himself, leaning up against the wall, his arms folded, an alert, watchful look on his face.

Roll call hasn't changed much over the years: a short lecture by the Lieutenant about errors in report writing or signing out subpoenas, hot spots of illegal activity, BOLOs—be on the lookout fors— and just basic riding-your-ass reminders like wear your hat, keep incidental chatter on the radio down, stay in your zone. Depending on the lieutenant, roll call is either straightforward boring, or a mixture of joshing, fingerpointing, and veiled threats. Then the squad sergeants throw in their two cents, and units are assigned to their designated zone and told to get out there and go 10-8, in service.

Despite our jitters and the parade of faces and information, we all agreed later that two people stood out from the moment we entered the precinct: a big linebacker of a coonass with a broken front tooth and a kettledrum voice, and a tall slender woman with dark hair done up in a tight French braid, thick eyebrows, and makeup so artfully applied that her uniform was a jarring contrast.

One of us, Mark Denux, was assigned to ride with the linebacker coonass, a Vietnam vet named Joe Boudreaux. And one of us, Richard Marcus, was assigned to ride with the tall woman.

It took a minute for the name to register. "Marcus, you'll ride with Cippoine," the Sergeant said, and both Richard and the woman nodded.

It wasn't until she came toward us, a shotgun propped against one shoulder, and we saw her nameplate—K CIPPOINE—that we truly believed that this was the Katherine, Johnny's Katherine, our Katherine.

Perhaps we imagined the flush on Richard's cheeks, the quick downward glance as Katherine approached. But not the crack in his voice.

"Got a name besides Marcus?" Katherine asked. Her voice was huskier, more coarse than we'd expected.

"Richard, ma'am. Richard Marcus." The words sputtered out soft, his drawl deeper than normal. He no longer leaned against the wall.

Her face twitched, and she smiled, a megawatt smile. "Oh shit, please, no ma'ams. You'll make me feel ancient. Katherine is fine."

Richard nodded.

"Well," she said. "Come along, Richard Marcus."

And then we heard no more between them as we each met our assigned partner and scattered out onto the back lot, listening to the various instructions as to how we were expected to behave ("follow my lead," "let me do the talking on calls," and "don't get in the way," were the most consistent admonitions). But not before one of us overheard Beth Sanderson, an older woman with short bleached hair and sunblasted skin, mutter, "There goes her latest," as Richard and Katherine passed in the hallway, a comment that carried little weight until much later.

We envied Richard. But we were also relieved. The next week would be a test of our character, a measure of our suitability as police officers. How could you stay inside your own skin if you were assigned to ride with a living legend?

Not well, as it turned out. Not even for someone like Richard Marcus.

These days most of us veteran officers, the ones who've been on the force fifteen years or more, bemoan the lack of camaraderie and closeness on the squads that compose a shift. "Everybody's out for himself," we say with a shrug. "Not like the old days when you could count on cops covering your ass." Some argue that eliminating two-person units contributed to fewer enduring partnerships and shift choir practices, two essential elements for any good squad. Others claim the move to straight shifts from rotating shifts created competition and hierarchy. But the truth is, there have always been close-knit shifts and shifts that never jelled.

The shift the six of us were assigned to was unusually close; most of the officers had worked together for over a year, an anomaly back then as officers seemed to be transferred regularly for no good reason other than the whim of the Uniform Patrol Commander.

So we frequently saw Richard and Katherine those first few nights: on calls as backup, at coffee shops and convenience stores, in deserted parking lots around 4:00 or 5:00 A.M. when officers met to joke, exchange information, stay awake.

It quickly became evident that Joe Boudreaux and Katherine Cippoine were the driving force on the shift. While Joe was loud, blustery, opinionated, and physical, Katherine was steady, contained, mostly quiet except on calls when she seemed to fill up the room. Despite the unexpected obscenities that frequently escaped her lips and the coarseness of her voice, which indicated a childhood lived in some East Coast town, we relished the occasional real smile that transformed her from simply lovely to stunning.

We didn't mingle much with the officers at first, spoke only when spoken to. We listened and we watched. And we talked among ourselves, standing off to one side to compare notes about the calls we'd worked, the partner we'd been assigned.

"What's she like?" Denux asked Richard. Denux was short, skinny, and nearly bald, but he'd flipped all of us with ease during takedown training at the academy. Richard was closer to him than anyone else in our class; they often ran neck and neck on the firing range and during PT, and both seemed to enjoy the good-natured competition.

"Good," Richard said.

"Yeah?"

"Tough. Professional. She pushes hard. Like a drill sergeant."

"She given you any push-ups yet, buddy?" This from Hawkins, a scraggly fellow with a huge Adam's apple who was generally considered the academy washout. We all looked at him, incredulous.

Richard pushed his hands into his pockets and looked down at the ground. "Every moment's a test. 'Where are we now,' she asks me twenty times a night. 'If something happens to me, you need to get backup and you need to know where you are.' Stuff like that."

"Yeah, Boudreaux's doing that to me too. Gets pissed off when I don't get it right," Denux said.

"She doesn't get angry," Richard said. "She doesn't say a word."

"Nothing?"

"Just moves on to something else."

"Like what?"

"How to watch hands and eyes, see in the dark, how to hold a flashlight, how to approach a car, use your hands, the way to talk to people, stand in a room."

Hawkins frowned. "Sanderson's not telling me much of anything, except don't touch the mike and stay in the car. Goddamn dyke, if you ask me."

"That's a bit off base, Hawkins," Richard said.

We all looked over at Beth Sanderson, who was talking to a couple of guys from her squad, and wondered who had the rawer deal: Sanderson for having to ride with such a dipshit or Hawkins for having to ride with a woman who seemed habitually grouchy.

"Hell of a lot more interesting than the academy," Denux said.

Richard nodded. "They both have their place."

We were all silent for a moment.

"She ever mention Johnny?"

"Jesus, Hawkins!"

Richard shook his head, grimaced slightly. "No."

"You gotta admit," Hawkins pressed on, "she is something else."

Richard nodded slowly and changed the subject.

By the third night we felt more relaxed and, through some unspoken invitation, became a part of the semicircle of six or seven units parked in an old run-down high school parking lot off Evangeline Street. It was warm and humid, as most nights are midsummer in Louisiana, and some of the officers had taken off their bulletproof vests, laid them on the hood of their cars beside their portable radios.

It seemed that when cops weren't working calls, they're telling stories. Sanderson was telling about Hawkins leaving his flashlight in the car on a burglary alarm ("You got night vision, boy?" Boudreaux asked.), and pretty soon the officers started telling stories about other officers, mostly the ones who'd done something funny or stupid like Hawkins.

"Remember that rookie Boudreaux had a couple of years back, Jack something or other?"

"Holy shit, that boy was a fuckup from the word go," Joe said. He played a coffee straw around his broken tooth as he talked. "Fresh out of the academy and we're chasing this 42 suspect down Acadian Thruway, and the boy asks me at what point do we load our guns. Shit! When do we load our guns. He's running around with an empty goddamn gun."

We all laughed, shot glances at one another, wondering at poor Jack something or other's stupidity. Hawkins giggled like a girl.

"He didn't last long after that," said a corporal named Akers who looked like an eggplant, both in color and in size, and whose voice faintly resembled Darth Vader's. "What, another couple of months?"

"Didn't make it through probation," Katherine said.

"Should've had you as his training officer," Sanderson said. "You'd have gotten him in line."

"Let it the fuck go, Beth." Boudreaux's tone was cutting, but his body language never changed.

"Fuck you, Joe." Sanderson's fingers curled tightly around the buckle on her gun belt.

"That's a whole lot of goddamn fuckin' going on," Katherine said mildly, looking up at the night sky.

A short burst of air escaped Boudreaux's lips.

"Hawkins." Katherine looked at him, and his whole body lurched forward like a marionette. "Why'd you join?"

"Ma'am?"

"Why did you join the police department?" She spoke slowly, enunciating each syllable.

"Well, ma'am, my granddaddy was a Texas Ranger." He looked everywhere but at Katherine as he spoke.

"Oh sweet Jesus," Akers snorted.

"And he's the one who taught you to call women less than ten years older than you 'ma'am'?"

"Ma'am?" Hawkins squinted at her.

We all laughed, even Katherine. Hawkins smiled hesitantly.

"What about the rest of you boys?" Boudreaux asked. "Why'd you want to become the po-lice?"

Our answers, delivered mostly in a shy, offhanded way, hardly varied: to do some good, to give back to the community, to help people. Richard didn't say a word.

Bemused smiles greeted our answers. The officers cut glances at one another, lifted eyebrows, nudged one another. Only Katherine watched us silently, her fingers playing with a small pearl earring in her left ear.

"Well, that'll get shit out of you within the first couple a months riding the streets," Joe said. He lit a cigarette and pulled hard on it, expelling the smoke in a sharp exhalation. "Doing good and helping people is crap, lemme tell you. All we do out here is answer calls, cover our asses, and try not to get hurt."

"That's about it," Akers said, nodding, the flesh under his chin jiggling slightly.

"And what about you, Richard?" Katherine brushed a stray strand of hair behind her ear, and we caught a faint whiff of perfume, something fragile and sweet.

Richard looked around and smiled. "The adrenaline."

"Now there's an honest answer!" Joe reached over and slapped Richard lightly on the shoulder. "Katie, we've got us a keeper here."

"Could be," Katherine said. "You a fuckin' cowboy, Marcus?" Her enunciation was just as studied as it had been with Hawkins.

"Do I look like a fucking cowboy?" Richard spoke quietly, but his tone was tight.

We all gaped.

"She only wishes," Sanderson muttered.

Katherine inspected the toes of her boots, lifting one up slightly to catch the streetlight. "Beth, you want to start exchanging tales, you better ask yourself what I know."

Joe pitched his cigarette. "Whether or not—"

"I killed a man when I was fourteen," Richard said.

"Well hello," Akers muttered.

The 5:00 A.M. train rattled down Choctaw in the distance. We all looked at Richard.

"Man broke into the house. Just my mom, my little brother, and me. My daddy'd disappeared not long before. Another woman, we figured." Richard looked only at Katherine as he spoke. "He had a knife; I had my daddy's shotgun."

"Well didja now." Boudreaux smoothed a thumb across his mustache, looked Richard up and down. "God bless shotguns. They'll trump a knife any day. Sounds like a clean kill to me."

"It was a mess," Richard said flatly.

"They usually are, boy. But it felt good, didn't it?" Boudreaux grinned at him.

"Headquarters, 1D-84." The dispatcher's voice was impersonal and no-nonsense.

Sanderson scowled, creating even more wrinkles than we thought possible, and pulled the portable radio out of its case and up to her mouth. "1D-84, go ahead."

"Got a signal 45, possible shots fired, Starling and 12th. Code 2."

"10-4; enroute." Sanderson moved toward her unit as she spoke, gesturing sharply at Hawkins to join her.

Boudreaux keyed his mike, moving rapidly toward his unit as well. "1D-79 enroute as backup."

Starling and 12th—still a place that gives a cop pause. Back then there were pockets of danger—the Sip and Bite off Acadian that most cops called the Shoot and Stab; a pool hall off Greenwell Springs; Gus Young and 39th; a trailer park off Harding; individual houses and blocks off Plank Road and North Foster—there are even more spots today. But twenty years ago, Starling and 12th was the pucker-up zone: you didn't go in there without backup, even in daylight.

So no one was surprised when Sanderson called for more backup as she and Hawkins arrived. Even with Boudreaux and Denux behind her, realistically she had only one officer as backup. Denux and Hawkins had no guns and little authority. But then Boudreaux's voice came booming through the radio seconds later, calling for more backup *now*, a note of agitation so unusual that Katherine, already in her unit, flicked a look at Richard and told him to buckle up and hold on as she hit the red lights and siren. Four units followed close behind her.

When a second call for backup came from Boudreaux, most of us were only two minutes away. But two minutes can feel like two hours when you hear someone like Boudreaux shouting, "Signal 63, possible CU, Signal 100." And in the background, behind Boudreaux's words, a ragged mass of voices yelling and cursing.

Signal 63—the call that opens the adrenaline floodgates and shakes any officer's gut. Not just that help is needed immediately, but that bodily injury or worse is imminent. Very few officers abuse this call for help—they don't last long on the streets if they do—and someone like Boudreaux probably uses it only three or four times during his career.

The dispatcher's calm voice came right back, clearing the frequency for emergency traffic only. "Headquarters all units, 10-33. Any units available respond Code 3, Starling and 12th. Possible riot situation, possible sniper situation. This frequency is 10-33."

Starling and 12th is one of those strange intersections where five streets converge and create a weird geometric layout that no doubt some traffic engineer way back when thought was classy, brought a little élan to this then blue-collar, white neighborhood of wooden shotgun houses. It hasn't been white in decades. Blue-collar either. The drug dealers like it because they can flee quickly in any number of directions, if they choose to flee rather than dropping their cache in the weed-choked ditches. The cops like it—if any cop can truly claim he or she likes that intersection—because there's a fairly clear view, a quick snapshot of who's where doing what, no matter which street you approach on.

Three blocks away we could see a crowd converged around the two police units and up in the yard of what must have once been a yellow house but now could only be described as dingy. A crowd of thirty-five to forty people, mostly black, of every age, the number growing by the second. It was not a friendly group.

Boudreaux stood on the steps, a shotgun in one hand, his other hand, palm flat, out behind him. Denux was up on the porch beside Sanderson, who was bleeding heavily from a gash in her cheek, her hand firmly gripping the forearm of an emaciated-looking young man the color of café au lait, who looked both frightened and defiant. Hawkins was nowhere to be seen.

Katherine squealed to a halt just on the edge of the crowd, along with the other units. She slid a shotgun out of the dip between door frame and seat, handed it over to Richard.

"Use it if you need to. You'll know. Stick close and do not—DO NOT—get hurt." And she pulled another shotgun, the department-issued shotgun, off the rack on the wire mesh screen behind her.

What we would learn that night, and in the years to come, is that you get thrown into a situation without understanding all the pieces—like entering a movie already in progress—and all you can rely on is your gut, instinct, experience, and, if you're lucky, the officers around you. And only after it was over could you piece together what exactly had happened and why.

At the time, the next eight minutes were mostly a blur, a series of quick snapshots, impressions, and sensations barely coherent for us cadets.

We pushed out into the crowd, Katherine holding her shotgun perpendicular to her body, saying, "Clear the way, move back, back up" as she walked, her voice devoid of emotion but clear and authoritative even over the angry hive of noise. Richard walked sideways behind her, the top of his head just even with the back of her neck, shotgun pointed somewhere between the night sky and the crowd of people folding back around him. Two officers on each side moved forward parallel to them, cutting a small path that additional officers tried to hold open along with a few of us cadets who also held guns, although not shotguns, that our partners had suddenly slapped into our hands as we arrived on the scene, cautioning us to use them only if our lives were in danger.

Up on the porch, Sanderson was swearing profusely. Denux held a small .38 at his side, his mouth a tense line as he sheltered part of her body with his. He looked out at us with a mixture of glee and alarm.

Boudreaux shouted, "One round fired, not sure from where. Chipped out a piece of the railing and hit Beth."

The eight of us moved into a semicircle on the steps, Richard just one step below Katherine as she leaned into Boudreaux. "The neighbors don't look happy, Joe."

"Perp shot up the house," he said. "Didn't hit anyone. Took a swing at Hawkins."

"We got to get off this porch," Akers growled.

The crowd pressed in, shouting, "Let Clay go, man," and "Damn police fuckin' with people."

"Where's Hawkins?" Katherine said.

"Inside," Sanderson yelled. "Gonna whip his pansy ass."

"You, with me," Akers said, pointing a finger at Richard as he moved past him up the steps.

"I'm with her, sir," Richard said.

"Boy, move your goddamn ass."

"Sir, I'm not leaving my partner." Richard never took his eyes off the crowd as he answered Akers.

"It's okay, Marcus," Katherine said.

"I'm not leaving you."

"Denux," Boudreaux shouted. "In the house with Akers."

Within seconds Akers and Denux returned to the porch, each with a hand on Hawkins, pushing him forward. Hawkins squinted, lifted his elbow away from Denux.

"I'm gonna kill you," Sanderson snapped. "If we get out of here."

"We're moving, now," Boudreaux yelled. "Everyone."

Wood spit up from the side of the house as the sound of a shot cut through the crowd. Everyone ducked. Except Katherine. She racked a round into her shotgun, pointed it in the direction from which the shot seemed to come, and yelled, "GO!" For several seconds she stood alone, upright, like a single reed in a field of flattened grass.

Then Richard stood up, pulled Katherine in front of him and pushed her shoulders down as she stepped off the porch. He fired off a round into the air, cracked that night sky wide open with a KA-BOOM, racked another one into his shotgun, and waved it across the crowd. "MOVE BACK NOW."

"Here we go," Boudreaux shouted, grabbing Richard by the arm, nodding down at him for one brief instant.

We pushed forward slowly, steadily, a tight phalanx with guns drawn, pointing outward, as we crab-stepped toward units, shoving back against sweaty bodies, ignoring spit and worse hitting our faces and uniforms.

And then it was over. More officers arrived as we tumbled into our units, but we shook them off with the universal sign for okay and twirling index fingers, Code 4'd the call, pulled away, and headed to the holding cell at the precinct. Two units remained on side streets to make sure that the crowd dispersed, that they didn't take their anger and frustration out on property or people, hoping to find a possible hint of the sniper's identity.

On the sweaty, jittery ride to the precinct, we were counseled not to mention one goddamn thing about having guns or Richard firing off a round, at least not around supervisors, and *never ever* to the academy training staff.

"Didn't happen, understand," we cadets were told. We understood. Cops would lose their jobs, and we'd be out of a career.

Most of the shift arrived back at the precinct, pumped from the aftereffects of adrenaline, high on the sweet rush of being alive.

"This damn sure calls for a choir practice," Boudreaux said to vigorous nods all around as Sanderson left for downtown booking. Her cheek would require stitches, but only after she'd processed and booked the perp. She left Hawkins behind, and the Lieutenant suggested, none to kindly, that Hawkins go ahead and check out for the night.

And so we attended our first real cop choir practice in a sparsely furnished one-bedroom apartment off Woodward. It's an old practice, still common today. An apartment complex manager makes a deal for extra security and a police presence in exchange for an empty apartment. Usually a cop, and sometimes his family, will live in it, but back then, more often than not, a group of officers, generally on the same squad or shift, used it as a second home—whether during shift as a place to kick back, eat, or use the bathroom, or off shift as a place to sleep during turnarounds or for what's vaguely referred to as "fooling around" and specifically means cheating on one's spouse.

The apartment housed the basic necessities: liquor, sodas, and coffee; a couple of broken-down couches; floor pillows, a boom box, and giant bags of pretzels, chips, and cookies. Toilet paper seemed to be in short supply. Gun belts, shoes and boots, uniform shirts and bulletproof vests were discarded; we walked around in T-shirts, socks, and uniform pants. Beer flowed. The storytelling—and retelling—began. We talked in loud edgy voices, eager to hear what happened to Hawkins (he panicked with the first shot that ricocheted into Sanderson and retreated into the house), to learn more about the perp (he struggled, and his girlfriend ran out into the street screaming that the police were beating him up), to speculate about the sniper (calls would be made to Narcotics to shake down a few confidential informants), to relive Katherine standing on that porch wide open to whoever was taking potshots at the police ("hell of a thing to see") and Richard pulling her down in front of him ("gonna make a hell of a cop").

By the time we popped the tabs on our third or fourth beers, a bunch of us were leaning up against the counters in the alleyway of a kitchen, and the rest crowded around the door.

"You did good, boy," Boudreaux said, slapping Richard on the back hard enough to make beer flip up out of the can he held. Richard grinned, his whole body relaxed in a way we'd never seen. "That was something, you up there waving that damn shotgun around like John fuckin' Wayne."

"Goddamn Rambo, he was," someone said.

"Motherfuckin' Godzilla."

"You're lucky I don't write up your ass for not obeying an order," Akers said in a mock growl. Richard winked, raised his can toward Akers.

"Ah hell, you'd of done the same," Boudreaux said.

"Hell, yes," Akers said.

"You sweet goddamn cowboy," Katherine said, and leaned over and kissed Richard on the cheek.

Richard's face flushed; he tipped an imaginary hat at her without directly meeting her eyes. "Anytime, ma'am."

"Oh freaking Jesus." Katherine laughed, looked at Boudreaux. "They're all out to make me an old woman, Joe."

"Never, Katie," Boudreaux said.

"No ma'am," came from several officers.

We don't know when Richard and Katherine slipped out. One moment they were there with us, sprawled out on the floor, and the next they were gone. No one mentioned it, really, although we cadets talked about it plenty among ourselves in the days to come.

But after they'd gone, on about the eighth rehashing of our adventure earlier that morning, we lingered again over Katherine's moment on the porch.

"That woman," Akers said, a beer balanced on his considerable chest. His tone conveyed both admiration and reservation.

"Wasn't one of her wiser moves," said another officer. "Still, hell of a thing to do."

"That's Katherine," said an older, gray-haired officer.

"No one else like her," Boudreaux said. He sat against a wall, his legs stretched out in front of him.

"Seems she'd know better," Denux muttered, his words slurring slightly.

Boudreaux lifted his index finger and shook it at Denux. "Don't go where you don't understand, boy. She's a damn fine cop."

Separating the truth from myth, the reality from wishful thinking, the facts from the fabricated is a delicate undertaking, sometimes impossible. Over time stories take on their own life as details are discovered and carefully added to the whole or discarded when the evidence doesn't match up; any first-year cop can tell you that after working a few crime scenes. But who's to say which details are the truth? Everyone has his own perspective. What's been blurred and forgotten? What is highlighted and exaggerated?

Perhaps it doesn't matter what the exact truth is, if the skeleton is fact, the emotional core is real.

It took us years to piece together what happened between Richard and Katherine before we came up with what we considered the whole story, or as close to the whole story as we were going to get: snippets of information from Richard, seemingly indifferent questioning of cadets who came after us, observation among those of us who worked the same shifts as Katherine and Richard, casual asides from veteran officers, sifting through the rumors about personal lives that inhabit every precinct.

But the story we pieced together, the one we consider true, is one we keep mostly to ourselves. Even now we protect the story of Katherine, as so many officers have before and after us, smiling when we hear the tale of her and Johnny, knowing there is more but reluctant to share it. Protecting Katherine. Protecting Richard. Mostly, though, protecting ourselves, the selves we were so long ago: eager, optimistic, naïve.

There was another empty apartment in the complex to which Katherine, along with some of the other officers, had keys. She took Richard there, his brain softened by more beer than he was accustomed to. A place, she would have told Richard, where just the two of them could talk in peace and quiet. He carried a six-pack of beer in one hand and his cadet uniform shirt crumpled up in the other. Katherine rested her hand on Richard's shoulder as they walked, hips bumping up against each other on the narrow walkway, her gun belt, bulletproof vest, and uniform shirt slung over the other arm.

And they did talk for a while in low, thoughtful voices, mostly about their childhoods, about other cops, about the call at Starling and 12th. And there was silence as well, a comfortable silence, although Richard felt his heart beat more rapidly each time she leaned in close to him, each time she laughed. And he would have still tasted the aftereffects of the adrenaline rush from earlier, that need to feel again how alive he could be.

At some point she would have reached out a hand, slid it along his cheek and up into the hair above his ear, her fingers gently raking his scalp; then she'd have smiled that liquid smile and pulled his face toward hers, told him, "Don't think, cowboy, just kiss me."

And who among us could have said no, her body pressed up against ours, hands traveling down our back pulling us closer, the sweet intoxication of her tongue deep inside our mouth, the feel of her breasts, her hands fumbling with the buckle, then the snap, then the zipper on our pants, that quick shucking of clothing, the headiness of flesh wedded to flesh, slow and fast and again and again.

Who knows how long they stayed there, talking and kissing and touching, Katherine playing with the hair on his chest, her head resting on his shoulder, his hands stroking the skin on her waist and hip, how very white her skin was under that uniform. And no one knows what he said to Ellen, his fiancée, when he returned to their apartment later that day—or even if he did return.

We do know Richard arrived at the precinct that night looking tired, subdued, his eyes tracking every move Katherine made. She sparkled, laughed loudly and frequently, said, "Come on, cowboy" to him when roll call ended.

"Jesus H. Christ, Katherine," Sanderson said as we walked to the back lot, a large bandage covering the hollow of her cheek. "Keep a lid on it."

"Oh, Beth," Katherine said, her voice light and playful, "go home and kiss your kids." And she handed Richard the keys, brushing up against his shoulder as she told him to do the unit check before they left the lot. He smiled at her, a slow smile both tender and defeated.

Later that night, after another impromptu shift gathering in an abandoned gas station parking lot that Katherine and Richard attended only briefly, Katherine seemed so soft and giddy that Boudreaux told Denux after they left, "She's something when she's happy, isn't she?"

"Even when she's not," Denux said. "Seems a little wired at times."

"That's Katie. Comes and it goes." Boudreaux shrugged. "You won't find a better cop, though. She killed a man once, didn't blink an eye about it. Tough gal. Damn good training officer too. She used to train only rookies, but a couple years back, she started working with cadets." He gave a short laugh, shifted in his seat. "That woman was a cop from day one, even as a cadet. Johnny and I knew."

"Her husband Johnny?"

"Yep, he and I were partners out of Broadmoor. Katie rode with him during thirteenth week when she was in the academy. You didn't know? That's how they met. She was so sweet and so fierce at the same time. She adored him. He trained her when she came out of the academy too. Hell of a cop, Johnny was. Never should have died." Boudreaux flicked his cigarette out the window. "Let that be a lesson to you, boy. It can happen to any of us, no matter how good you are. And he was one of the best."

Denux was tempted to ask more, but he resisted. As he told us later, "It was just all too frigging weird."

The following week we returned to the academy, feeling even more constrained by the classroom after our time on the streets, bursting with the desire to be done with this. The next ten weeks dragged on in some ways—hour after hour in our seats, taking notes, trying to listen, the sky so blue and promising outside the high, small windows. But it also became more intense and focused as our goal grew closer. Richard mingled with us more frequently, despite seeming distracted. He came alone to some of our parties and drank heavily; we didn't ask about his fiancée, Ellen. His grades dropped some, but he pushed himself hard in the gym and out on the firing range. We never mentioned Katherine, although we saw her on occasion, slipping in during lunch to sit with Richard for a few minutes out in the breezeway. The cadets who hadn't been on our shift tended to find excuses to walk down the breezeway past them for a soda or a cigarette. Richard and Katherine always nodded hello, but that was all.

With only three weeks left until graduation, Hawkins washed out as expected, unable to avoid the reality any longer of less-than-passing grades and poor evaluations from his thirteenth-week ride-along. He'd never been particularly impressive on the firing range either. And he truly was a dipshit. Still, we all patted him on the back, said we were sorry to see him go, suggested he try again.

That was around the time Richard turned morose and short-tempered; circles appeared under his eyes, and he often sat blankly during class, staring at the far wall above the instructor's head. Sergeant Jackson gave him twenty push-ups one day at roll call for an unacceptable uniform. Katherine no longer visited at lunchtime.

Who knows at what point she started to withdraw, or when she actually ended it, but we know it was before graduation. We learned over the years that her pattern was consistent: she selected one male from the academy class and always ended it before graduation. She would have let Richard down calmly, matter-of-factly, just before she'd handed him his graduation present, the graduation present she always gave.

"Early, I know," she might have said. "But this is it, cowboy, between you and me, and I want you to have this before I go."

Did he say anything as she took the tiny St. Michael's medallion out of its box, slipped the silver chain around his neck? Or did he just stare at her, stunned and bewildered, his heart skittering hard against bone?

"There," she said, adjusting the medallion on his chest, her fingers lightly brushing his skin. "You know who St. Michael is, don't you? The patron saint of police officers. You don't have to be Catholic. He'll keep you safe if you do the rest." And she reached down and kissed him, a soft lingering kiss, before she stepped back and began to dress.

"Nice while it lasted, cowboy, but it's over and no harm done. Go back to your fiancée. Go be a good cop."

Did Richard plead, cajole? Or was he more stoic, laying out a rational argument? Did he explode in frustration, tell her he loved her, wanted to be with her? Whatever his approach, he would not have accepted her dismissal. He would not have walked away; he would have laid himself even more bare. Of this we are convinced.

And why would her reply to him be any different than the reply she gave all the cadets who came before and after him?

"So you fucked the legend, Marcus. Congratulations. Now let it go."

And so we graduated and hit the streets. It seems long ago. And it was, nearly twenty years now. Over half our original class has left the force—quit, fired, disabled. Two are dead, but not from the job. The rest of us are sergeants, some even lieutenants, working in departments as varied as Homicide, Auto Theft, Criminal Records, the Chief's Office. Some of us still work uniform patrol, but we're supervisors and rarely go out on the streets. Richard's in Planning and Research, down at Headquarters, after a long stint in Armed Robbery. He's married, but not to Ellen, and has two sons.

Katherine died seven years after we graduated. The last the dispatcher heard from her, she was out with a Signal 34, a prowler, on St. Ferdinand Street. It was a busy night, full moon Friday, and when another unit finally arrived ten minutes later to back her up, it was clear she'd put up a fight: slashes and cuts, some of them deep, covered her arms and face and legs; blood gushed from her femoral artery. The perp lay partway on top of her, the barrel of her gun resting against his cheek; Katherine had managed to blow his head off, even as he stabbed her repeatedly, hepped up on PCP. She was barely conscious when the officers got there, whispering something they couldn't understand. They threw her in the backseat of their unit and hauled ass down North Boulevard to the BRG, but her heart had stopped and she'd lost too much blood.

Her funeral was something to see; the line of police cars stretched over a mile on the way to the cemetery; the department bugler played taps. We all saluted her casket.

Her picture is up on the wall at Headquarters when you first walk in, behind a glass case. The Wall of Honor, we call it: all the Baton

Rouge city cops who've died in the line of duty. Far too many of them. After you walk in and out of there day after day, you tend to pass by it without really *seeing* their faces; the wall becomes more of a twitch deep beneath your skin that can't quite be ignored as you turn down the hallway to the evidence room or crime scene division, or wherever your business may take you.

Still, sometimes we do stop and linger, needing to study the too-long parade of faces—good cops we knew like Carl D'Abadie, Chuck Stegall, Warren Broussard, Betty Smothers.

Does Richard occasionally pause here as well, we wonder. Is his eye caught by Katherine's face, more serious and far younger than we ever remember? Does he look at her, and look at Johnny, the two Cippoines up there on the wall? Does he stand here, like we do, and remember when the world seemed good and bright and we were all so alive and full of possibility.

LIZ

"Who speaks for the dead? Nobody.
As a rule, nobody speaks for the dead, unless we do."
—Detective Andy Rosenwieg,

from *A Cold Case* by Philip Gourevitch

LEMME TELL YOU SOMETHING

Mango-colored sawdust spits and floats, filling the air as George cuts deeper into a stubby limb on the massive, twisted mulberry in my front yard. He has refused my offer of a ladder, and so, as he reaches the chainsaw above his head, his navy sweatshirt hikes up to reveal the gentle swell where back becomes buttocks and dives into a dark inverted Y. I grin and look away.

Although he is only fifty-nine, George resembles an eighty-year-old walrus and moves as if his knees are permanently fused. Every morning and every afternoon, he walks his ebony pug past my house in a slow shuffle. I know he has a wife, though I've never seen her. I know he's retired, but from what I can't say for sure.

"Lemme tell you something," he said by way of introduction several weeks after I'd moved into the neighborhood. "I like most cops. You gotta hard job. Most people don't understand, but I do."

I'd thanked him politely, agreeing silently that the job was hard, but not in the way he might expect.

"Nice work you've done here on this house," George had continued, barely stopping to take a wheezy breath. "Most people don't care. They'll let everything go to hell. I can tell, you're not that kind of person." He tucked in his lips, puffed out his cheeks, and nodded, his jowls jiggling, as he took in my newly tilled garden, just washed windows, recently edged grass. I squinted a little at my house, the yard, saw it through his eyes, and relaxed my shoulders, straightened my spine. Yes, I thought, I'm not that kind of person.

I've lived here five months now, and I've learned that George likes to tell people something, sometimes several somethings, each time he sees them.

Like this morning, for instance.

"I'm gonna tell you something, Liz. Now, I'm not telling you what to do, but that mulberry will rot if you don't cut those limbs flush and paint 'em. Simple thing, really. But your business is your business." The last wisps of his hair flip-flopped willy-nilly in the breeze.

I'd nodded, looking at the tree, thinking how Andy would have hated this kind of chore; we'd divorced just before I joined the police department eight months ago. Maybe one of the guys on my shift would lend me a chainsaw, show me how to use it. Or my sister's husband, a man who seemed born to hold a hammer and pound a nail. A chainsaw, a gun: What's the difference? They're both just tools to be mastered. I'd flexed my fingers, imagining the quivering machine clamped between my hands, the crisp, cool cuts I would make, smoothing out the lines of the tree. A task that, when finished, would actually show the effort.

But George had other ideas. Despite my protests, he was back in ten minutes with his chainsaw, his whole body tense with delight.

"At least show me how to do it, George," I'd begged.

He'd brushed off my request. "No need for that," he responded, a smile skittering quick as a mouse across his lips. "My contribution to public service. This'll be done right quick. Won't take but half an hour."

I relent, and he is happy.

As he works, George tells me things. Actually he tells me something for fifteen minutes, then cuts for five minutes, then tells me something else for twenty minutes, and so on. I glance at my watch, stifle a yawn. This is not going to be a right quick job. I have to be on shift in less than two hours.

He tells me about the weed eater stolen from his driveway. "Hell, if they'd of asked, I woulda given it to 'em. But stealing. Sheesh." He shakes his head in disgust. "But I don't have to tell you, Liz, do I?" And he fires up the chainsaw, cuts another limb.

He stares at the ground or the tree as he talks. He tells me about mowing the lawns of three neighborhood widows, relates the deaths of their husbands: heart attack, pancreatic cancer, Alzheimer's. "Fine women, a real shame." About the history of his German chainsaw. "Don't make 'em like this anymore. Never breaks, not like that stuff they sell you these days, lemme tell you. People think they can save money, buy something on the cheap, then it breaks on them six months later. Ha!" About the property he's bought outside Baton Rouge in Greenwell Springs. "Thinkin' of movin' there. Real soon. City living has gone all to hell. Anybody steals from me, I can shoot 'em, no problem."

I don't know whether he's trying to get a rise out of me or whether he really believes this, but I can't let the comment pass. So I keep my tone neutral and mention that I believe shooting somebody is a problem no matter where you live, whether that somebody is stealing from you or not.

His lips fold inward, his jaw juts forward, and he glares at the police unit parked in my driveway before he starts in on another limb high above his head. The inverted Y appears again, a much deeper view. Swear to God, it's all I can do not to giggle. This will be a good story to tell the guys at work.

After the limb thuds to the ground, he turns and looks me straight in the eye. "Lemme tell you something. I killed somebody once. Over in Vietnam, was there three years. I killed Vietcong, yes. But I'm not talking about that." George moves closer, and I smell the rankness of his body. It takes all my willpower not to step back.

"I'm talking about putting a gun upside someone's head and pulling the trigger. An American. Army fellow like me." His cheeks expand like a chipmunk, and he expels a long breath. "Was raping a little Vietcong girl, no more than eleven or twelve. Just a little girl that never did no harm to nobody." His gaze drifts away. "Couldn't abide by that. So I killed him. And lemme tell you, I may have night-mares, but I don't regret it."

George fires up the chainsaw, rises back up on his toes. The blade bites into the limb, sawdust fills the air. This time I don't grin, and I don't look away. I study the wide expanse of his flesh, really study it, the ripples and hollows, the caterpillar trail of hair. I'm startled by the sudden urge to reach out and gently pat his half-bare bottom.

But I don't. I just stand behind him, sawdust floating around us like fireflies, taking it all in: that exposed flesh, the deep crack, our broken secret hearts.

FINDING A PLACE

It's been two years since I left. Some days I miss it so badly, the ache is so deep, that I think I must know what amputees feel like, reaching for that part of themselves no longer there. I miss the laughter, the stories, the camaraderie, the adrenaline.

In the last four months I've finally been able to move my gun from under the pillow to the floor beside my bed. I've passed the point where I stood transfixed in front of my closet, bewildered by choices: Black skirt and halter top? Blue jeans and white linen shirt? Flowered sundress?

"Your face has softened, Liz, really it has," my sister tells me. But I don't see a difference.

I still bark "Hello" into the phone, still stand with feet slightly apart and hands on hips, still get up at least once a night to check a suspicious sound, still habitually distrust just about everyone's motives, still am more aware of what's happening around me than most of the human race. I still have nightmares, and I still wonder about the color of that boy's eyes.

I don't know what to do with the bulletproof vest, the men's black shoes, the brass polish, two sets of handcuffs, nightstick, six-cell flashlight, PR-24, precinct pins, and silver breastplate engraved in block letters L MARCHAND. Or the metal ticket holder, report clipboard, plug-in spotlight, dozens of scribble-filled pocket-sized notebooks recording the details of nine years worth of calls.

I envisioned shedding that life as easy, something I stepped out of into something new. I didn't realize it had permeated my skin, blood, cells, brain chemistry—how irrevocably the work altered my DNA.

People ask me why I left: acquaintances at school, men I'm dating, strangers I meet at cocktail parties. Swear to God, I don't know how to respond. Their expression always throws me, that look they give me and the cane clenched tightly in my hand. Their eyes are so eager. They want dirty, horrific, appalling viewed from a distance; they want a sense of their own mortality made safe.

Usually I shrug the question off, say, "I was in traffic division most of the time, working wrecks and writing tickets. Pretty boring stuff." That often does the trick; they launch into their own story about how some cop wrote them a ticket and "was an asshole" or how they were "only three miles over the speed limit," or they wonder why cops write tickets when there are "real criminals to catch." They ask me for tips on getting out of tickets. "Be nice," I always say, "don't make any sudden moves, don't argue." And I smile inside, a tight little smile, because often the person will turn right around and argue with me, pressing home their case for why the cop was in the wrong and they were in the right. If I'm feeling particularly patient, I might explain that more officers are killed on traffic stops each year than any other type of call, that more officers are killed or injured in car wrecks than from guns or knives.

Sometimes, when someone asks me why I left, I gesture toward my leg and cane, say, "Would you do it, be a cop?" and change the topic.

"You're really defensive," men will say. "You're a very angry woman." They don't ask me out again.

My sister says I need to work on my social skills. "You didn't do anything wrong, Liz. I don't know why you dance around it. Tell them there was an accident, it wasn't your fault, but you'd had enough. It's not a complex question needing a complex answer."

I love my sister. She's a banker with four kids and an endless supply of practical optimism, one of those people who says, "Have a nice day," and means it.

But my accident, the one that landed me in the hospital for six weeks with my leg strung up like a marlin on display, isn't the real answer, just the easy one.

The truth is, I'd already pretty much decided I was leaving before that middle-aged suburban mom out running errands plowed into the side of my patrol car. There were the usual cop burnout reasons: poor pay, lousy equipment, disgruntled civilians, jackass chief, the sheer weariness that comes from doing the job. All a part, but not the whole.

When I ask myself that question, I see gloves, stiff with blood, stuck to the dashboard of my police car; this one particular night, six months before my own accident, plays out in my head every time I search for the moment my heart shifted gears, and I began to leave.

It was the last tour of dogs, midnight to eight shift, on a crisp, cold February night just after Mardi Gras. I'd recently been transferred out of the traffic division into uniform patrol. It had been quiet for the most part—some disturbance calls and family fights, a couple of thefts earlier in the shift. About four in the morning I backed my police unit up against a deserted Exxon station. I was filling out a few reports, kind of dozing, smoking cigarettes, and waiting for daylight to roll around. It's nice at that time of night. You're cocooned in this little world of your own, just the occasional chatter of the radio to break the silence; otherwise, it's peaceful. Kind of holy if you're the religious sort and want to see it that way.

Headlights turned in suddenly, and I tensed, ducked a little, squinting, then the lights were killed and another unit glided in smooth and quiet next to me, driver's side to driver's side. It was Gary, a short, compact man with a skittery laugh and porcupine eyebrows. We sat there, slouched down in our seats, letting the night wrap around us, talking some and silent some, listening to distant voices on the air.

We're sitting there, and pretty soon a couple of other units pull in, and before you know it, most of the shift was in that parking lot. There are only so many places you can hide from supervisors. Even Frank and Larry from K-9 and a couple of guys from ARAB, Armed Robbery and Burglary, were tucked in among us.

We leaned up against our cars, hunched into groups against the cold, talking low and laughing, swapping stories. We complained about the new uniforms, which seemed a pale imitation of those worn by the State Police, and generally agreed that this year's craw-fish season was likely to be lousy. Mona and I debated the hot rumor about the new guns the brass wanted to issue to female officers; they thought the new .357s were too much gun for our hands. We made all the guys hold up their palms so we could compare width and length. Everyone, except Sid and Gary, agreed that our hands were definitely bigger than Sid's and Gary's.

I remember it as being a good night, one of those easy, graceful shifts where there was no tension, no stress. No one pissed off at any-one else. It was a night where it felt good to be a cop, and you knew when you went home that morning, you'd actually sleep, probably not need that shot or two of scotch to get you there. It was one of those nights where we were laughing at ourselves, genuinely liking our job.

Bart was telling about Cookie finding a big toe in the back of his unit, up under the matting. Swear to God, it was just a toe, with lots of hair on it. Long toenail, kind of yellowed. Obviously male. We were offering suggestions about what had happened to the person for-merly attached when the dispatcher called for any unit in the area of the interstate split.

We went quiet and looked at one another. We were only six, seven minutes away; two minutes if it was a Code 3 call. But no one was going to volunteer for anything at that time in the morning.

Dispatcher calls again, says it's a major 52 up on the interstate. Mona looked at me and grinned. "He's gonna ding you, Liz." I shook my head and prayed.

The problem was, at that time of night it's one of two things. Either a drunk with a slightly banged-up car—which meant waiting on a wrecker and then trying to decide whether to run the silly jerk on the PEI to see if he's over the 1.0 limit, which meant too much time involved to get off shift on time (of course, you could just drive the drunk home instead, but the possibility of piss and vomit in the back of your unit was extremely high). Or, it really was a major accident—which meant time at the hospital, relatives to deal with, and too damn many forms to fill out. Either way, no one wanted it. So we waited to see who the dispatcher would nail.

"2D-78," he said. "Can you copy?"

Mona elbowed me, and I sighed, pulled out my portable radio. Each unit is assigned a zone to patrol, and the interstate split was mine.

"2D-78, go ahead."

"I got a one-car, major 52, eastbound, right after the interstate split. Car's supposed to be off the roadway. Advise on ambulance and support units."

I acknowledged, told him I was enroute, and headed toward my patrol car, grumbling disparaging comments about the dispatcher and wrecks in general. Everyone stirred around, moving away from my car, laughing, telling me to give them a call if I needed assistance. Sid said, "Can't escape those traffic calls, Marchand." I gave him the finger. Mona asked if I wanted her to ride on up with me, but I said no, the car was probably abandoned, and I'd be back in a couple of minutes.

I pulled out of the parking lot, tires squealing—mainly for the effect—and flipped on my red lights and siren as I headed for the interstate. Traffic was almost nonexistent, and I made good time: engine racing, pedal floored to the mat, steering wheel vibrating.

As I slowed down coming off the Interstate 12 overpass, I saw the skid marks and debris that marked the path of the lone car, sitting upright but misshapen, ahead of me. The driver had lost control in the turn coming off the ramp and flipped three, maybe four times.

I parked about fifty yards back so my spotlight flooded the area and told the dispatcher I was 10-7 on the scene. I got out of my unit slowly, walking wide and left of the blue Toyota as I approached. I couldn't see anyone in the car, so I alternated between watching the car and scanning the shoulder and nearby woods as I walked up. It was possible the driver had been ejected as the car rolled, but none of the debris so far had looked like a body.

The shattered windshield of the Toyota was flecked with blood and bowed out on the left. Half the hood was caved in and had tangled about itself. It wasn't until I stood even with the driver's side door that I saw him. The halogen lights on the interstate reflected off the bright, shiny surface of his skull. His brain quivered and throbbed between jagged pieces of bone, pumping blood onto his neck and shoulder. Brain fluid seeped through his dark, curly hair. He lay alone, against the driver's door, his legs sprawled out across the bucket seats. Glass shards glittered in his clothing. There was stubble on his cheeks, and his eyelashes were thick and long. He was eighteen, maybe twenty.

I pulled off my glove and reached to feel his pulse.

"2D-78, Headquarters." I used my other hand for the portable radio on my hip. "Major 52 here. One vehicle. Male subject with massive head injuries. Get me EMS, 10-18. Fire department, supervisor, and rescue van—he'll need to be cut out."

The dispatcher acknowledged my transmission. The boy's pulse was weak and broken. But it was a pulse.

I took a deep breath, then spread my hands as wide as possible and grasped the torn fragments of his skull, applying pressure over the bleeding holes and gashes. My bare thumb rested firmly against his brain.

I stiffened my arms and pulled his neck back and upward slightly. Tiny red-flecked bubbles appeared at his mouth with each exhalation. Alcohol permeated the air. I counted four beer bottles strewn about the car. His inspection sticker had expired. The left turn signal beat a steady monody, and on the radio, swear to God, an oldies ballad by Billy Joel who loved us just the way we were.

Time slowed; I became aware of each passing second. The night air was crunchy cold and whipped about us. A vast expanse of deserted interstate stretched out before my eyes as the flashing red lights of my unit bounced off the trees. There was no movement, no life anywhere, except between my hands.

Half leaning into the car, wedged up against the door, I felt my pulse slow to match his. His blood trickled down my arm as I whispered an old lullaby my mother used to sing to soothe my childish fears, to scare away the bogeyman. I watched his face, peaceful and unmarked from the brow down. I wondered what color his eyes were and whose lips had last touched his.

Gradually, a siren's lonely, plaintive keen drifted through the night and surrounded us with its wail. EMS had arrived.

The scene became a hive of activity. Pressure pads were applied, intravenous injections given, neck brace put on. The airway was supported open and oxygen fed in. Blood pressure and vital signs were taken. Radio hookup to the hospital was established. The technicians moved quickly, efficiently, spoke in short, clipped sentences—all their attention, all their skills focused on stabilizing the body before them.

"Keep upward traction. Don't move," they told me.

I hadn't intended on giving up my place. The boy and I still breathed as one, but there was a distance between us now, and I felt the urgency more acutely.

Other officers arrived. Gary walked up, stopped, his eyes widening. Briefly he glanced at me. Then, delicately, we began the task of removing the boy from the car. Extraction tools were needed. An officer wedged the prongs of the Jaws of Life into the door, flipped the switch, and peeled the metal back. Glass popped and shattered as I shielded the boy's head with my own. Two officers eased his legs out while a paramedic supported his back; another held his neck steady. Even as we moved him to the stretcher, my hands remained anchored to the boy's head.

Mass shock trousers—inflatable rubber pants to keep the lower body stabilized and slow any internal bleeding—were put on, then we rolled him to the waiting ambulance like hermit crabs scuttling sideways with precious cargo. Gently we lifted him into the ambulance's waiting embrace. I crouched inside and hollered at Gary to pick me up at the hospital.

I half stood to maintain traction, bracing my hip against the interior wall of the ambulance. A metal safety clip dug into my leg. The driver talked to the hospital via radio; the other paramedic started a second IV. My arms began to ache and burn. The inside of the ambulance was an alternate world—the glow of yellow and red lights played across our faces. I watched the boy's face. We went around a corner, and I locked all my muscles in place, trying to retain my balance. A stream of blood came off the stretcher at the next turn, and I moved my feet, trying to avoid getting it on my pants. The attendants laughed. I smiled. Inside, another part of me withered. A boy was dying, and I didn't want blood on my uniform.

Pulling into Lady of the Lake Hospital, he was still alive. My arms were two long knitting needles of fire; there was a sharp pain in the middle of my back. We moved him quickly into the emergency room. People stood to look as we passed through the lobby. Ahead, in the emergency bay, a doctor was waiting with several trauma nurses; they surrounded us as we came through the glass doors.

Before I could register anything, my hands were empty; a flow of blood pooled up from where I'd held his head and dripped onto the floor. The nurses worked feverishly to stop it.

I stood in a corner and watched; when they cracked open his chest and even more blood collected on the floor, the doctors and nurses shuffling through it so as not to slip, I turned and walked out of the room.

"Fresh coffee, honey, if you want some," called the admissions clerk. We knew each other well from nights such as this, but I shook my head.

Outside, the wind had died down; thin clouds spackled the sky. I watched the attendants hose out the back of the ambulance as I lit a cigarette then stared at the red smears from my glove on the filter. I pitched the cigarette, peeled off my glove, and called Gary on my portable radio.

"I'm done here," I said. "Come get me."

"Can't," he said. "On my way to another 52. Mona's on the scene."

Mona couldn't leave the scene unsecured, and no supervisors were available to pick me up, so I begged a ride back to the scene with the ambulance crew.

"Pretty messed up, that boy, huh?" the driver said.

"Be a blessing if he just died," said the other paramedic.

"No worries there," the driver muttered.

Mona's unit was parked near mine. She was getting ready to leave even as I exited the ambulance, waved my thanks to the driver and his partner.

"You ever notice how all hell breaks loose just before it's time to get off shift?" Mona asked. "Tow truck's on its way."

I nodded and watched her drive off to another call, burglary in progress or something.

I stood there a minute, hands tingling and sore. I checked my watch: just after 6:00 A.M. The sky was starting to blend back into blue in the east.

I turned to the job at hand: measurements to be taken, vehicle to be inventoried, debris to be collected and cataloged. I threw my bloody glove on the dashboard of my unit, removed a plastic bag from the glove box, pulled the flashlight out of the ring on my belt.

I was alone on the roadway; the red lights of my unit reflected off the shattered remains of his car. The lights made a shush . . . click . . . shush . . . click sound as they revolved. I bent to my task. Slowly, I picked up the small pieces of brain and skull along the pitted blacktop.

I thought of that boy a lot as I was lying in the hospital after my own wreck, how peaceful his face had seemed. I replayed his accident as much as I replayed my own, putting myself in his driver's seat, wondering if he too had that moment where he realized there was absolutely nothing he could do to prevent what was about to happen.

But of course I wasn't drunk, it wasn't nighttime, I didn't die. And, as my sister likes to point out, it wasn't my fault.

I was just driving down Capitol Heights Boulevard, headed toward the school zone near Catholic High to write a few parking tickets. I saw the green van ahead, on the street off to the right, perpendicular to me. The van slowed for its stop sign; I had the right of way: no stop sign, no slowing down. But the van lurched forward. Accelerated. That moment before impact, a hesitation of breath. The air thickened, and I was suspended in time. A long glide: one, two, three seconds elongated, stretched like hot-blown glass and became minutes of sailing across the road.

Real time returned with a rush. I smashed my right foot onto the brake pedal, locked my knees and hip as though that would stop me in time, turned the steering wheel hard to the left to deflect the impact. Metal thuds, scrapes and screeches, the downpour of shattering glass. There was a time lapse of sound, as though I heard everything two seconds after it actually happened.

My body was whipped left to right, something sharp entered my knee, my calf, my ankle; then I was whipped to the left again. There were jolts back and forth, until my unit came to a stop in the intersection. Dazed, I lay against the door, head down.

Dimly I reminded, then demanded my muscles to relax. I needed to get on the radio, get units and an ambulance out here; I needed to get out of my car, check on the other driver. After a moment, my hands unclenched the steering wheel. My leg muscles loosened and the pain, the pure white piercing pain rushed in and took my breath away again.

I moved my head slowly to the right and studied a shoe on the floorboard, near the radio console. The sunlight was bright and the shoe, a black Red Wing just like mine, appeared three-dimensional, popping out of a flat background; everything surrounding it was flat. It was bloody, the shoe. I should have been able to smell that blood, it looked so real.

I looked at the leg attached to the shoe. It was familiar, yet not. Someone's leg was twisted around and wet-white bone poked out, a good inch jutting forth, sharp and foreign to the air.

Then everything happened too fast. People talking, running up. "Ambulance," I heard. "I've called the police." "Doesn't look good." And, "Oh God, she's bleeding too."

I couldn't seem to move, my head too big, my arms numb and detached. I whispered to a figure standing near my window, "The other person?"

"Don't you worry," a voice said.

But I insisted, mumbling the question over and over. Finally, the voice told me the other driver was just fine. Later I learned she died on impact, face through the windshield, skin peeled back like the husk off corn. Traffic investigators determined her shoe had been wet, slipped off the brake pedal and punched the accelerator instead.

She wasn't wearing a seat belt. But then neither was I. Neither was that boy out on the interstate. I wonder if it would have made a difference for either of them.

Something about that boy's accident has stuck with me, although I've worked other accidents just as bad. Cops remember most calls they work; I remember every murder, every suicide, every fatality, and it colors everything I do. But you compartmentalize and joke those calls into a tame and distant place. I can't find a place for that boy.

Anyway, enough stories. It happened long ago, in another life.

In this life, I walk with a limp and have blinding, white-pain headaches. The doctors tell me I'll recover fully, some day. My sister says I'm lucky. She says I need to move on, suggested I take classes at the university and get my degree. And so here I am, surrounded by vibrant young men and women; when I meet them in classrooms or walking under the live oaks that dominate the campus, I study their faces and look at the shadings and depths within their eyes. I am glad to be among them, although I have no idea what or who I'll be in this new life.

I try to avoid that stretch of interstate, but it's hard. This is a small city, and when I find myself there, especially at night, I feel him again, warm between my hands. I've been thinking about going out west—maybe Idaho or Colorado. Someplace where the sky embraces you and the hours are slower. I've been reading about firewatchers, people who sit up in these rickety little cabins all summer, high above the rustling trees, searching for signs of smoke. I like the idea of that.

MONA

The truth is rarely pure and never simple.
—Oscar Wilde

UNDER CONTROL

This is what I see the first second into the room: The hands of the three men are empty.

Then: The gun, a blue steel .357 across the room in front of me, there on the floor, lying next to the body. Dispatcher said, Man with a gun; possible shots fired. She was right.

Next: The face of the man near the gun, a quick study of his features—eyebrows, forehead, mouth, cheeks, jaws: muscles, it's all about the muscles in the face—his body language. A threat, but not imminent, not at this particular moment.

Last detail: Blood. Lots of it. Two additional doors, both on the right side of the living room, one in the back corner, one toward the front. A quick glance back over the six hands of the two living and one dead. Yep. Still empty. I check the body's hands last; I've had bodies come back to life and start shooting. But this body is a body. Bet my life.

Finally: Process everything. Old man in a raised hospital-type bed in front of the door in the corner closest to me. A gaunt, withered celery stalk of a man. Oxygen and IV attached. Hasn't moved a muscle except his eyes since I arrived. Mouth open in a perpetual twisted smile. Paralyzed.

Other man, late forties, stands near the body. Blood on his shirt. Upper left side of head caved in—missing?—old injury?—maybe birth defect? Fresh bruises, large welts on his face and neck. Wailing, agitated, early signs of shock. Over and over he chants softly, "Mommy's gonna be mad, so mad, mean mad." He is too damn close to the gun on the floor.

As I sweep the scene again with my eyes, the room twists and blurs; a parallel world slips in and I see my brothers and my father in place of the three men. They are all grinning at me, even the dead brother, I think it's my oldest, he's grinning, too.

What the fuck you think you know, my father yells.

I blink. Quickly. Knowing it will go away, this vision.

There are three strangers, a gun, and too much blood in front of me. I am first on the scene. My father is not here. I am his daughter, empowered to protect the living and keep the peace. Officer in charge.

First, lower potential violence. Defuse. I slide my revolver back into the holster, leaving it unsnapped. I put both hands out, palms down, close to my body. "Move away from the gun. To your left. Move!" I speak firmly but softly.

The man pauses for a moment, frowning and sniffling. Almost as though he's listening to something.

"No!" he screams, throwing his hands out. "Lady, you go away. You go away now."

Four slow steps back into the hall foyer, three-quarters of my body tucked tight behind the door frame. The front door is open behind me. My right hand, fingers spread wide, hovers gently above my holster.

"All right," I say, calmly, cajolingly. I am good at this. It is amusing yet bewildering at times: me, twenty-one years old, and they, decades older, hand over their lives for inspection, correction, solutions.

Too early to tell which way this one will go. My portable radio's breaking up, and there's no chance of anyone just swinging by. Too shorthanded. Everyone's on call already, and most supervisors won't move from the office without a Signal 63. Dispatcher should send backup when she doesn't hear my Code 4.

"Okay, mister. It's all right." I tilt the palm of my gun hand toward him, gently pressing the air between us. If he was kneeling here in front of me, this gesture would be a benediction: thou art forgiven.

He squints his eyes, lower lip thrust out. "Everything's all bad. Go away. No more hurting." His voice is high and breathy, like a child's. He wipes a sleeve against his nose. The lower half of his face is much larger than the upper half. Something about this guy is not all there. More than the stress, the emotion, the killing.

"No one's going to hurt you. I'm here to help." I croon it like a lullaby.

I will help you, I tell my mother, he hits you again.

The man is crying. Tears stream down his puffy chalk-white face. It is cool in here, a weather warp from the ninety-degree day outside. A ceiling fan wisps in lazy circles overhead. The old man's eyes are rolling around and around in their sockets, darting back and forth. The gun is closer now to the living, pacing, crying man's foot.

"I really didn't mean to. He kept coming at me, miss. You saw, Daddy. I couldn't. I had to." He pounds one fist against his chest, the other arm thrown wide.

A father and son—sons? Where's Mom?

Where's Mom? I say to my father. I am ten. He tilts his head toward the hall closet. I unlock the door, sit on the floor beside her, watch the door swing shut, hear the latch turn.

"Okay. We're all right here, now." I speak slowly. "I didn't catch your name. What's your name, sir? I'm Officer Burnnet. Mona Burnnet."

This is the first step: soothe, lull, distract. It's been maybe two minutes. We have all the time in the world. I take off my hat, toss it on the floor behind me. I want the man to see me, not the badge, not the gun.

"Victor. That's my name, miss. My name's Victor Franconi, and this here's my brother. We don't look much alike, I know. Everyone says so."

A hard point to dispute; one of them is dead.

Victor has backed up against a table and is rocking from the waist. He keeps glancing at the gun on the floor. "My only brother, Frankie. Frankie Franconi. I hurt him bad. Yes? I didn't mean to."

"Of course you didn't mean to hurt him. We'll get it straightened out, Victor. But first I need to check on your brother, see if he's still alive."

Victor stops rocking and looks down at the body. "Oh, he's dead, miss." His voice has gone flat; there's a metallic taste to the tone. "Dead as my turtle. Dead, dead, dead. Shot him three times, maybe four. Had to make sure. He wouldn't stop."

His voice rises. "You saw him, Daddy. You saw, I had to stop him, miss."

"I believe you, Victor. You had to defend yourself. It happens. It's going to be all right."

The dad's eyes are still rolling, but they are fixed on me now. I wonder about the twisted, frozen smile—what was he doing when this illness caught up and squashed him? What was so funny?

Suddenly I sense movement. Behind the door blocked by the dad's bed. I watch the door swing inward, seven inches or so. I watch Victor. I watch the door. My hand is sweaty, gripped tight around my gun. I relax the muscles in my legs and prepare to drop back, to my knees, away.

I see eyes, tiny brilliant blue eyes, eyes with depth to them on a doll-sized person, the face framed by a wad of paper white hair. The mother? She watches me, the back of her hand up against her mouth. I shake my head slightly: No, I am telling her, stay put. She nods and turns her hand around to put a finger to her lips.

Victor is pacing again, mumbling to himself, throwing wild-eyed looks my way. What I'd like him to do is throw himself at the dad's feet—beg for mercy, cry, whatever will erase from his mind the possibility of the gun nearby. I could rush him, I could pull my own gun and advance into the room, but I don't want him to go for the gun. I don't want to kill anyone. As is, Victor's thinking too much; there is the potential for choices. Shoot himself? Shoot Dad? Me? There are either one or two bullets left.

The first time my father pulls his gun on my mother I am twelve. My oldest brother tackles him from behind. The gun flies from his hand, slides along the floor, and rests at my feet. My mother yells at my brother not to hurt my father. I kick the gun away.

"Victor," I say. "Victor, think of your father. Let me come check your brother. Step away from your brother, Victor." I begin to ease myself slowly around the door frame and into the room. My hand still caresses the air above my gun.

"My daddy's a devil, miss. He's a mean, ugly, stupid, old man. He'll never die, that's what Frankie said." Bits of spittle burst from Victor's lips as he moves closer to the dad. "You want to know something?" His voice drops to a whisper. "I hate them. I hate both of them."

Your father's a good man, my mother says as I drive her to the hospital. I have just gotten my learner's permit. He just lives harder than some, she tells me. Her nose is broken, and she needs three stitches above her left eye. They have to shave the eyebrow.

I nod at Victor. "Of course you hate them. I understand." It really doesn't matter what I say, what lies I tell. Tone is everything. Tone and presence.

I am overly aware of the mother, of her restrained restlessness behind the partially open door. She is like a high-pitched whine: constant and just loud enough to bug the hell out of me. I swear I hear something like chuckling from behind that door.

"He hurt me," Victor whispers. "They both hurt me all the time."

The body on the floor is large—mostly fat. I can't see the face. Blood has pooled beneath the body and in the low spots of the floor. It has begun to coagulate. The smell of gunpowder has dissipated into the thick, sticky smell of released body fluids. The ceiling fan continues to circle lazily overhead, cutting arcs of air down on us.

"I know," I say. "I'm here now. You don't have to be afraid."

Victor is slumped over, and his face sags like Silly Putty. "So hard," he says. "It's so hard to be good when they hurt you." Victor points his finger at the dad. "He hurt me most of all."

My father has me pinned to the wall, his hand raised, poised to descend again. I am nineteen. My voice is steel: Hit me again and swear to God I'll file charges. He is startled for only a second, then he laughs, pats me on the cheek, and turns away.

I look at the dad, but he is rolling his eyes at the ceiling: pale blue, watery eyes, large but recessed, focused on nothing. The eyes remind me of something, someone. This man can hear though; I know he can hear. Despite the eye rolling, I bet this old man doesn't miss much. Paralyzed, his presence still eats up part of the room.

Again I glance the mother's way, over the bony points of the dad's body. She is sipping something from a flowered teacup. A teacup with a saucer. She has one son dead on the floor and the other trying to decide what to do with a gun. She is very quiet as she drinks.

"You see this?" Victor points at his head, the dented-in place. He moves closer. He looks at the gun, then at me, then back to the gun. I force myself to relax, project nonthreat in my body posture.

"Daddy threw me up against the wall when I was three because I was crying too long. Now I'm not right. Frankie wasn't either. None of us are." He smiles slightly at me, then looks down at the floor. "I did a real bad thing, didn't I?"

"If he hurt you, Victor, if you were threatened, then you have the right to protect yourself."

Victor nods. "That's what Frankie always said."

I sense movement before I hear it and pivot to my left. Victor lets out a startled, "What?"

I quickly turn back. "It's okay, Victor. It's EMS, the ambulance people. They're here to look at Frankie and take care of you."

"Stay back." I speak low, barely moving my mouth to Roger, the med tech standing behind me. Victor is six, maybe seven feet away and can't see him.

"You ain't gonna find me in there, babe." I hear the grin in Roger's voice.

Victor is shaking his head. "I don't know. I don't know."

"Victor, he won't come in until you're ready," I say. "We can talk some more. No rush."

I check my watch: six minutes since I hit the door. "Any other units out there?" I whisper.

"Just you, me, and Harold who's driving, babe," Roger says, much too loudly.

A quick sting of irritation: cut the "babe" shit. "Get him to call

Headquarters and send me a backup. Tell 'em we got one dead already."

"Gotcha." Roger moves quickly away from the door.

"WHAT ARE YOU SAYING ABOUT ME?" Victor yells.

"Nothing, Victor. I just told him to go away, that you didn't want his help." I turn back full face to him, both hands out, a welcoming embrace. Victor is lightly slapping both hands against his face. His eyes are on the gun. For a second, less really, I see a slight resemblance to the creature in the hospital bed.

"I don't want him here. I don't like him. I like you."

"He's left. I told him to wait outside."

The dad has his eyes on me again, and that's when it hits me. Killer's eyes, that's what they remind me of. No feeling, all hate. The mother has ditched the teacup and has her face pressed against the opening in the door, one hand knuckled under her chin. She nods at me as if in encouragement.

"What were you talking about?" Victor's voice is heavy with accusation.

"The ambulance man and I are worried about you, Victor. You need to get ice on those bruises."

He touches his face and winces. "Always hurting me, him and Daddy."

"Yes."

"Too much hurt."

"Well, no one will hurt you now."

"He can." His voice trembles as he nods his head toward the dad. "He can get out of his body. He walks around. It's all a big act, him lying there, you know. Him and Frankie would gang up on me, hurt me. Now it's just him."

I can barely hear Victor's low monotone. I'm getting pinpricks on my neck, blood pumps down to my fingers. I ease my right hand gently, so gently, onto the butt of my gun. This has gone on too long. Where is my backup? Just one more unit to go around back and come in from behind and we can Code 4 this call. Without any more bodies.

"Frankie won't hurt you anymore."

"No. But, miss lady, he can." We both look at the dad, lying there watching us, laughing his timeless laugh.

Aw, hell. I feel it coming. Something in his face alters, a quick ripple under the skin, his eyes shift, and I see him make the decision.

Before Victor has completed his quick, almost graceful step backward and grabbed the gun on the floor, my own gun is out of the holster, barrel pointed at Victor's forehead. I have dropped back to my knees, half hidden by the door frame, which, if I stop to think about it, affords no protection whatsoever.

"Bye-bye, Daddy." Victor has the gun pointed at the dad.

"VICTOR!" I snap his name like a bullwhip.

"Oh, damn," Roger mutters behind me.

Victor looks at me, and the gun swings slightly my way. "I'm not gonna hurt you, miss. You've been nice to me."

"DROP THE GUN. NOW!" I use the command voice they taught us in the academy. Deep from the diaphragm.

"I can't." He has started to cry again. The gun is shaking, wavering somewhere between me and the dad. "I have to stop it."

I tighten my index finger on the trigger. "Victor, this isn't the way. PUT the gun DOWN."

"Ya got backup pulling in now," Roger whispers.

"Tell them round back. Hurry." I only hope the backup isn't some damn John Wayne rookie who doesn't know how to read a scene.

"Victor, we got other people coming now, Victor. They aren't gonna be as patient as me. Come on, Victor."

"I won't hurt you, miss. I promise. Just him."

"VICTOR. NO." Squeezing back on the trigger. Do not make me do this, Victor.

"Victor!" A new voice, tiny, frail. From Dad? No. From behind Dad. Oh God, it's the mother making her debut.

"Mama?" Victor starts to whimper.

"Lady," I yell. "Get back."

The small, white-haired woman, hunched over but solid and mobile, quick-steps daintily out into the room, toward Victor, toward the gun.

"Jesus, lady. Get down. VICTOR, DROP THE DAMN GUN!"

Then my backup, Sergeant Burnnet, my father, rounds the corner through the door at the back of the room, behind and to the right of Victor. He is four or five feet back from Victor, and his gun is drawn, pointing dead on at the back of Victor's head; he braces himself against the far wall. For less than a second I am out of my body, away from this, watching, disbelieving.

"DROP IT, MOTHERFUCKER!" my father bellows.

"Mama?" Victor's eyes are startled moons, his mouth slightly opened.

"WAIT," I yell at my father. He cuts his eyes over at me, then he's steady back on Victor.

With that flick of dismissal, the realization hits me, leaves me breathless, in a vacuum: my father is a perfect burly target over my sights. The anonymous silhouette figure at the end of the firing range with the bull's-eye that wins you the prize, your life, solid three hundred. If I moved my gun slightly to the right I would be smack on, in the middle of his forehead, the yellow-gray curls a frame for the perfect kill zone; just a sixteenth of an inch more pressure on the trigger and I could have Victor and my father. I could have my father. He taught me himself, out at the range, to shoot two rounds at a time. Everyone would understand: of course it was an accident, and what a terrible burden for his daughter; but he was rather close, almost in the way, he should have known better.

He is right there, across from me, and it would take less than a heartbeat.

A noise, like a train whistle with too much air, comes from the dad in the hospital bed.

I jump, gun swinging right onto the other dad then back quick as a finger snap on Victor. My father readjusts his stance, gun still steady, his chin tucked into his shoulder, sighting down his arm. Victor swivels, a sluggish wide arc of both arms, and pulls the gun toward the dad again. The mother crosses in front of my line of fire. I snap the gun up, pointing the barrel toward the ceiling.

"Oh, lady," I moan. I watch my father; he is only half-seconds away from shooting. I have seen that look before.

She marches up to Victor, her neck about even with the gun in his hand. She stands blocking the line of fire between my father and Victor. I'm squeezing back on the trigger, my sights on Victor's chest.

"Victor, you're trying my patience. Gimme that gun 'fore you hurt yourself." The mother holds out her hand, palm up. The other hand holds the saucer from the teacup.

One heartbeat. Two. It's hot in here. Too hot.

"Get the situation under control, Officer." My father's voice is harsh, unforgiving, familiar.

Such a simple decision, really: shoot to kill. I move the gun slightly to the right. I wait for the bullet to leave the chamber. Let the shot surprise you, he'd tell me at the range; steady pressure back on the trigger.

"Victor, listen. Gimme the gun now," the mama shrills.

Victor's hand moves slightly, wobbles; his eyes shift.

BAM! BAM!

The gun kicks tight and familiar in my hand; the fresh smell of burnt gunpowder fills the air, bites my eyes and nostrils. I have pulled the gun up at the last moment, giving my father's life back to him. I want to laugh—this is funny, a weird horrifying funny—but I'm still too stunned. My father's face is blank, his mouth slightly opened. Sweat beads his upper lip. And a tic I have never seen before, there is a rapid tic under my father's left eye. It quivers, the flesh folded beneath his eye. It is the only part of him moving.

Victor sags to the floor, unhurt, leaving the gun in the mother's hand. I am already standing, moving toward her and Victor.

My father looks at me. It is a look I am more accustomed to seeing as a child when I would face myself in the mirror.

"Oh-oh-oh. Bad boy. Bad, bad," Victor whimpers.

The mother turns to me, and I meet brilliant, piercing bird's eyes. I take the gun from her outstretched palm. Her hand is trembling, as is her voice. "It weren't necessary to shoot up my good room, Officer. Victor was coming round to minding me."

I watch my father locate the two bullet holes in the wall, three inches at most above his head. He looks back at me, then at the wall again. He stumbles getting to his feet.

Two officers come skidding around the corner. I holster my gun and nod toward Victor. "Cuff him. Gently. And Code 4 this, will you? My portable's down."

I cross over to the body, Frankie, and check with two fingers for a pulse at the neck. No pulse. "Roger," I holler. "It's safe now."

He sticks his head around the corner, grins, then walks toward the body, his partner behind him.

The adrenaline kick starts to ease, and I feel one knee start shaking rapidly but ever so slightly, not enough for anyone to notice. I expel a deep breath, then turn back to the mother. She stands by the dad. They are both watching me.

"He's dead, ain't he?" she asks.

I nod. "I'm sorry."

"I suppose you gonna take Victor from us, ain't you?"

One officer has cuffed Victor and they lead him past me, out to a unit. Victor doesn't look at me; his eyes are on the ground, his face expressionless.

"He's got to be booked, Mrs. Franconi. But you can get him out tonight if you want. If it was really self-defense, no jury will convict him."

She nods, twisting her head to look up at me.

I take another deep breath, and my anger curls out into the air between us. Anger at her, at the dad, at myself, at my father. I am conscious of my father watching and listening. And the dad; his eyes have stopped rolling. This close to the old man I smell his death, lingering close by, waiting. He is watching me too. They are all watching me.

I see Victor's face again, distorted and panicked, and I am weary.

"Tell me, Mrs. Franconi. Did your husband really throw Victor against the wall when he was a child?"

She hisses air through her teeth. Her eyes snap up at me. "Your question's got no business bein' asked."

"I'd say it was extremely relevant to the matter at hand." I keep my voice tight but soft.

My father walks up behind me, clearing his throat before he speaks. "Mona." His voice is still gruff and imposing, but with something new in it, something I can't identify. "A moment?"

I hesitate, then nod, lifting my index finger up to Mrs. Franconi as I turn to face my father. He still holds his gun loosely at his side.

"That was close," he says.

"Perhaps." My knee no longer quivers.

"I applaud your restraint with a gun." He rocks slightly on his heels. Some color is returning to his face; red blotches ripple over his cheeks and forehead.

He wants me to say I won't try it again; he wants a guarantee, a capitulation. I look at him, the sweat, the blotches, the tic. I meet his eyes, and I let him see it all. I let him see his daughter.

He breaks first. His gaze shifts. "Well—" the gruffness, the newness to his tone still there.

I smile. It spreads into a grin. Unable to stop, I laugh quietly. Reaching out, I barely touch him on the arm.

"You can holster your gun now. I've got it here," I say, then slowly turn my back, take a pen and notepad out of my shirt pocket.

I hear the squeak and whisper of leather. My father's gun slides back into the holster, and the strap snaps closed.

CLEANING YOUR GUN

You are cleaning your gun. It is an ordinary, early spring afternoon, and you should be at work. Protecting the public. Instead you are here in the kitchen, drinking rum from a plastic cup, suspended without pay. It is not unusual to be sitting in this straight-backed chair with your gun on the table—bristle brush, bore rod, and oily rag nearby—listening to the hum of the refrigerator and the uneven drip of the kitchen sink. Except your husband has taken your daughter and left you. You light another cigarette and savor the familiar smell of gun oil and smoke as you admire the shine, the straight cold lines of the gun, the lethality of something so simple.

You walk around for eight, maybe ten hours a day with that gun bumping and rubbing against your hipbone. There is a permanent bruise on the skin; the area stays sore and discolored. Your gun is a natural extension of your body. It was not always this way. At first, you couldn't figure out how to hold your right arm down by your side—the gun got in the way. So you tucked both thumbs into the front of the gun belt and rested your forearm on the gun and holster. But you are told this is dangerous: you are unprepared, you can't draw your gun as quickly. So you try resting your palm on the butt of the gun, but this is awkward, uncomfortable, and threatening to the public. You return to letting your right arm dangle out at an angle over the gun. As you walk, the grip chafes a small, oblong spot on the inside of your forearm the color of grapefruit. This becomes as natural to you as breathing.

You pick up the gun from the kitchen table and let it lie in your hand. The weight is soothing, the gun as familiar as your daughter's face. You pop open the cylinder and check for the third time that it is indeed loaded. Six little lead circles stare back. Push the ejection pin with your thumb and watch the bullets tumble out and roll out across the kitchen table. Stand them up in a neat row, then close the cylinder with a snap—the sound echoes coldly through the empty kitchen. Do this several times: thumb open, flick wrist, snap closed.

It would feel good to scream right now. But you don't. You resist the urge. Like you should have last night.

You raise your eyes. Your daughter's stuffed lion stares back. It sits on a corner of the kitchen counter where you threw it last night, before you hit her. Study the yellow quilted lion with its chewed legs and fraying mane as you begin loading and unloading the gun by touch alone. You have learned many ways to handle this gun. You can break it down and reassemble it with your eyes closed. It is as familiar to you as your husband's hand—every bump and scratch and groove.

Your father was a cop too. He trained you to use and respect a revolver, a shotgun, a rifle. He let you hold his matching pistols with inlaid Mexican silver and promised that one day they would be yours; never mind your brothers, he said, they don't have the discipline. You stood watching him at the pistol range and mimicked his every move.

Look at this gal, he'd tell his buddies, she's a natural.

Just like her old man, they'd throw back in reply.

And you expanded under this strange warmth, wanting it to last forever. When he started drinking, you pulled yourself inward, trying to become invisible as he took on a new smell, one that choked off the usual mix of whiskey, metal, and sweat and became a vague pungent odor, thick and seething.

Your father has a difficult job, your mother would say, usually after he had hit her. She was always slightly out of focus, a blur of cooking, fresh sheets, too-soft hands, a washed-out voice. This is what you knew: she was afraid of loud noises, the night, guns. Sometimes your father. Nothing frightened you more than those occasions when your father said, a slight smile coating the disgust on his tongue, You're just like your mother.

Once, long before he died, your father took you on a hunting trip up in the Texas hill country during dove season, a rare father-daughter trip. You were seventeen and felt warm and safe watching the fire play across his face, the trickle of water over stone nearby. Your mother is a good woman, he said, so softly it might have been your imagination, a man needs someone to quiet the voices. You think of her broken nose, the shaved eyebrow, her black eyes. You want to love him. You want to believe.

Then he shrugged and reached for a beer, throwing you one. Let's see how you handle your liquor, he said, his laugh an echoing clarion noise that opened up the sky and pushed back the night. That evening you sat under stars, drinking beer and cleaning your gun, thinking maybe things would be different from now on.

You move out of your father's house for good when you are nineteen and suggest your mother does the same. She doesn't. Two years later you join the police department; your father pins the badge onto your uniform shirt at graduation. Just like your old man, his buddies say. You can barely meet his gaze. Five years after that he stops a fugitive on a traffic violation and dies from the blast of a double-barreled, sawed-off shotgun. They say he never felt a thing, but in your dreams he lies on the pockmarked cement, conscious of the blood streaming from his chest, unable to act, unable to save himself. The irony of it does not escape you.

Your mother said soon after, Perhaps now you'll quit that job, give up this strange fascination with guns. She buys you a bulletproof vest when your daughter is born. You always wear the vest. You have learned many things from your father.

You are still loading and unloading your gun by touch alone. A cigarette dangles from your lips, burning your eyes. You hold your head at a funny, half-canted angle to avoid the smoke.

You wish your daughter were here right now, as she usually is when you sit cleaning your gun. She would talk: half-formed words, slurred, jumbled baby talk. Her voice would rise in a lilting song— perhaps the alphabet song, or "I'm a Little Teapot." You would sing along with her, if she were here. You would talk about the birds outside the window, and she might begin the "what dis" game. Momma, what dis? And you would answer her: That's a chair, that's the stove, this is my nose, those are your hands, that is Momma's gun. After each item, she would ask over and over, maybe four or five times, What?

If she were here right now for you to hold, to inhale her warm baby-shampoo odor, maybe you would lock up your gun and the two of you would share a bowl of ice cream. You would laugh and giggle, play tickle and tag. And if you had to go to work, if you weren't on a thirty-day suspension for roughing up a prisoner, maybe you would call in sick and spend the time rocking her back and forth. Momma's girl, you would croon, you are Momma's special girl. If she were here, if last night had not happened, perhaps that's what you would be doing now.

Instead, you are cleaning your gun.

You walk a fine line between the reality of yourself and the reality of the streets—back and forth, in and out, a shadow dance along the fringe. You are afraid, terrified at times, a terror that wells up from your soul. Your childhood bogeyman awaits you in the quiet hum of a brilliant summer day or in the freezing rain on a darkened stretch of interstate. You will never know when, where. In the suffocating darkness within a vast warehouse, your gun clenched tightly to your side, your heart racing upward to a dry mouth, your inner voice trembles forth: Momma, I don't like being here. And suddenly, that is where you would give anything to be—in her lap, her hands—dusty with flour—clasping your head tight against her chest, her honeysuckle perfume enveloping you. But only for an instant. The larger part of you always takes over, and you push past the fear, triumphant at having won again.

You do not share these fears with anyone. There is a vague unwritten rule that forbids the discussion of fear and anxiety. You share moments with other cops, but they are moments centered on fighting: swinging nightsticks, high-speed chases, drawn guns. Your common language is one of profanity, technical information, and terse commands. You trust them with your life but not your frailties. Cops aren't supposed to be frail.

You can spend hours with these men and women discussing the peculiarities of other people, but you don't touch upon your own. You have slowly lost your civilian friends. They see only your badge and gun; you are sure they cannot comprehend the brutality of your world. So you draw closer into the circle where other people's pain and secrets are an everyday occurrence to be dealt with. Your own are tucked away.

Silence presses in. You push away from the gun, from the table, stand up slowly, and brace yourself at the kitchen sink, bury your head in a wet dish towel. Over and over you lift cold water to your face, as though the chill will carry up to the brain and freeze forever the events of last night, the last month. You are stopped by your image in the small silver mirror hanging near the door, the mirror your husband bought on your honeymoon in Mexico. Everyone says you favor your mother: the widow's peak, the sharp chin, the dimple in your right cheek. But it is your father's eyes that stare back at you, dark and bloodshot, full of an angry, familiar pain.

Gratitude washes over you. Your daughter has her father's eyes.

*   *   *

You spend ten hours a day, four days a week, working in a world of mostly men. You are their buddy, their partner, their backup. You are your father's daughter.

One day you fall in love. With a cop. With his steady intelligence, his fierce devotion to right and wrong, the long second before he laughs, the taste of his upper lip. His disdain for violence first intrigues, then amuses you. He is a cop, but not a cop. He carries a gun, but his work is in the labs, part of the crime scene division, analyzing violence already committed. His is a safe job, but you would never tell him this.

You aren't sure why he falls in love with you. He smiles when you swagger your female appropriation of macho-male copness. He calls you pet names. And he holds you tight to his chest in the quiet of the bedroom.

As time passes, you laugh at his frown or pretend not to notice his disappointment when you drink too much or talk of bashing heads. He walks out of the room when you snap in anger or scream in frustration. He puts a sign on the kitchen door: LEAVE THY WORK BEHIND. You laugh and attribute it to his sensitivity, something your father would agree with if he were alive.

Your father was the job and nothing more, your husband says.

He was a good cop, you say.

But he wasn't a good man. He wasn't a good husband or father.

But he was a good cop, a damn good cop.

He looks at you, your husband. And that's enough for you?

There is now a single bullet in the chamber, and you are spinning the cylinder round and round with your thumb, popping it back and forth. You palm it closed and open your eyes, wincing when your knuckles hit the edge of the table as you reach for another drink. They are raw from being punched through Sheetrock last night, after he walked out.

Turn your head and bury it in your shoulder—inhale. You are wearing one of his old T-shirts smelling of sweat, gun oil, and baby powder, a hint of the aftershave he wears. The smell cocoons you in his gentleness. He is a gentle man, your husband the cop. Everyone says so.

Put the gun up flat against your cheek. Let the tip of the barrel rest against your nose. Blowing off a piece of your face would not begin to atone for last night. So the question becomes, What would? You think of your father and the way he steadied the rifle on your shoulder, the stock tucked tight against your cheek as you took aim at a target.

With one hand you reach out for the bottle of rum and pour more in the glass. The gun never wavers in your grip, flush against the soft contours of your face.

Last night he said you were dangerous. As he threw you back against the wall, he said you were out of control. Screaming in your face, he told you that you were a lousy mother and a lousy wife and a lousy cop. As he yelled, you watched your child, yours and his, become even more rigid and wild-eyed. Drawing within herself, becoming invisible.

Then he went rigid and quiet too, barely quivering in his anger. My God, he whispered, the words reverberating long after he left, What have you done to us? A muscle fluttered along his jaw as he stared at you. And you stared at your daughter. Then he turned and scooped up your child, yours and his, and walked out. And you don't know where they are. And you don't know if they'll be back.

But she had been chattering so. On and on, weaving in and out between your feet. Questioning this, wanting that, whining, bumping up against you, twirling that lion round and round with arms out-stretched. And you felt like a real lion, pacing in this kitchen, drinking too much, smoking too much. She chattered on and on and pulled and tugged at you, holding on to your legs, weaving in and out, around and about you. Every step you took, there she was, underfoot, wanting something. She wanted to know how come you hadn't gone to work like Daddy and was it true you'd been a bad girl and how come she had to have peas for supper, she'd had those last night, and she wanted Daddy to feed her and Momma she wanted more juice *now* and you whirled, slapping her—very hard and very fast.

Not as hard and as fast as you hit the prisoner last week, the thirty-day-suspension blow. Too many recent incidents of unwarranted aggression in your folder, they said, too many complaints. You need to learn to restrain yourself. You have a problem with drinking, Officer. You have a problem controlling your temper. Never mind that the prisoner you backhanded had just set his four-year-old son down on a lit stove burner. You should control your emotions, Officer. You aren't the judge and jury on the streets, sweetheart. Maybe you should seek some help, they all said.

To hell, you had yelled back, to hell with all of you. I'll take the thirty days.

You slide the gun along your cheek and place it against your lips. The danger is that your aim will be off just enough so that you won't die instantly but do considerable damage and bleed to death. Or live. It all depends on the angle of the gun when you put it in your mouth.

You feel your heart thudding, taste the staleness, the dryness in your throat. You place the gun in your mouth and tilt it up slightly so the bullet will slice through the brain instead of following the curve of your skull. The gun tastes bitter and oily; it is heavy against your teeth. Close your lips around the cold metal; it is unbearably, soothingly foreign. A thick, wet silence wraps around you, drifts into your ears, fills your skull.

You tighten your right thumb on the trigger, hold the gun with both hands, your left thumb hovering above the hammer. A distant voice tells you steady pressure on the trigger will ensure a perfect shot with little recoil. Continual, steady pressure, the familiar voice says, don't anticipate the sound of the gun going off. And you see your father again in that moment before the trigger gives, a quick montage: his hand raised, descending; his head framed in the sights of your gun; his flesh twitching just below his eye; his body twisted and bleeding, dying alone on the barren strip of roadway, fingers clawing the cement. Turkey buzzards circle overhead in sync with the revolving lights of his unit. Just like her old man, you hear the whispers, echoing voices across the stretch of years as the trigger releases, the hammer flies forward.

The pain of the hammer hitting the thumb of your left hand is as sharp and sweet and real as the gentle folding inward of yourself, this giving in to life.

The gun grows heavy in your hand. Your lips and cheeks feel bruised. Ease your thumb out from under the hammer. Slowly pull the gun back out of your mouth. Open your eyes and look at the gun. Carefully push it away. Listen to the hum of the refrigerator, the uneven drip of the kitchen sink. Briefly, for an instant, another vision: your mother leaning toward you, offering you your daughter's stuffed lion in her outstretched hands.

CATHY

It is in our darkness that we find our truth.
—Kenneth Robinson

SOMETHING ABOUT A SCAR

The first time I saw Marjorie LaSalle she was kneeling on her bed naked, hands gripping the sheets to help support her weight, a nine-inch steak knife embedded deep just above the spot where the flesh parts to rise and become breast; the place where a child or lover would rest his head in grief, in need, in utter devotion; that place the tips of fingers caress and feel both implacable bone and sweet, full softness—a place of promise, of absolution, the center of ourselves.

Her house was impossibly full of men, overly loud voices, and too much artificial light for 2:52 in the morning. All those police officers—five out in the yard, three in the living room, two talking in the hallway, one taking pictures of the nightstand, another speaking into a portable radio by the walk-in closet—and not one touched her or sat by her or held a sheet to cover her. Only two paramedics hovered nearby, talking briskly and efficiently as they set up an IV and discussed how best to move her to the gurney. They eased her onto her back as I finally stepped into her bedroom, handling her body, it seemed to me, as though it were separate from her soul.

There wasn't much blood, and this small detail bothers me even today: a smear on the portable phone, the sheets wet with red in places, but not drenched. When the phone rang, wrenching me out of sleep, and the flat male voice said, "We got a VS request on a stabbing and sexual assault in Southdowns," I'd expected to walk into a small pond of blood. Half awake, I'd stumbled over my still slumbering dog and put on old stone-washed jeans and a black polo shirt with my name, CATHY, and VICTIM SERVICES embroidered on the front, clothing that could handle cold-water soaking and heavy detergent.

On the short drive into Southdowns, I rehearsed the Victim Services' list of rules in my head: do not touch anything, do not interfere with the police officers, do not make judgments or offer opinions, use a soothing voice, do not volunteer information about yourself, do not touch the victim without asking the victim first, do not ask what happened; focus on active listening, compassionate support, and contacting the friends and relatives the victim wants notified. This was my first solo call out, and I still believed in the rules.

As soon as I turned off Perkins Road, I knew I was close to the scene: taillights, spotlights, and flashing red and blue lights punctured what should have been dark, calm, sleepy: a simple middle-class neighborhood in the heart of Baton Rouge where during daylight children rode bikes, dogs trotted aimlessly in neighbors' yards, couples bickered lightly on porches, and lawn mowers puttered every weekend. Generally a safe place, or as safe as any place can be.

But now police cars lined the block, along with a fire truck and ambulance. Some neighbors stood on the edge of their driveways or in doorways, peering toward all the activity, dressed in hastily thrown-on clothes and bathrobes. I felt a momentary thrill that unlike them, I would walk into the crime scene; unlike them, I would have access to the intimate details.

The intimate details were this: Marjorie LaSalle awoke to a thud on her chest—the sound, she would say later, was what woke her—then pressure, a sharp pressure that made her think the cat had landed on her chest, claws digging deep. "Huh?" was all she managed before she saw him, a thin, shadowy outline at the side of her bed. And even then she thought she was having a waking dream, until she smelled him, heard him, felt his hands on her legs, and she sat up. He stepped back, to the doorway, turned on a flashlight held high, shone it in her face. She squinted, swallowed a scream, scrambled backward, her spine crammed against the headboard.

"Don't hurt me; please don't hurt me," she whispered.

The light changed directions, traveled down the hallway, and he was gone.

She got slowly to her knees, panting, realizing suddenly *holy mary mother of god* that she had a knife in her—so deep, the doctors would tell us later, that the blade tip was embedded in her spine, that it took such force to remove it, even after carefully cutting away all the tissue, muscle, tendons around each serrated edge of the knife, that her body came up off the surgical table.

She called 911, whispered her address over and over in a high-pitched voice—because she knew that's what they'd need first, how they'd find her—that she was hurt, that she needed help, the words tumbling on top of one another in a clatter of syllables, indistinguishable.

The dispatcher told her to be quiet. "*Be quiet*, ma'am. Just calm down now and let me find out what's going on."

Something clicked inside her, shifted, and Marjorie came back into her body, eased herself down onto the bed.

She spoke her address into the phone, quick clenched words, and her name when she was asked, and that she was bleeding, a man had hurt her, when she was asked what happened, and then there wasn't time for anything more because *oh sweet jesus* the man returned, came to the side of the bed, pulled her knees apart.

"Shuddup, or I'll kill you," he said as she whispered into the phone, "He's back."

The dispatcher asked, "What's happening?" and she said in a voice soft but clear, "His hands are on my legs."

The dispatcher said, "Do you know the man?"

But Marjorie never answered, because the man hit her, hard, and the phone went flying, disconnected. He pried her legs open, his knees holding her down, two fingers fumbling to find her, trying to guide himself into her but unable to; her crying and fighting to stay conscious, knowing she had to stay conscious to live; him getting more agitated, pushing down on one shoulder, still probing with his fingers; her trying to remember whether the children were here at home or with their father, and, oh the relief, yes, they were with their father; him pushing, pushing, pushing.

She came up to her elbows, tears running down her face, breath catching in her throat, her throat was so dry, thought, *Okay, this is going to happen; this is happening; I need to not fight him; I need to see him and remember.* She squinted against the darkness, half blind without her contacts, and tried to see.

Black male, no shirt, long chest, thin build, tall, young, short nappy hair, small wire-frame glasses.

And what came out of her mouth then was so ridiculous she admitted later, over and over, so very ridiculous, but it's all that came to her mind because if she lived through this, she didn't want to die from AIDS.

"Are you wearing a condom?"

A long pause, him breathing into the darkness, the stale air from his lungs washing over her with the faintest hint of tobacco and spearmint. And then he was gone again, this time for good, the front screen door slamming hard behind him.

More slowly now, she moved back to her knees, carefully slithered onto the floor, found the phone, didn't want to bleed on the antique rug her mother had given her, got back up on the bed, onto her knees. *Stay conscious,* she told herself; *stay alive.* Dialed 911 again.

This time she was calmer, her voice high and skittery but clear. Said, "I'm bleeding" when the police dispatcher, a different dispatcher, answered. Said, "I've been stabbed." Repeated it again when he transferred her over to EMS, gave her address to the EMS dispatcher, said, "Please help me, please hurry" many times. The police dispatcher told her to stay on the line.

A slight pause and then the police dispatcher asked her questions, many questions, and you can hear her on the tapes that are now a part of the official case files answering softly with just the occasional hitch in her voice: no, the man was gone, just seconds ago; yes, she lived in a house; her age was thirty-seven; no, there wasn't anyone else in the house; no, there weren't any weapons in the house; are the police on the way; no, he hadn't penetrated her;

please send help; no, there was just one man; is someone coming; yes, she'd stayed conscious; yes, she was still bleeding; no, she couldn't move to get a towel, she was afraid, the knife was still in her (and the dispatcher's incredulous voice coming back, the only time you hear any emotion in his voice, "The knife is *still in you?*"); okay, she'd wrapped the sheet around the knife; no, she didn't know what kind of knife it was; please hurry; no, she didn't know how he'd gotten in; no, the front door wasn't unlocked, oh, wait, she thought he might have left through it, so it was probably open. Please help me, she said, please hurry.

But I didn't learn any of this until much later.

"Please," was the first thing she said to me when I walked over to the far side of the bed. "Hold my hand, please?" Her green eyes wide, her teeth chattering, her hazelnut hair cut just below her ears and slicked tight down one side of her cheek. Three tiny diamond studs traveled up one ear lobe. Her arms and shoulders were muscular, like a swimmer's.

"I'm Cathy," I said, kneeling down on the floor so I could meet her eye to eye, so I wasn't looking down and seeing the knife too. Her skin was rough and moist. The paramedics barely acknowledged me. "With Victim Services."

"Just hold my hand," she said, her words more short snaps of air than sound. One eye was slightly larger and darker than the other.

"Yes." I wanted to cover her nakedness but knew that definitely constituted interference.

She nodded back at me, her stare intense. There was fear in her eyes, huge fear, but also something else, a kind of steel glinting at the corners that wasn't anger but something deeper. She smelled like laundry detergent and another, stronger, more acidic odor I couldn't place.

I gently squeezed her clenched fist. "It's okay."

"Yes?"

"Yes," I said, trying not to look directly at the knife—all I could see was the hilt flush against her flesh—but drawn to it in spite of myself. One paramedic held a huge pressure bandage around the edges of the knife while he adjusted the flow on the IV drip; the other talked to the hospital via radio, using medical terms and acronyms I didn't understand.

A plainclothes officer with short, sandy blond hair, lightly pock-marked skin, and rimless glasses came into the room carrying a small black leather bag in his plastic-gloved hand. He was handsome in an uncommon way; his energy and confidence filled the room. I smiled and nodded, but he ignored me.

"What's that?" Marjorie gasped. "I can't see."

"A purse," the officer said. "We found it one house over."

"He wanted money?" she said.

"We need to move her," one of the paramedics said.

I stood, but Marjorie didn't let go of my hand.

"I'll be with you all the way. Don't worry." I smiled at her again and carefully removed my hand.

The plainclothes officer took several steps back. "Where did you leave your purse, Ms. LaSalle?"

"The stereo speaker, just inside the door." Her shoulders flexed forward with the effort to bring forth each word.

"You sure?"

Her head bobbed once as the paramedics eased her to the edge of the bed. "Always in the same place," she said.

"I do that too," I said and immediately regretted allowing such inane words to come from my mouth.

The officer looked at me without raising his head. "You new?"

"Cathy Stevens. With Victim Services."

"Yeah, kind of guessed that from your shirt." He wrote something in his notebook. "Young, aren't you?" he said, more dismissal than interest to his question. "There is no sign of forced entry to your house, Ms. LaSalle. Are you sure your front door was locked when you went to bed?"

Marjorie's face went momentarily still, the knife hilt moving with each inhale exhale. "I, I think so, I'm almost positive."

"Well it isn't now," he said. "The responding officer found it ajar when he arrived."

"We need a hand here," a paramedic said, and two uniformed officers stepped forward. Marjorie's face twisted as the men bumped her onto the gurney. One of them finally pulled a sheet up over her, leaving just her left breast exposed.

The plainclothes officer shook his head, wrote some more. "All your windows are locked; the back door is unlocked but with no sign of tampering; we haven't found any blood transfer yet; nothing seems to be missing but the contents of your purse." His voice was devoid of emotion, almost as though he were dictating into a tape recorder. I wondered if he was this way on all his calls, what made him so detached. "Kind of strange."

Mucus ran from her nostrils. I came around the bed, pulled a tissue from my back pocket, reached across the gurney and wiped her nose.

"Don't touch anything," the plainclothes officer snapped.

I flinched, stepped away, wondering if he meant Marjorie or the bed.

"I don't understand." Marjorie's hands gripped the edge of the gurney.

I smiled, whispered, "It's okay."

"Actually, it's not," he said.

"Okay." I fought to keep my voice from quavering, cursed the flush I knew had just appeared on my face. Did he not like women or just people in general?

"I," the officer said, still writing in his notebook, "am the detective in charge of this case." He clipped his pen to the top of the notebook and folded his arms. "Robileaux. Detective Ray Robileaux. With Homicide."

"Homicide?" The word slipped out before I could stop it. Robileaux gave me a long, steady look but didn't answer.

"We're out of here," a paramedic said, and Robileaux nodded, asked, "The General or the Lake?"

"She said the General; she's got privileges there."

"Privileges?" Robileaux's forehead folded into confusion.

"I'm a psychologist," Marjorie said, each syllable coming slowly. She looked at me and fresh tears welled up. "I work with teenagers."

"A psychologist," Robileaux said, and jotted something down in his notepad.

"You're coming?" She twisted her head slightly to look at me as the paramedics maneuvered the gurney to the door.

"In my car. Right behind you."

Another, younger plainclothes officer with an ample stomach

came to the doorway and whispered something into Robileaux's ear. His black hair was slicked back, and he wore a cream-colored polo shirt under his brown jacket. Marjorie watched them, panting through an open mouth.

"Have you found something?" she asked. "Have you found him?"

"Detective Hebert, ma'am," the younger man said. "We found the contents of your purse." His voice was soft, and, unlike Robileaux, he actually looked at her while he spoke.

"Everything except for cash," Robileaux said. "Do you remember how much you had in it?"

Raised voices came from the front of the house. "I need to see her," a man's voice said sharply.

"Cesar?" Marjorie lifted her head, tried to look past the paramedic. "I called him. Please let him in."

"You called him?" Robileaux said.

"After I called you."

Robileaux hesitated a second, then barely nodded to Hebert.

"Let him come on back, Charlie," Hebert hollered.

"Cesar, that Mexican?" Robileaux asked.

A small, compact man hurried down the hallway, dressed in black jeans and a blue T-shirt. His hair was long and curly, his complexion dark.

"I'm here." Cesar leaned over the gurney, but didn't touch her.

"Look what happened to little Pollyanna." Marjorie brushed his arm with the back of her hand. It struck me as an odd thing to say.

"How did this happen?" There was only a hint of an accent to his voice.

"We've got to move this woman now," a paramedic said.

Cesar nodded and turned to follow them, but Robileaux reached out a hand. Cesar looked at the officers, his face frantic. "What happened? I need to go with her. Is she going to be all right?"

"Well, sir, that's what we're trying to determine. What's your name?"

"Cesar Campos. Will she be all right?"

"When did you last talk with Ms. LaSalle, Mr. Campos?"

"Earlier today. Well, when she called me tonight, but I saw her earlier today, at her office. She was fine then."

"I'm sorry," I said, not knowing how to interrupt or leave gracefully. I introduced myself, told Cesar what hospital Marjorie was going to.

"This is really unbelievable." Cesar stood stiffly, his hands jammed in the back pockets of his jeans.

"I think you're done here, Miss Stevens." Robileaux's look was unnerving, and I felt myself flush again.

Detective Hebert rested a hand lightly on my back. "Why don't you come with me, ma'am."

"Cathy," I said, pulling away from his touch.

"Josh Hebert." He extended his hand when we reached the living room, and I took it reluctantly. It was smooth and warm, and he smelled faintly of a cologne I recognized. "We always appreciate having someone from Victim Services, Cathy."

"I don't think he appreciates my presence much."

"Ray? Oh, he can be a bulldog, but he's a good detective." Hebert opened the screen door for me, and I shivered, even though the night air was heavy and close.

"First time for something like this?"

"Yes." I looked out at the street. Most of the neighbors had gone back inside.

"It's always unsettling the first few times."

"Do you get used to it?"

"Not really." He smiled, and a dimple appeared high on his cheek, under his right eye. "But you learn to see it in a different way, not feel it so much."

I rubbed a thumb over the outside seam on my jeans. "And how do you do that?"

He shrugged. "You just learn. Happens over time." He slapped a thin spiral notebook lightly against his leg. "You got everything you need here?"

I nodded. "Thanks for walking me out."

"We'll probably see you over there in a bit. And don't worry about Ray. He's just having a rough night."

Not as rough as Marjorie LaSalle, I thought, standing beside my car after Hebert had gone back inside. An errant blue jay chirped from a huge magnolia tree across the street. The ambulance and fire truck had left, along with some of the police cars. By morning, you'd never know anything had happened here, the neighborhood back to normal. Except the woman who lived in this house, of course. I wondered how Marjorie LaSalle could ever return here. If she lived.

I'd wanted to work in law enforcement since I was a child, probably the result of too much television. I'd watched *Mission Impossible, I Spy, Streets of San Francisco, Police Woman, Cagney and Lacey,* and *Hill Street Blues* with a passion bordering on religion. My favorite characters were Christine Cagney, and Sergeant Lucy Bates on *Hill Street Blues*—they seemed the most realistic: tough, independent, smart. And they had integrity; they held their own in a man's world.

I graduated with a degree in criminal justice from LSU, despite withering comments from my older sisters, my father's bewildered "But what are your goals, what do you want to do with this?" my mother's quiet "If that's what you want to do," my grandmother's "You'll never marry into a good family doing that," my friends' puzzled looks. Five months ago I'd taken and passed the required battery of psychological and physical agility tests, the civil service and physical exam, the interviews necessary to be accepted as a police cadet. In less than two months, I would enter the 50th Basic Training Academy of the Baton Rouge Police Department.

But I wanted more experience, something beyond classroom learning. So I'd enrolled in the training for Victim Services, an eight-week program designed to help victims of crime or crisis. Mostly we soothed, provided a friendly face, allowed the professionals—the police, firefighters, paramedics—to do their job without having to attend to civilians' emotional needs.

What I wanted was to *see*. I knew nothing about the world. My life had been relatively calm and safe, sheltered even. A friend dead in high school from an overdose, another friend's father murdered, a waitress at work robbed at gunpoint—but these events affected me only peripherally. I needed to see the unspeakable now, if only to reassure myself that I could see.

But what do you do with the feelings, I wondered, as I pulled into the crowded ER parking lot. The sight of Marjorie LaSalle hadn't made me sick to my stomach, hadn't sent me fleeing, hadn't made me probe my own vulnerability or made me frightened for my safety as a woman living alone. I'd felt responsible for her, a fierce, hot responsibility that arose from some deep, unfamiliar place.

A nurse directed me to Marjorie's cubicle. I walked around the corner and stopped. She lay naked on the bed, the curtains to her area thrown wide, visible to anyone walking by. A catheter tube ran from between her legs. A police photographer took pictures of her, close-ups. Two doctors and four nurses were crowded into the tiny space, and she tracked their movements with her eyes, barely turning her head. She had a gorgeous body, if you ignored the knife hilt protruding from her upper chest.

"Just this one stab wound to the left subclavicular thorax. Looks like a slight left to right angle."

"*Just?*" A nurse shook her head.

One doctor probed her breast. "We got another wound here, about two inches deep, under the left breast," he said.

"Really?" Marjorie said. "I don't feel it." Her words slurred, and her right hand twitched, as though she were tempted to locate the injury.

"Must have just missed the major aortic branches."

"X rays show the lungs are clear."

"Won't know until we get in there."

"Okay, let's get her prepped and up to surgery."

The room cleared out somewhat, and I moved so I was in Marjorie's sight line.

She squinted, turned her head slightly. "Who's there?"

"Cathy," I said. "From earlier, at the house." Before I'd finished talking, she extended a hand.

"Kind of laid out for the whole world to see, aren't I?"

"I'm so sorry."

"Doesn't really matter. Just the body. They're doing what they can." Her breathing barely moved the knife now. "It's started to hurt, really hurt. Funny how it didn't hurt until I was in the ambulance."

"It's the shock."

"You've been very kind."

"It's what I'm here for."

"No. It's you. I can tell."

I patted her hand. "What are these scars here on your arm?"

"Gymnastics," she said. "Fell from the high bars when I was four-teen." Her eyes almost closed, and her voice sounded thin. "Guess I'm going to have a whole new set now, aren't I?"

I patted her hand again, and for a few minutes we stayed like that, in silence, as two nurses worked around her.

Before they whisked her down the hall to the elevator, I took down the names of the people she wanted contacted: her parents, ex-husband, someone at work. I promised I'd wait. That I'd be there when she got out of surgery. I had no idea what I was promising. She was in surgery over seven hours, and I didn't see her again until just past noon when those of us who had been waiting—her parents, all four of her brothers, an amazing number of extended relatives, and me—gathered outside her room in Intensive Care to hear the doc-tors' report.

The doctors told us that only in surgery had they discovered her esophagus had been completely severed as well, and so they had gone in through her back, collapsed her lungs, and sewn it back together. That the knife blade had been situated between the right subclavian and the left common carotid vessels, with the serrated edge directly abutting the aortic arch. That a great deal of force was required to remove the knife, which had been embedded in the deep tissue along the paravertebral region. That, basically, it was amazing she'd sur-vived—both the stabbing and the surgery.

Marjorie was woozy and disoriented, but she smiled at us.

"My daughter never gives up," her father said, his tall, lean frame bending over to kiss her on the forehead. A tiny gold boxing glove dangled from his neck, brushed her cheek. "Never," her father repeated.

When I visited her two days later, winding my way through the labyrinth of the hospital's icy pink halls, I stopped, puzzled by the name taped to what I thought was her door. Celia Flores. Had they moved her? Had I forgotten her correct room number? Then the door swung open and a nurse stepped out, Marjorie's voice trailing a thin "thank you" behind her.

The head of her hospital bed was barely elevated, the TV turned off, the room filled with baskets of flowers, stuffed animals, cards, and one big heart-shaped balloon. Tragedy made cheery. For the first time, Marjorie LaSalle looked exhausted.

"What's with the Celia Flores on your door?" I asked.

"Did you see the paper this morning? They printed my name in it. My name! And the name of the hospital. In the paper, that I'd been stabbed, sexually assaulted. What if he sees it, what if the man who did this sees it and reads that I gave a description of him to the police and comes looking for me here?" The words tumbled out fast, like a child's anxious recitation.

"No!" I sat in the chair beside her bed, put my hand on her arm. The paper never printed rape victims' names; it just wasn't done.

"So they've given me a new name, taken my name off all the public records. I told them they had to do something. I'm so scared. What if he comes back?"

"You're safe here," I said automatically. I didn't mention where my mind had immediately gone: her name, in the phone book. But then he already knew where she lived, didn't he?

"My brothers are at my house. Packing. I can't live there anymore." She shuddered, closed her eyes. "Robileaux's meeting them. He was here earlier. Asking questions. I don't like him much."

"Me either," I admitted.

She opened her eyes, and we grinned at each other.

"Why are all the cute ones jerks?"

"Genetics, I suppose," I answered.

"Ummmm. Celia Flores. That's a pretty name, isn't it?"

"Very pretty," I said.

"I like how it feels in my mouth. Celia Flores." She said the name slowly, rolling the vowels around in her mouth like a cat stretching.

"How are you doing? Much pain?"

She nodded. "Some. I'm just so scared." She closed her eyes then snapped them open again, grabbed my hand. "You believe me, don't you? You believe me?"

"But—well, of course I do." I stared at her, puzzled.

"Breathe, just breathe," she whispered and took deep, long breaths. "I'm alive, and it's over. The worst is over, isn't it?"

"Yes," I said.

*   *   *

Detective Ray Robileaux decided that Marjorie LaSalle's injury was self-inflicted.

I didn't learn this from him, of course, but from Marjorie when I visited her at the hospital during her eleven-day stay and then for weeks afterward when she'd call me, often late at night, long rambling phone calls during which she was weeping, infuriated, or tightly calm. I simply listened. Perhaps I was foolish to give her my phone number. But I couldn't say no to her.

Robileaux based his decision on a number of facts. His suspicion started with the lack of evidence at the crime scene to substantiate the claim of an intruder. No sign of forced entry, but okay, maybe she'd forgotten to lock her door; happened all the time. No fingerprints were found—not a single one, not Marjorie's or her children's or her ex-husband's or Cesar's—the house was clean. No fingerprints even on the second, smaller kitchen knife lying on her nightstand. This was quite strange, alarming really, both the existence of a second knife in that location and the absence of fingerprints. No blood transfer; the perp had to have gotten blood on him someplace, somehow, stabbing her, handling her body. But there was no blood on her purse or anywhere else in the house except the phone and the bed. No evidence of her crawling across the bed to retrieve the phone from the floor—shouldn't there have been blood on the rug? This too was quite strange, a strong tip-off that things might not be the way they first appeared. And the intruder's MO was unusual: he stabbed her once brutally, didn't rape her, left, came back, perhaps with the second knife, and what? Just nicked her breast? But there was no blood on that knife, no fingerprints. Why would he have come back; he didn't hear her on the phone? It was odd he fled simply because Marjorie asked him if he was wearing a condom.

But crime scenes are funny; they don't always follow the rules or what's expected or the way other, similar crimes have looked. So Robileaux tucked these details away as something to puzzle, to probe, to take out and examine again and again.

Then he found the letters in an envelope on the nightstand when he returned to her house two days after the stabbing. A long typed letter from Cesar, written in a grandiose style, accusing Marjorie of discomfort over his ethnicity—his father was Hispanic, his mother African American—of being embarrassed to have her family know him; he wrote that her family didn't like darker-skinned people, that she didn't respect him and truly want him to be a part of her life. An extended separation was called for, he wrote. Cesar told Robileaux that he'd gone to her office and given it to her the day before she was stabbed, that they'd had a brief, heated verbal altercation, and he'd left. Also inside the envelope was a short note Marjorie had written Cesar later that day, but had not yet given to him. In it she apologized for being rude and abrupt with him, explained that she wanted him to know her children and her family but now realized that was impossible. Their differences were too great. She ended with "I'm so tired."

Robileaux dug into this like a hound. All the odd, unexplainable details of the crime scene shifted and fell into place. She was despondent, he decided, over a relationship gone awry. She was suicidal or, worse, she'd staged the whole thing for attention from her family or to get Cesar back. He thought about the Pollyanna comment she'd made when she saw Cesar, how coherent she seemed given the situation. He wondered how familiar she was with anatomy.

He talked to the doctors at the hospital. No, they'd found no evidence of bruising about the legs or vagina, consistent with an attempted rape. The smaller cut under her left breast could be a hesitation cut, he decided, often common when sharp objects are used in suicide attempts. He found it strange that Marjorie claimed not to remember this cut, when she remembered so much else, that she couldn't explain the presence of the second knife on the nightstand. And the angle of the knife in her chest seemed inconsistent with her report of what happened. In fact, each time he talked to her over the next four weeks, her version of what happened changed slightly, small changes, but Robileaux found them significant.

And there was the composite drawing. Marjorie, frustrated with what she perceived as slow movement on her case, went to State Police Headquarters and enlisted the help of a prominent sketch artist. The artist, a woman younger than Marjorie with a gentle demeanor and crooked teeth, had her look through a number of face, eye, nose, and mouth shapes. Then, working off the selected shapes, to refine the drawing and make it as accurate as possible, she had Marjorie get down on the floor, reenact that moment again in her bedroom when the intruder leaned over her.

"The body will help remember what the mind might have forgotten," she told Marjorie. "I want you to see it again, as closely as possible."

What her body remembered was panic and terror, Marjorie told me later. And so, as she lay there on the floor, seeing and feeling it all again, her knees spread apart, her arms outstretched, she whispered, "Okay, make this real, this is real." To encourage herself to get back to that moment, she told me, to stay strong.

But this wasn't the way Robileaux read it when he talked to the sketch artist later. And it wasn't the way she read it, either. She told Robileaux she thought Marjorie was too nervous, that she was deceptive at times, sincere at others. That she worried mostly about Marjorie's children, that she thought Marjorie might at a later time take the children's lives along with her own. But Marjorie didn't find out about this until weeks later. She left the sketch artist's office believing she'd taken a positive step to help find the man who'd stabbed her.

Meanwhile, Robileaux interviewed her parents, her ex-husband, Cesar. All seemed stunned that Marjorie might have done this to herself.

"But anything's possible, I guess," her ex-husband said at the end of a lengthy, intense interview.

"Do you think Marjorie would take a polygraph exam?" Robileaux asked him.

"She'll probably say they aren't reliable," her ex-husband said.

Which is exactly what Marjorie LaSalle said, two raw, thirteen-inch scars now gracing her chest and upper back, when Robileaux asked her to submit to a polygraph exam five weeks after her stabbing. But she agreed, infuriated with Robileaux's insinuations. The polygraph examiner asked her five questions, three of which pertained to the night of July 13.

"Did you stab yourself at your house?"

"No."

"Did a Negro man stab you at your house?"

"Yes."

"Have you made up any part of your story concerning a Negro man stabbing you?"

"No."

The examiner's finding? Marjorie was answering "deceptively" to the relevant questions.

Detective Ray Robileaux set up a meeting with Marjorie at the Homicide office and asked Hebert to join him. Without her knowledge, he arranged for the interview to be videotaped. He confronted her with the lack of evidence and pointedly accused her of stabbing herself, said her kinesics, or body language, clearly indicated her guilt. What body language that was, he refused to say. Hebert remained mostly quiet throughout.

Whatever shred of calm Marjorie had left, she lost. She yelled, she was sarcastic, she held her hand out and said "Stop" each time Robileaux interrupted her, which was frequently. She looked at the ground or the table or Hebert as she talked. She accused Robileaux of bias against women. She said the investigation had never been carried out properly. She told him she could prove she didn't stab herself but that would cost her money and energy, neither of which she had. That what he accused her of was so exotic in interpretation that she felt a new sense of violation—she was being victimized by the police who were supposed to be helping her. The interview ended abruptly.

But Robileaux had one more step to take. He took the videotape to the police psychologist, McCants, and asked him to review it, his report, and all the witness interviews and statements. McCants asked to talk to only one person—Marjorie's ex-husband. And then he called Robileaux and said, "I agree. All evidence points to deceptiveness. I'd say your findings are accurate."

And so the investigation was halted and the offense changed from attempted capital murder to attempted suicide.

Later that night on the phone, Marjorie told me Robileaux had said that no one would know the final disposition unless she told them. But if she took this any further, if she took it to the media or publicized her dissatisfaction with the way the police were handling the case, "all the quirks will be pulled out."

"I just find it intolerable, unbelievable," Marjorie said. "He's threatening me. He's saying my alleged instability will be leaked and damage my position and viability as a professional psychologist."

I made murmuring noises to acknowledge I was listening as I threaded my fingers through the hair around my dog's face. Increasingly, I'd been avoiding her phone calls, letting my answering machine screen calls. I just didn't know what to say to her. I'd started out wanting to help a woman who had been brutally attacked and who had somehow survived, a woman who had the strength to live and stay coherent through an unimaginable horror. I'd admired her. I still admired her. But this had swirled out into something much bigger than I could comprehend. Or handle.

"I told him," Marjorie continued, "that I pride myself on three things. My integrity, first and foremost. And my honesty—I always tell the truth, well, except to my parents when I was a teenager, but as an adult, I always tell the truth, I don't lie. And third, being a mother. I'm a good mother. I would *never* leave my children without a mother. I just wouldn't do it."

"I'm so sorry," I said.

"You believe me, don't you?"

"Of course," I said, remembering the knife buried deep in her chest. I knew people killed themselves, I knew people tried to kill themselves, but not like that. They didn't do it like that, did they? They shot themselves or cut their wrists or hanged themselves or took pills. But they didn't bury a knife deep into their own chest.

She was silent a moment. "You know, I always believed in the police. I always told my kids, the police will help you, they're there to protect you and keep you safe." She started crying. "But that's not true, is it?" she whispered.

"There are lots of good cops."

"I'm not so sure."

"Hebert seemed very nice."

"But he didn't *do* anything." Marjorie's voice rose.

I stared at my dog, thought about Hebert's comments out on the porch. He'd seemed kind, genuine. Did he believe Marjorie had stabbed herself? Was there something I wasn't seeing? I felt the edges of a headache coming on.

"You've gone awfully quiet," she said.

"Sorry."

"I keep feeling there's something you want to say and aren't."

My head started throbbing in earnest.

"Cathy?"

"You probably should know, I'm entering the police academy in a couple of weeks."

"Oh." She was quiet for a long time. My dog nudged my hand with his nose. "Have you talked to them?" she asked.

"Who?"

"The police, Robileaux."

"No! Why would I talk to them?"

I heard children's voices in the background, the sound of dishes clattering before she said, "I wish you'd told me before."

"You just seemed so down on the police, I didn't want you to think . . ." I hesitated.

"You've been planning this for a while, haven't you?"

"Yes."

"Since before you met me?"

"Yes."

A deep sigh. "You know you're the only one I've been able to talk to about this, really talk about it, besides my therapist. I haven't wanted to burden people. But I've burdened you, haven't I?"

"No," I said, not sounding convincing even to myself.

"Well." Her voice turned brisk. "You'll be a good police officer, I'm sure."

"I mean to," I said quietly.

Our conversation didn't last much longer. There really wasn't anything else to say. After she hung up, I buried my face in my dog's side. I felt old, confused, relieved. I doubted she'd call me anymore, and I was right. She never called my house again.

The next six years were good to me. I graduated the police academy in the top third of my class, qualified as an expert marksman, and went straight into a two-year tour of uniform patrol out of Broadmoor Precinct. Did over two years in Juvenile as a detective, got transferred to Scotlandville Precinct, got married, bought a house in Central, and then

was selected for my current assignment: community liaison, the brain-
child of the new police chief, a man I'd served under out of Broadmoor.

"Civilian complaints are rising," he'd told me in his airy, light-
filled office. "We want a fresh, objective eye. Someone they can connect to. Your job is to determine whether a case should be reopened,
reexamined and by whom, or whether an officer should be investi-
gated by Internal Affairs. You aren't Internal Affairs," he stressed.
"You are a liaison between civilians, the police attorney, IA, and the
Cold Cases teams."

I'd nodded hesitantly, thinking cops would view me either as a
rat, out to get them, or as a buffer, out to protect them. It would be a
fine line to maneuver, and if I hadn't trusted the Chief and believed
in his motives, I would have said no.

"I'm asking for a two-year commitment," the Chief said. "Mostly
days, some evenings. If you agree, it'll be you and George Donovan."

It was tempting. No fighting to stay awake at 4:00 A.M., none of
the blurry tension that came from working in the never-ending dark,
no wondering what horrors the night might bring. That, and teaming
up with George, clinched the deal for me, and I'd agreed with the
promise that I'd be transferred into general detectives at the end of
two years.

I liked the job for the most part. It exercised different muscles,
and it allowed me to listen, something I'd always been good at. People came in angry and frustrated, and I soothed, explained, investi-
gated; sometimes I made them happy and sometimes not.

George and I ruffled some cops' feathers, but that was to be
expected, especially when family members were involved. Nepotism
was the norm in the BRPD. It seemed half the department was
related to one another: husbands and wives or siblings and cousins,
or sometimes the whole family—mother, father, sons (but rarely the
daughters)—working in various divisions. Even George and I had
family in the department: my husband worked in Auto Theft; his sister worked in Communications. It really wasn't a problem. We didn't
have the final say on any case; there were always higher ups—the
police attorney, the Captain in Internal Affairs, and sometimes the
Chief or Civil Service Review Board composed of civilians, police
officers, and firefighters—who evaluated our findings.

Still, our decisions were rarely overturned. George and I were a good team. We were overworked; civilians filed requests for reviews constantly, some dating back years before my time in the department. But everyone in the department was overworked. It was simply one of the factors of the job you accepted.

So when the police attorney, Lou Cox, came into my office and threw the file down on my desk, I barely flinched. Barely. It was close to quitting time, and my mind was occupied with what my husband was fixing for dinner. He'd promised crawfish étouffée.

"This one just came in. Interview's set for Friday." Lou tugged his silk tie even looser, then jammed his hands deep into the pockets of his linen trousers.

"You can't be serious." I looked at the stack of files already on my desk. "Give it to George." I nodded toward my partner, who had his feet propped up on his desk, reading glasses perched low on his nose. Red reading glasses with yellow polka dots, my spare pair because he'd forgotten his somewhere earlier today. I was tempted to giggle every time I looked at him, and I looked at George a lot. He was one of the handsomest men I knew, like an older Denzel Washington but with salt-and-pepper hair and mustache.

"Don't shove that shit off on me." George's lips barely moved.

"She wants a female officer, Stevens. You're our female officer. I think." Lou looked over at George, who never stopped reading but slowly raised his hand and gave him the finger.

"Generally that would be me," I agreed. "But two days to prepare?"

"It's just an interview," Lou said. "Do the rest afterward."

I rested my chin in my hand and looked at him. After seven months in the liaison office, I'd learned we did things on Lou's schedule. Depending on the case, that was usually yesterday. Still, I had other plans for tonight, tomorrow was packed with appointments and cases to follow up on, and tomorrow night I'd intended more of what I had planned for tonight. I hated when my husband and I were on opposing shifts, and I guarded my time with him ferociously.

"Ray was the lead investigator, but the complainant's emphatic about a female handling the case," Lou said. "George'll have to review your findings."

"Sure." I stared warily at the file on my desk.

Lou thumped his hand against the door frame before he left. "Won't be a problem, right?"

"Hasn't been before," I said to his back.

"Good ole Ray Robileaux," George said softly.

I reached for the file and read the complaint date, said, "Wow, an old one," scanned the heading, *Attempted Capital Murder/Reassigned: Attempted Suicide*, saw the complainant's name, and felt my body lock up.

"What's a matter, girl? You gone a bit white there," George said.

"I am white." It was an old joke between us.

"I didn't mean nothing by it."

"What?" I was still staring at Marjorie LaSalle's name.

"About Ray," George said. "I like him. He's changed."

I looked at George. He'd taken off my reading glasses. "You say that a lot, George, that you like him."

"Well, I do."

"I know he was an asshole; I know he's changed."

"Maybe you should give me that file."

"You'll get it soon enough." I pulled the file back in front of me, glanced at my watch, called Ray and told him I'd be running a little late, then settled down to read my husband's final nineteen-page report and accompanying notes on the stabbing of Marjorie LaSalle.

Ray Robileaux was legendary in the department for three things: his ability to read a crime scene, his high case clearance, and his drinking. Not that the drinking was that much of an anomaly. Back in the old days, when we had a police chief without much spine, cops, especially the detectives, often drank on duty. You could walk into the Pastime Lounge and find on-duty detectives eating a slice of pizza and throwing back a beer at lunch- or dinnertime. After 10:00 P.M., it was the Shipwreck Lounge, tucked into the back of BonMarche Mall, a dark, dirty dive with a loud juke box full of country-and-western tunes and songs from the 1960s. The Shipwreck was mostly frequented by off-duty uniform cops, the whole crew from ARAB—

Armed Robbery and Burglary—and a scattering of detectives from Homicide, Sex Crimes, and Juvenile. There were lockers at the front entrance to secure your gun.

Ray Robileaux was a regular at both the Pastime and the Shipwreck. By the time I'd graduated from the academy, his marriage had ended in a ferocious divorce, he'd lost custody of both his kids, and he'd been busted down to Communications—just one step above the Governmental Building security detail or the Booking Desk, in terms of punishment. Ray's drinking days were over if he wanted to keep his job. He checked himself into a rehab program at the Tau Center, started attending AA meetings, and dipped below the radar of department gossip.

Three years later, I was working Juvenile, and got a call out on a 65 that involved two juveniles. A young teenage mother, stoned, fell asleep on the couch with her six-week-old son. She rolled over in her sleep and smothered the baby.

When I walked into the tiny, generic apartment on Flannery, I stopped, my usual professional words of introduction caught in my throat. The young mother's face was blotched, startling shades of red and white; she veered between wild hysterics and glum defensiveness. She wasn't the surprise. It was the uniformed officer. I barely recognized the man I'd last seen at Marjorie LaSalle's house. Ray Robileaux, now working uniform patrol out of Broadmoor Precinct, paced slowly in front of her, his face shuffling among dismay, tense concern, and what fleetingly looked like panic. Every line in his body was unassuming. He was much thinner than I remembered, but still handsome in that uncommon way.

"Well, I'll be damned," I said, words finally uncorked, rising up out of my mouth drenched in sarcasm before I could stop them. "Ray Robileaux."

He paused in midstep as though he'd been slapped before his shoulders slumped, his fingers relaxed, and he faced me full on. He looked oddly embarrassed.

"Detective Stevens." His voice was melodious and polite. He gave me the facts of the case, one finger tapping softly against the small green notepad he held in his hand. When he'd finished, I didn't even give him the courtesy of a nod.

"I believe you're done here now, Officer Robileaux," I said, a half-second after he'd finished speaking.

Two weeks later he came into the Juvenile office and sat down in the chair beside my desk, took a pear out of his pocket, and put it gently on the blotter in front of me. "This is for you," he said.

I stared at the pear and then at him. His uniform was too big, and his shoes needed polishing. His eyes were the color of tin. Finally, he rubbed the edge of his index finger along his nose and said, "I must have done something to piss you off."

I nodded warily.

"I'm here to offer my apology, for whatever it was."

I folded my hands in my lap, leaned back in my chair. "Okay."

He nodded slowly, got to his feet, and quietly walked out of the office. I sat there for a long time, looking at a poster of the FBI's Ten Most Wanted list on the wall beside the door, until the phone rang, jerking me back to work.

Over the next several months, Ray continued to drop by the Juvenile office, sometimes putting a cup of coffee, or a beignet, or a piece of fruit on my desk and chatting briefly for a few minutes before he left.

When he asked me out six months later, his request so tortured and awkward that he blushed, I said yes.

I waited until Thursday evening to tell Ray that I was investigating his old case.

I'd asked Josh Hebert about the case once, soon after Ray and I started dating. Josh was still working Homicide and sat on the edge of my desk contemplating his hands when I asked him if he thought Marjorie LaSalle had stabbed herself.

"It was Ray's case," he said.

"C'mon, Josh, you worked it with him."

"We differed on some things."

"And?"

"And it was an odd case. No fingerprints, no blood transfer. A hard one to call, I'll give you that. But things aren't always as they appear." He looked at me without expression. "Aren't you learning that with Ray?"

"He was a different man then," I said.

Josh shrugged. "There you have it."

"But do you think she did it?"

"What I thought then is pretty irrelevant now, isn't it?"

I'd shaken my head, frustrated with his ambiguous answers. "At least Ray takes a stance," I'd said, and Josh nodded slowly, looked as if he was going to say something else, then shrugged again and left.

Now, watching Ray clear away our plates scattered with shrimp shells and corn cobs as I started on my second Abita beer, I wished my husband was more open to doubt, allowed more room for the gray areas where most of life, I was learning, played out. I thought about the videotape I'd watched earlier that day, the 911 recordings, the crime scene photos, the police psychologist's report, the witness statements. Ray's report was clear-cut: Marjorie LaSalle had stabbed herself, and he'd carefully laid out every piece of incriminating evidence he had. Which was a lot.

I took a swig of beer and watched Ray rinse off some strawberries, put them on a plate. He came back to the table with his own beer, a nonalcoholic one he'd been nursing all evening, took off his glasses, kissed me, and popped a strawberry into my mouth.

"Ugh. Strawberries and beer don't mix." I wrinkled up my face.

"You'd rather champagne?"

"I'd rather wait on the strawberries."

He lifted my feet up into his lap and began to massage my right foot, his thumb digging hard between my toes. "Tough day?"

"You remember when we met?" I said.

He smiled. I loved his smile; it had such depth to it. "When we worked that juvenile homicide off Flannery and you gave me hell."

"You deserved it."

He worked his hand down around the ball of my foot. "Probably."

"I mean the very first time."

"Ah." The lines around his mouth tightened slightly.

"Remember?"

His hands stopped moving, and he peered at my foot as though the answer—or escape—was buried between my toes. "Why are you bringing this up again?"

"She's coming in tomorrow afternoon. She wants the case reopened."

All warmth evaporated from his body. "After six goddamn years?"

"What options did she have before now?"

"That woman stabbed herself, Cathy, and you're never going to convince me otherwise."

I picked at the beer label with a fingernail. "Think of all the weird cases you've worked, Ray. Isn't it just possible, on this one, that you're wrong? Women don't stab themselves like that. Look at any of the statistics."

"You've always had a soft spot for that woman. You've never been able to look at it objectively." He studied the table with great interest.

"Did you?"

He put my foot down and swept both hands across his face and through his hair, a gesture I knew well. "Are we going to fight about this?"

"I don't want to."

"Me either." He drained his beer and stood up, headed toward the back door.

"I just wanted you to know," I said softly.

"Now I know," he said, the door closing behind him with a gentle click.

I stared blankly at the door for a minute, then downed the rest of my Abita and went to the kitchen sink and started washing the dishes. Ray stood on our patio, smoking a cigarette, my dog crouched down at his feet, tail wagging, begging for a ball toss. Ray ignored him, but the dog didn't give up. Smoke curled up into the darkening sky, and I felt a momentary longing to join them. We'd both quit a year ago, but Ray still slipped, and more often than he wanted me to know.

I leaned on the counter, chin in my hands, and looked at his back, his hair just lapping the collar of his shirt, his cop stance of barely locked knees and feet at shoulder's width. I thought of his quiet tenderness, the way he treated our relationship like one of those sand dollars he loved to collect on our trips to Perdido Key, his lack of selfishness as we negotiated our way through the dailiness of living with each other. Love is a mystery, I thought, not for the first time. A giddy, difficult mystery. My husband was human—he could still be arrogant and short-tempered at times, he had a hard time admitting when he was wrong, and his sense of humor was decidedly off kilter—but I loved him. Sometimes that was as much a surprise to me as it was to him.

But even during the height of his drinking, the worst of his marital troubles, I knew Ray had been a good detective, prejudiced sometimes and bullheaded often, but he was usually thorough and precise.

Which brought me right back where I'd started: thinking about Marjorie LaSalle's stabbing.

Friday was rushed with appointments, hearings, and interviews, but I found it hard to concentrate, thinking about Marjorie's file sitting on my desk like the gecko lizards my dog loved to bark at—defiantly immobile, definitely there despite the camouflage techniques, and quite capable of biting when provoked. And I felt like a metronome: back and forth. She couldn't have done it; maybe she could. What was I missing? No, she couldn't have done it, but then . . .

I found myself mentally rehashing a case I'd handled out of Broadmoor, about a year after I'd graduated from the academy. My partner, Charlie, and I went out on a shots-fired, man-down call about 6:00 in the morning, just before end of shift, at an apartment off Sharp Lane. A hysterical woman in her forties greeted us at the door dressed in a plaid bathrobe that gave us glimpses of her ample nakedness underneath, her hair so overbleached it looked like a horse's mane. Her boyfriend was in the bedroom, lying on the right side of the bed wearing a mud brown T-shirt and white boxer shorts. His right hand flopped over the edge of the bed, a gun on the floor below it. The back of his head was blown off. Blood and brain matter covered the headboard and fanned out across two of the walls and down onto the carpeting.

He'd been despondent for days, she told us, talked about suicide. But she hadn't thought he was serious until the shot woke her.

"I was *right* there, on the bed beside him, sleeping, when he did it," she wailed. She alternated among fury that he'd done this to her, hysterics over reliving the moment, and heart-stopping grief that he was dead.

By the time Barker and Cowan with Homicide arrived, we'd got-

ten her calmed down somewhat, found his prescriptions for antide-
pressants, had the name of the counselor he was seeing at the V.A.
Hospital in New Orleans. Straightforward suicide, we told the detectives. Bizarre, but straightforward. The detectives agreed.

While we waited on the coroner and crime scene guys, the victim's girlfriend decided she'd get dressed. But she didn't want to go
into the bedroom, so I retrieved some clothes I found tossed on a
chair and handed them to her through the bathroom door. A second
later we heard a shriek so abrupt and piercing that we all jumped.
Charlie put his hand on his gun.

"Ma'am," I said, knocking on the bathroom door. "Ma'am? Are
you all right; what's going on in there?"

She opened the door, mascara running down her cheeks, and
handed me her bra. "It's got him on it," she screeched.

I looked down at the bra. Bits of brain clung to one of the cups.

"Jesus. Sorry." I hurried into the bedroom to get her a clean one
from the dresser, horrified at my mistake.

When Charlie and I left an hour later, she was still crying,
despite my best attempts to console her, and Barker and Cowan were
getting ready to transport her downtown for a statement. Charlie and
I drove to the Mister Donut a block away so he could pick up a dozen
for his kids, and we sat there waiting for a fresh hot batch, drinking a
cup of coffee, saying very little.

"Never fucking seen anything like that." Charlie sat hunched
over the counter, one foot tapping against the foot stop. He'd been in
the department for over ten years and was about to make corporal.
"Shooting himself in the bed while she lay sleeping beside him."

But both of us went slack-jawed two weeks later when Barker and
Cowan arrested the woman for murder. They'd followed routine procedure on a shooting: the Atomic Absorption Test, a fancy name for
a simple test that checks for gunpowder residue on anyone who was
at the scene. She'd tested positive; her boyfriend's hands had been
clean.

"Get out of here," Charlie said when Cowan told us. I couldn't
say a word. I felt betrayed. I also felt stupid. I resolved then and there
never to put myself in that position again. And for the next several
months I played out my interactions with her over and over again,

trying to figure out what clues I'd missed, what I hadn't seen. I questioned Charlie and the detectives. They all shrugged, said you can't always read the truth.

But, I thought, that was an easy call after the Atomic Absorption Test came back positive. The evidence was irrefutable. Marjorie's case, on the other hand, was as murky as my husband's gumbo.

"You're looking at that file like it's going to start talking to you," George said, startling me out of my reverie.

I put my palm up to my forehead and pressed hard. "I wish it would."

"I'm headed over to Armed Robbery, then I'm going home," he said. "You about done?"

"Just this last interview." I grimaced and pulled Marjorie's file over in front of me.

"A hinky one, huh? Want to talk it through? I got a couple of minutes."

I cupped my chin in my hand and looked at him. "Sometimes I hate this job."

"That Ray's case?"

I nodded.

"I looked over it earlier today, quick, but I got the jist of it."

"And?"

"He's not the man he used to be, Cathy."

"Jesus, George, enough already. I know."

He squatted down on his heels in front of me, concern deepening the lines in his face. "What I'm trying to say, but you keep taking my head off, is that Ray could have been wrong on this one. There's some compelling evidence to indicate she might have done it—lack of blood transfer and fingerprints, the polygraph, the psychologist's statement. On the other hand . . ." He shook his head slowly. "That's a hell of a wound to self-inflict, and I'm not sure I buy what Ray pinpointed as her motive. I need to spend more time with it, but it's okay to think that, you know? You aren't betraying the man you're married to now by saying he handled a case poorly six years ago. The worst that could happen is Cold Cases reopens the investigation, and he gets a letter in his file. It's an odd case. But there's no malfeasance, right?"

"Technically, no."

"What does Ray say?"

"He won't talk about it."

George stood, stretched his arms back behind his back, and shrugged. "No problem, I'll interview him."

"It's just . . . hard," I said.

"Go with your gut. You've got good instincts."

"What if you don't trust your gut?"

He grinned and winked at me. "Then you punt it, girl. Let someone else decide."

"That would be you," I pointed out.

"Then it's me." He slipped his shoulder holster on, then his suit jacket, and patted me on the back as he headed out the door. "You think too much."

Why, I thought, do men always tell women they think too much?

I glanced at my watch and gathered myself up to go out to meet Marjorie LaSalle.

My first thought was that her hair was prettier: softer and lighter and longer. She looked happy, and younger than when I saw her last, if that was possible, comfortable in her skin despite a fluttery nervous tension as I said her name. Three bulging brown folders rested in her lap.

When she stood to face me, I struggled not to stare at her chest. She wore an olive-colored blouse, the first three buttons undone, and her scars, one long vertical line and two short curved ones, were visible and distinct, snaking across her tanned skin and trailing down into the V of her breasts. They were hard to ignore, those scars.

"I'm Officer Stevens." I extended my hand. "Why don't you come on back to my office."

"Don't I know you?" she asked, when we were seated at the small, round table George and I used for interviews. "Did you work on my case?"

"Sort of," I said, smiling. "Victim Services."

"*Oh my gosh.* Cathy, isn't it? Cathy Stevens." She reached forward and gave me a hug. "Oh, I'm so glad it's you. I feel so lucky. Look at you, you look great. And you're married," she said, picking up my hand, fingering the ring. "Who is he?"

"A cop." I smiled slightly and hoped she wouldn't press for a name.

"I'm married, too. Just over a year."

"Cesar?"

"Oh no. I met Eric a year after my stabbing."

"Congratulations."

"You too." She ran her hands across the folders in front of her. "It's been a long time, hasn't it?"

"Yes."

She grinned, and I found myself grinning back. The old admiration rose up, and I pushed it down. In another life, she and I might have been friends. And I guess we were once, in a way, briefly.

"So," I said. "Your case."

She nodded, and her face lost its softness. "I want it back in attempted homicide where it belongs." She fingered a small necklace she wore around her neck, one with an intricate, delicate design that looked faintly religious and rested at the point where her three scars converged. "You're the one who decides?"

"I'm the one who makes a recommendation; other people will review it as well."

"Do they take your recommendation?"

I nodded. "Usually."

"Ah." She leaned back and put her hand on her chest, closed her eyes briefly before she looked at me again. "So. You'll reopen it?"

"You've seen the police report?"

"I got copies of everything through my lawyer."

"Then I'd like to hear your version, where you feel the police investigation was problematic."

"Where it went wrong was Detective Ray Robileaux accusing me of doing this to myself," she said firmly.

I nodded but kept my face impassive.

"You were there, after it happened. You know."

I opened up the file and slid my notebook on top of it, picked up a pen. "Well, let's go through it again. I understand you have a list of points you want to cover. Why don't we start there."

She looked at me intently, then shifted in her chair and sat straighter. She pulled out several typed pages and began reading off them, glancing at me now and again to speak extemporaneously or when she wanted to stress a point.

Why, Marjorie wanted to know, had the police never finger-printed her, Cesar, her ex-husband, or her children to match them up with any fingerprints found at the scene? And how could it be that the police never found any fingerprints? There was fingerprint pow-der residue in the house, she said, but not much and not in all the places she would have expected. Could it be that the police didn't do a thorough job dusting for fingerprints?

Possible, I thought, but not likely.

Why weren't neighbors questioned as to what they might have seen or heard? Marjorie had talked to her neighbors, and although Robileaux said the neighborhood was canvassed, most of her neigh-bors said no one from the police department had talked to them.

I nodded, thinking how funny it was that victims so often zeroed in on witness statements, not realizing that most witnesses are fairly unreliable, and canvassing is usually done only in homicide cases. Which, I reminded myself, this case had been. An attempted homi-cide. At least initially.

The report was wrong, she said; there was blood on the rug. Not much, but she had a copy of the cleaning bill. And there were incon-sistencies about her purse. Robileaux said the contents were scattered across a backyard. Then why, Marjorie wanted to know, was every item precisely where she'd put it when it was returned to her? She always put everything in the same place, she was very organized that way, and she found it unbelievable that Robileaux or some other officer had managed to put the items back in exactly the same way. And about the lack of fingerprints on the purse: Robileaux told her they couldn't dust for prints because there was too much dew on it, which inhibits finger-print detection. Yet his report stipulated the purse was picked up that night—and didn't I remember Robileaux himself brought it into the house—so it wouldn't have had time to collect dew.

I did remember, distinctly, Ray holding the purse in his gloved hand.

And her comment about being a Pollyanna? That was a ludicrous interpretation by Robileaux, that it was evidence she wanted atten-tion. She *was* a Pollyanna, or had been, always believing the best of people, believing the world was good, absentminded about locking her doors and windows. "And isn't that a joke now," she said, "given how the police treated me, how Robileaux was?"

I kept my body language positive, open, and nodded.

"Do you remember how awful he was?" Marjorie said.

"Ummm." I fought to keep my eyes from drifting from hers.

"He was biased from the first moment. He went looking for things that fit his bias." She tapped her finger on the table.

I thought of Ray's incredible anger toward his first wife; manipulative, he'd called her, said she'd played all the emotional colors of the rainbow. How much of that had been projected onto Marjorie?

"Detective Robileaux can be challenging at times," I said.

Marjorie looked at me, surprise and puzzlement clouding her face. "I seem to recall you didn't like him much either."

"What I thought then, Marjorie, is really irrelevant now," I said carefully.

"Really!?"

"I was just an observer, someone there to help you, that's where my focus was, not on the scene."

"Oh." She leaned back and her eyes narrowed. "That's right. You're a cop now."

I shook my head. "I just want to hear your side. I'm not passing any judgments."

"Please don't make this a waste of my time."

"I hope you don't think that's what this is."

For a minute I thought she might get up and leave, but after a long silent stretch during which she studied her list, she looked back up at me. "The 911 tapes." Her voice was clipped.

She'd listened to the 911 tapes, had them right here with her, and she didn't understand why they weren't sent off to the FBI for electronic enhancement so they could pick up the sounds of the man talking or hitting her. Maybe he hit her first, the phone disconnected, and then he said, "Shuddup, or I'll kill you."

I stifled my reflexive response: this was not the kind of case where we would ask the FBI to analyze a tape. The backlog of material they had already was dizzying enough. And dismaying. Our own fingerprint division had a six-month backlog of felony cases. But no complainant wanted to hear her case wasn't big enough or important enough. So I remained silent, nodding, as Marjorie continued.

Why was it so amazing to Robileaux, she wanted to know, pointing a finger stiffly at her chest, that she didn't remember the second cut on her breast; how could he see that as evidence of her guilt? She was terrified. And why was she supposed to explain the presence of the second knife; she wasn't a police officer, she didn't know why the intruder did the things he did. And he fled probably because he realized that she'd been on the phone, that she'd called for help, not because she asked him if he was wearing a condom. How was she supposed to explain the intruder's supposedly weird MO? And Robileaux saying that her story changed slightly each time he interviewed was ridiculous and a flat-out lie. She told it the same exact way each time; it was written down in his report wrong, another indication that either he wasn't listening carefully or was choosing to hear only what he wanted to hear.

I thought of the minor inconsistencies Ray had listed in his report and wondered how much he'd taken into account the emotional and physical stress she'd been under.

And of course there was no bruising on her legs. "I wasn't going to fight him with a knife in my chest. I just wanted it over with and him gone," she said, her voice growing agitated. "In Robileaux's mind, it was up to *me* to explain the irrational behavior of an unknown psychopathic murderer-rapist on a given summer night, and in his mind, it was evidence of my guilt that I could not. The fact of my being asleep when having the knife plunged into my chest, and my awakening in an adrenalized and disoriented state of shock didn't seem relevant to Detective Robileaux."

She'd been precise and emphatic during her point-by-point recitation, but now she teared up, and I reached over, handed her a tissue.

She wiped each eye slowly several times. "It's just hard, you know. Every time I go back there, my terror returns, and then the unbelievable accusations of Robileaux, and I'm just—"

"Let's take a moment," I said gently. "Can I get you coffee, water?"

"I'm just frustrated. And traumatized. Still, six years later. That's why the polygraph wasn't accurate. Every time I think about that night my heart starts thudding, and I'm back there, terrified. None of this is right. I didn't stab myself. I wouldn't do that to myself; I wouldn't do that to my children. I have letters here from people attesting to that." She pulled out several sheets of paper and slid them over to me. "There's one from a doctor here that says based on my injury it was *extremely* unlikely I stabbed myself. Extremely unlikely. I don't know where Robileaux got that the angle of the knife indicated I might have. And the fact that I have no history of self-destructive behavior was irrelevant to him. Statistics concerning self-destructive behavior clearly indicate that self-stabbing in the chest is not a female form of self-destruction and in fact requires substantial physical strength to perform. Given that it took such force to remove the knife that I was lifted off the surgical table, well, how could I have done that?"

I nodded. Exactly, I thought.

"And then," she flipped through pages and pointed to the penultimate paragraph in Ray's report. "He keeps saying my kinesics, my body language, clearly indicated guilt, even in that final interview, that interview that, I must add, was taped without my knowledge and done clearly to sabotage me."

"That was—"

"But the only kinesics my body displayed was that of a woman with two fresh scars on my chest and back, still burning from thoracic surgery four weeks earlier." She sat back, took a deep breath, and traced a finger along the scars on her upper chest.

I watched the movement, gestured slightly toward it after a moment. "I was surprised, the scars," I said quietly.

She looked down, and her face softened. "I covered them up for a long time. I hated them, thought they were ugly. Then a friend said they were like a necklace. My scar necklace. I haven't tried to hide them since."

"Your strength has always amazed me, Marjorie."

She leaned forward, put her hand on my knee. "I did not do this to myself, Cathy. I need you to believe that."

I nodded slowly.

"Do you believe me?"

"You've got a number of good points here."

"But do you believe me?"

"There are troubling inconsistencies."

She sat back, her face tight and shut off. "You aren't going to answer that, are you." It was not a question.

I recrossed my legs, spoke carefully. "It's not my place to determine whether you're telling the truth, only whether the case should be reexamined."

"And what have you decided, can you at least tell me that?" A tinge of sarcasm colored her voice.

I gestured toward her file. "I need to look at that again, and my partner, George Donovan, will study it as well. If we decide to reopen it, investigate it as attempted murder, there is very little physical evidence for us to work with. But I need to check all the details, talk to the investigating officers, the witnesses. Our goal is to be fair and thorough."

"If you talk to Robileaux, he'll just say what he's always said."

"I know," I said, and then cursed myself silently.

She leaned forward, her voice both eager and angry. "You've talked to him?"

I pushed my chair back slightly from the table, put my hands in my lap. "Marjorie, I simply can't say anything more at this point. I'll call you next week, the following at the latest, and let you know the disposition. I'm just very, very sorry for all you've gone through."

"Well." The word came out flat and quick and hung in the air between us for several seconds. "I suppose I'm grateful that at least you listened and seem to care. It's more than I ever got from Robileaux or anyone else in this department. I suppose you can't take sides, can you? You cops protect your own, and you're not about to say Robileaux was wrong."

"I'm not protecting—"

"No." She held her hand out, palm facing me. "Don't try to explain. It wouldn't change anything." She stood up, gathered the files in her arms. "Funny how inadequate words can be, isn't it, given that all I have now is words?"

"Marjorie."

She tilted her head and almost smiled. "You're just doing your job. And I'm doing what I need to do. I'm thankful there could be some movement on this. It's more than I ever expected from the police." And then she did smile, a big crooked smile that suddenly showed her age. "I'm a brokenhearted woman with nothing to lose. And I won't stop."

I sat there a long time after she left, staring at her file, thinking about scars. About how some are so visible and some are hidden, even to ourselves, buried deep beneath tissue and muscle and bone in that ethereal place that makes us who we are. How both kinds mark us forever—knotty and twisted and painful to the touch even years later. But there's something about a scar that is so boldly, even proudly, displayed that makes it beautiful, luminous—a testament, and an honorable one at that, no matter the cause. And I wondered about my own scars, what new white snake was twisting into being deep inside from my inability to say, "Yes, Marjorie, I believe you; I have always believed you. Ray was wrong," as I scrawled *Reopen* across her file, tossed it on George's desk, gathered up my badge and gun, and headed home to my husband.

SARAH

*Don't tell us
how to love, don't tell us
how to grieve, or what
to grieve for, or how loss
shouldn't sit down like a gray
bundle of dust in the deepest
pockets of our energy, don't laugh at our belief*
—Mary Oliver

KEEPING THE DEAD ALIVE

She had been a woman who looked good in hiking boots. In the picture on the scuffed pine dresser, she wore khaki shorts, a Guatemalan shirt, and boots laced tightly above the ankle, the edge of teal green socks just visible. Her calves were muscular and brown. *Lithe*, I think, is the word some might use to describe her. Hazel-gray eyes curved up slightly, thin lips rested on a wide mouth, nose sloped into a gentle bump with a spatter of freckles and faint sunburn. A mole lingered between her brows. Deep auburn hair fell well below her shoulders, thick and frizzy with curl, the kind of hair that probably distressed her in humidity, made her dream of straight and simple, something that whispered just above her collarbone. She would have wanted my hair in the same way I envied hers. She had a sharp jawline and prominent cheekbones—both long enough to work in her favor. She was smiling, an impish grin, head tilted left to avoid the sun's glare.

From the picture I wouldn't have guessed she was so short, but the body lying between the bed and the wall was 5'2" at the most.

She lay on her back, naked. I was working on the assumption that this was the same woman as in the picture, although the only feature I could match for sure was the hair, and even that wasn't a safe bet. This woman's hair was clumpy with dried blood and matted across her face—if you could call the black, swollen flesh barely visible under the hair a face. Both arms were up in the defensive position, resting on her brow, as though her last moments were weary ones, not icy white terror, as though her hands and mouth had never been bound with duct tape.

Perhaps, I thought—a weak hope—perhaps she passed out early on before these last tortures. I couldn't tell. I knew she'd been alive for most of it; there was too much blood. Blood everywhere on and around her swollen corpse, already coagulated into thick, leathery pools and blackened at the edges. Dead bodies don't bleed.

She'd been alive. Shake that one out of your mind, go home and try to pay the bills, cook dinner, wash the laundry. She'd been alive when he took the pliers and tore off one of her nipples and yanked out two of her teeth. She'd been alive when he cut off her middle finger. She'd been alive for each of the five cigarette burns on her stomach and thighs. She'd been alive when he took the tennis racquet and jammed it up her vagina with such force that the handle was a purplish-blue hump just below her sternum.

In police work, just like life, "what-ifs" don't really pertain. It's already happened. That's the beauty of a crime scene, of any crime. It's pure fact. It's done. Inarguable. You play what-ifs to find the angle that will take you down the right path to solve the crime, what-ifs to ferret out the motive; but a crime, in this case a dead body, is exquisitely simple: there are no what-ifs. All the nuances of other possibilities—a right turn instead of a left, coming home ten minutes later instead of five minutes earlier—are obsolete. The robbery has occurred, the blow has landed, the person is dead.

It's one of the aspects I like best about my job. Wash away all the noise of motivations, clues that do or don't add up, guilt or innocence, and what you still have is fact: a crime.

Yet life is full of other possibilities, slight dimples in the texture of our days that change the course, sometimes forever invisible even to ourselves, of what might have been. And when an event becomes visible, something to take note of for whatever reason, being human we rewind the tape—hoping to put some logic to chaos, hoping to find the cause in order to make better sense of the effect. We look for meaning in coincidences. We try to connect the dots and discover some larger pattern at work. This practice has no great benefit except to soothe our pain or curiosity. It makes what is essentially nonlinear, linear for a moment. And then we can play what-ifs if only to understand our own control—or lack thereof—over our lives.

In the long, fevered weeks that followed, despite my best intentions and deep belief that addressing the facts, and facts alone, was the best approach to living one's life, I seemed incapable of stopping the what-ifs. And the place I came back to again and again was that morning, the start of day shift, a Monday, just before I found her body.

We'd already had roll call, a joke on any shift but especially the day shift. No one's totally awake at 6:00 in the morning; you wake up on your first call or on your fourth cup of coffee. Most of us that morning were somewhere between the second and third cup.

Despite how TV likes to portray roll calls with crisply dressed officers sitting or standing in tight rows listening to crucial information—or, even more amusingly, no roll call at all—roll call involves making sure you're there and some degree of finger shaking about whatever the Captain and Lieutenant have up their ass for that day. The real information exchange takes place out on the back lot, when one shift is packing up to go home and the other is loading shotguns, performing radio checks, making sure the tires are inflated and the siren and lights work.

Bobby had already told us about the latest rape on Tulip Street, the McCollough kids terrorizing their neighborhood, and the rumor that the Lieutenant was, once again, on the warpath about officers not wearing hats on calls.

It was a very regular morning.

Several of us lingered near our units, discussing the latest developments in Steve Darcy's case. Darcy had been fired recently for killing an unarmed burglary suspect. The department wasn't keen on our shooting unarmed people. Darcy was appealing the ruling. The general consensus was that it could have happened to any one of us, and Darcy was getting screwed.

I had my unit started, waiting for a break in the radio traffic to put myself 10-8, in service, when Gwen stopped and said the Sergeant wanted to see me.

"What for?"

"You think I asked?" she said, raising both eyebrows so high her hat rose with the movement. "Sarah." The way Gwen said my name, it had more than two syllables.

I smiled and shrugged.

Gwendolyn Stewart was tall, big yet muscular, and always had flawlessly applied makeup from Merle Norman, where she often visited when a shift was slow, dragging me along occasionally to check out the latest lipstick that she swore would bring out my eye color or the perfect blush to highlight my cheeks. She usually bought the lipstick or blush. But Gwen was persistent.

She'd been on the department twelve years, just two more than me, and was close to making corporal. She tended to be aggressive on calls and with people in general, which landed her in more fights than anyone else on our shift, except perhaps Doug Ledoux. She loved jewelry—diamonds in particular—and wore the biggest-assed diamond studs I'd ever seen on anyone who wasn't a socialite. She was a lapsed Catholic, her favorite expression was some variation on the word *fuck*, and she'd been married three times, the last time to an insurance adjuster. I didn't have high hopes for the marriage, and neither did she.

"Shoney's or IHOP?" I asked.

She waggled a piece of paper at me. "HQ gave me a 52 already. On the fuckin' interstate."

"Later then."

She snorted, said "Sarah" again. I knew her snorts well; she had three of them. This one meant, roughly translated, "Everyone but us is a dickhead." I have to admit, the sentiment frequently seemed apt.

We'd been night-shift partners over two years now, the first all-female uniform team working out of Highland Precinct, a sprawling area, bordered on one side by the Mississippi River, that incorporated the state university, estates that had been in the family for generations, rural homesteads, middle-class subdivisions, and the Bottoms—a high-crime, low-income neighborhood nestled right up against the precinct's back door. We shared a distaste for overblown authority, petty rules, panty hose, wool, and okra. She sometimes frustrated me beyond reason, but she was loyal and funny. And I trusted her without reservation.

Back in the precinct, Sergeant Mosher tapped his thick but well-manicured finger on a felony theft report I'd written the day before. "Forgot to sign it," he said, pushing it toward me.

I handed it back signed and dated.

"Noticed your ticket count was down last month, Jeffries."

I'd been working under Mosher for the last year, and I liked him as much as you can like a sergeant. He didn't crowd me often, so I nodded.

"I'll take care of it. Sir." Don't ever let anyone hand you any crap about cops not having ticket quotas. They are the great invisible rule on any shift.

I was almost out the door when Davy, the day desk officer, called my name. I wasn't fond of Davy. He was terrified of the streets, so he claimed a bad back. This from a man who ran a bush-hogging business on the side.

"Check this out, will you?" He handed me a call slip with a name and address. "Lady says there's something funny going on at her neighbor's. Wants to talk to an officer."

"You're an officer, Davy. You talk to her."

"Jeffries, she wants to *see* an officer." He grinned, and my stomach lurched at the sight of his broken-post teeth stained yellowish-brown deep at the gums. I resolved, once again, to stop smoking. Soon.

"Send it to HQ."

"You're here. I'll call and tell 'em you're taking it." Davy grinned again. "Unless you got something better to do."

I stared at a water stain on the wall above his head, thinking how tired I was of Davy, how he'd never pull this on a male cop, thinking how much I'd like to slap him silly. I took a deep breath and let what I thought was my better sense prevail. Davy was such an easy target.

"Define funny," I said.

"Huh?"

"'Something funny' at the neighbors. Can you be slightly more specific?"

He sighed and tugged his shirt down at the waist. Working the desk, Davy had gotten a little chunky. "She's worried."

"That's a start." I nodded encouragingly.

"Something about not seeing her neighbor for several days. Something about the back door."

"You're good on those details, Davy." I smiled sweetly, a smile that anyone who knew me recognized as the opposite of sweet. "So funny really means suspicious?"

"Look, Jeffries, you gonna take this, or you want me to pass it on to Mosher?"

"I'll handle it, Davy. You sit tight."

Which is where, many days later, my what-ifs took me back to: sloppy attention to paperwork, my own damned sense of superiority, and letting Davy needle me into taking a call that should have gone through HQ dispatch. It didn't make what came to happen any easier to understand, and I've never denied my own culpability. But it was a starting point.

The complainant, Doris Whitehead, lived in an older part of the city, near the Mississippi River levee and the railroad tracks. It was a run-down area with small houses on large lots crowded with pecan, oak, and cypress trees. Some of the houses had been slave quarters originally.

This time of morning a pinkish-gray fog hovered near the river. The sun was an eggshell orb already burning through the haze. There was a peaceful hesitancy to the morning, a rare and appreciated beauty. It was another plus to the job, seeing the city in all its various guises. Sometimes, I could love it.

As my tires loped over the railroad tracks, I thought of the skeleton woman. A year ago we'd found the remains of Val, a young coed, in the high grass down the bank from the tracks, near the university golf course. She'd been missing over four months. Went out for her regular jog early one morning and never came back. That's one of the downsides to working the job for ten years: your landmarks are crime scenes, and everywhere you turn, memories shimmer to the surface momentarily whether you invite them or not.

There was just enough left of Val's remains to tell she'd been sexually assaulted. That the perp had smashed in her head with a large metal object. Probably she died instantaneously. Probably. But that didn't ease the thoughts of what came before. That's what always froze me, set icy hot caterpillar nerves restlessly stirring; it's what I tasted. The just before.

Death is disgusting no matter the context. It rips the fabric of what is. Whether it's an elderly woman dying peacefully in her sleep surrounded by those who love her, a young boy killed in a drive-by shooting, or a drug addict dead from an overdose, death is singularly ugly. And sooner or later, whatever your personality or disposition, the exposure to death wrings life—that stuff that makes us who we are—from those who deal with it regularly.

I'd tried various ways to tame death, to compartmentalize the sheer human misery I dealt with day in and day out. Alcohol helped. So did sex. But then Tracy Skinner told me about the group—an informal gathering, she said, nothing religious, just a moment of acknowledgment—and invited me to join. The skeleton woman was my first.

We gathered at the site the night after Val's body was found. One o'clock in the morning with a cloud-soaked moon and the deep smell of wet mud and rotting grass drifting off the Mississippi, nine off-duty female cops picked our way carefully through tall weeds, one flashlight leading us to the edge of the golf green where we stepped over the yellow crime scene tape and stood in a circle. Marge, the responding officer, spoke quietly about the scene, described it in detail. And then for five minutes no one spoke, as we each, in our own way, honored the dead girl.

What happened next startled me. I'd only intended to wish Val's soul a safe journey, to swear we'd find the scum who did this. But standing there, shoulder to shoulder with those other women, the night air lapping against my skin, her terror inhabited me. I could have reached out a finger and traced her figure against the splotchy sky. I saw her hands raised, felt the raspy, acid gasps on my neck, heard the tumbled "nonononono"; his hands were on my breasts, the sexual stink of his body clung to my face. For five minutes, all my carefully constructed defenses collapsed, and I panicked silently, completely. Then I went home and threw up.

I shook myself away from the memory as I drove past the vet school and turned left onto River Road. There were goats in many of the wide yards, a few cows and horses. The lots became larger, the houses smaller, and the grass higher until I reached a small paved road that turned away from the river. I drove slowly, looking for the address Davy had given me.

A woman in her midsixties dressed in a faded denim skirt, purple LSU T-shirt, and white high-top tennis shoes stood at the end of one of the driveways. I stopped the unit so my open passenger window was even with her.

I leaned partway across the seat and nodded hello. "Mrs. White-head?"

"Doris. It's Jeannette next door," she said, her arms folded tightly against her chest. The woman's gray hair was chopped short, and her forearms were thick and corded with old muscle and fat. I looked in the direction she'd tilted her head toward, but I couldn't see a house for all the trees and underbrush.

"I'm Officer Jeffries. What seems to be the problem?"

"Haven't seen her in several days. I always see her leave for work; she passes right by my house, comes home this way too. She works 'cross the river at one of them refineries, regular like. But her car's in the yard."

"You've been over there?"

"Went up to the porch and knocked. Couldn't see nothing. She's always been meanin' to give me a key but never got round to it." She shook her head once. "I'm not a worrier, understand? But this is strange. Haven't seen her since the ruckus couple days back. Not like her, not at all." The woman's voice was firm yet soft. Her southern gravel reflected a long-time cigarette smoker and the skin around her nose a bit of indulgence in hard liquor.

"What ruckus is that?" I asked.

"It wasn't much. He's always hollering at her, regular like. Nothing strange 'bout that. 'Cept I haven't seen her."

"She lives with somebody?"

The woman nodded. "Her husband, Vince. Truck driver. Must be doing a route, his rig isn't there; but this isn't like Jeannette not to be passing by. She's a nice woman."

I took it from her intonation that Vince was not a nice man.

"Well, I'll go take a look, ma'am. You'll be here awhile?"

"Yup, I'm retired. Taught fifth-grade math."

I started to put the car in gear, then remembered Davy's comment. "You mentioned something funny about a door over there?"

For the first time the woman's eyes shifted away from me, and she rubbed the palm of her hand hard against her right ear.

"Flies," she said.

"Flies?"

"There's flies all over the back screen door and some of them windows." She spoke so softly I had to lean toward her. "Jeannette keeps a clean house."

I nodded slowly. "Okay."

"You'll come back and let me know?" She put a hand on my car. "Whatever?"

"Yes, ma'am. Whatever."

"Her last name's Durham," the woman said. "Jeannette Durham."

Jeannette's house was a small, sagging clapboard, with faded blue paint, sitting in a stand of magnolia and oak trees. I parked a good thirty yards back from the house on the shell driveway and put myself 10-7, on the scene, with HQ dispatch. I unsnapped my holster and kept my hand on the butt of my gun as I walked slowly, my footsteps crunching louder than I liked, the portable radio on my hip crackling faintly with transmissions. I stopped once to briefly touch the trunk of her car—closed and locked—scanned the interior—clean—and then touched the hood—cool.

There's always something faintly eerie about approaching a house this way with so many unknowns. Especially during daylight when everything appears normal, or at least what we perceive as normal, as safe. You get a hundred calls about someone missing or something not right, and the person almost always shows up, the mystery is no mystery at all. It tends to breed cynicism, a lackadaisical approach to the myriad calls you answer day after day. And then there's that exception. Someone says something like "flies," and your heart lurches.

The woman was right. There were an inordinate number of flies clinging to the screens on the windows at the rear of the house and side door. But even without the presence of flies I would have known something was wrong. After a while you can read the stillness, taste the texture of the air. Every sense processes a dozen different impressions that the brain computes and analyzes into one single pronouncement: something is wrong. It's what most cops live for, whether we like to admit it or not, that feeling of something gone wrong.

I hesitated only a moment, considering whether to call for backup. This seemed pretty straightforward: something was dead inside.

Blinds were drawn over all the windows except in the front, and the two doors were locked. But screens are ridiculously easy to pry off with a pocketknife, and people are generally lax about locking their windows, especially this far out of town. I got lucky on the third one off the front porch.

As I eased the window sash up, I smelled what the flies already knew: dead flesh. It is a distinct smell, thick and lush with the ecstasy of rot. It settles on your skin like a fine sheen of sweat and requires discipline to hold your imagination in check.

I stood there for a minute, listening. Nothing. Technically, I knew, I should announce myself. Not for my well-being, but for the protection of any civilians who might be inside—that was the official department reasoning. The department didn't want to get sued if you entered the wrong house, arrested the wrong person, shot someone you shouldn't have. You might get hurt, but God help you if a civilian did.

Some rules, however, are stupid.

Placing both my hands on the windowsill, I scrambled through the open window, very ungracefully but quietly, and sprawled on the wooden floor, gun in hand, and listened again. Past the wheeze of my own breath, past the slight buzz of flies, past the subtle sighs of a house in a morning breeze—searching for a rustle, a scrape, a sense that there was someone else here besides me and whatever lay dead in this house.

I rose slowly, wishing simultaneously that I had the silent grace of a tracker, that the search was already completed, that I had a scanner to detect signs of life-forms, that I'd called for backup, that I was eating breakfast with Gwen.

It's just like on TV, except you move slower and you don't say a word. You hug walls, use a sweeping two-handed grip on the gun, keep your knees bent, and move heel to toe. You toe-push doors open gently and pray that if something moves you have time to say, "POLICE, FREEZE," and make the right decision to shoot or not.

I worked my way back through the house toward the smell, doing my best not to contaminate the scene, noted the dirty dishes on the kitchen counter, the blood in the sink and bathtub, the reddish-brown smears on the hall walls, and the broken glass on the floor, until I came to the rear bedroom, saw her, checked the walk-in closet, and came back to the bed, looked down, and studied the remains of Jeannette, a nice woman who kept a clean house.

The most valuable aspect of SOP—standard operating procedure—is that while one part of your brain is reacting to and absorbing the scene or crisis, the other part of your brain is flipping through the index file of appropriate actions, accessing the correct ones, and activating the body until the rest of you can catch up. The longer you're on the job, the less time it takes to catch up and the more likely you'll react correctly.

I had the portable radio up to my mouth even as I began scanning the room, this time for evidence, for a sense of what went wrong here.

"2D-76 Headquarters."

"2D-76."

"Got a Signal 65 here. One female. Get me detectives, crime scene, coroner, DA, supervisor."

"That's a 10-4, 2D-76. EMS as well, 10-4?"

"10-4."

I sighed. It was asinine to send out an ambulance on bodies that were clearly dead and had been for some time. But in their infinite wisdom, some higher-ups had decided that a uniform cop couldn't determine for sure whether life had ceased, even with the obvious signs of rigor mortis and no pulse. So the med techs would come and say, "Nope, no pulse." And the detectives would come and say, "Yep, she's a goner." The assistant DA would arrive and say, "Looks dead to me." The crime scene guys would come and say, "Oh yeah, we got a ripe one here." One of the assistant coroners would arrive and say, "Yes, she's dead." And we'd all stand around and watch the final indignities: the photographs, the fingerprints, the prodding and probing and scrapping and bagging—and some of us, the autopsy.

The house would swell with mostly men, and they would stare at her; there would be jokes and raunchy comments, and later bootlegged copies of the crime scene photos would be passed around in coffee shops and parking lots. The official photographs would be included in the packet of photos shown to academy classes to prepare them for their first dead body, a one-dimensional illustration without smell and taste and adrenaline kick of what one human being can do to another.

And Jeannette, whoever she'd been before, would gently disappear, the texture of a whole life vanished into a series of cut-and-dried reports, and she'd be referred to, for years to come by people she never knew, as "that woman who had the tennis racquet jammed up her vagina."

After I replaced the two screens I'd popped off the locked windows, I sat on the porch steps and smoked a cigarette. I hadn't been particularly interested in staying with Jeannette. There was too much residual terror in the back bedroom for my taste. I'd seen a lot of dead bodies in my day, women in particular: beaten, strangled, raped, shot, stabbed, some even tortured. But the level and intensity of violence here, the sheer horror of what had been done to her body, eclipsed anything I'd ever seen before. And I'd learned early on that hanging out alone with a dead body could play tricks with your mind, that the essence of the dead person could come to life and swirl around in unsettling ways.

The first time that happened was nine months after I'd joined the force. We were dispatched to a shots-fired call in the projects off Nicholson. I arrived with two other uniforms so quickly we could still taste the acrid bite of gunpowder. A white male lay crumpled on his side, almost in a fetal position, gun resting in his hand as though it was an orange he'd just selected for lunch. One officer went back outside to call for an ambulance and detectives, the other followed him, and I'm there, alone in the kitchen, standing over the body and studying his face, wondering how he could look so peaceful with half his head missing, when I swore he shifted, that something of what he'd been started to rise up off the ground and speak. I clattered back out the side door, down the steps, and stood in the yard taking deep gulps of air. The other uniforms laughed at me, but I wasn't about to correct their notion that the body had made me sick.

Fact: The dead don't come to life again. Fact: Dead bodies don't stand up and speak. But the mind doesn't always like facts; it can have a sneaky desire at times to veer off into mystery and supposition. And that's where discipline comes in. The best I could do for Jeannette at this point was keep the scene clean and turn it over to the Homicide detectives when they arrived.

Before I'd finished my cigarette, a tan Ford Fairmont with a low front tire whipped in the drive with a blast of loose shells. Barker was driving, and Cowan was riding shotgun.

"Sarah Jeffries! What bundle of joy have you brought us today?" Cowan was a perpetually cynical and happy man, a weird mix that grated on my nerves sometimes, but mostly I appreciated how many cases he closed and how he didn't treat me like some dumb uniform.

"Torture, bondage, rape with a tennis racquet," I said, carefully stubbing out my cigarette and slipping it into a back pocket. "Not too pretty."

Barker winced and stretched his shoulders.

"Never is," Cowan said. "Keeps it interesting, though." His small frame vibrated with enthusiasm as he moved to the trunk to collect camera, plastic booties, gloves, and evidence bags.

"Anyone we like for this?" Barker wore a light green shortsleeve shirt that didn't improve his complexion. He had a voracious appetite—I'd watched in wonder one night when he downed three "cook's specials" at Steak 'n' Egg in less than a half hour—but he always looked pale and underfed. Unlike most of the detectives who'd gone to wearing belt holsters, Barker still wore a shoulder holster, his gun tucked up under one armpit, handcuffs under the other.

"There's an absent husband the neighbor lady doesn't think much of."

"Yeah, well, my neighbors don't think much of me, but I'm not about to go sticking a tennis racquet up my wife's box," said Cowan.

"You're divorced," I said.

"Exactly." Cowan grinned, took off his jacket, and tossed it on the backseat of the unit.

"What about this window?" Barker said, eyeing the screen I'd propped up against the house earlier, as he slipped on the plastic booties that ensured an untainted crime scene. Cowan stood in front of the house and started taking pictures.

"I popped the screen to get in. House was locked up tight otherwise. No signs of forced entry. Your evidence trail starts inside. I didn't touch a thing except the window and a few doorknobs."

"Not even the body?"

"It's kind of obvious she's dead," I said, giving him a look.

"Ungloved?"

"Yep."

Barker nodded, frowning. "Car?"

"Neighbor lady says it's the victim's."

"You got gloves?"

"In my unit."

"Check it if you get the chance. 'Preciate if you keep the outside scene secure until CSD gets here." Barker stuffed several paper and plastic envelopes in his back pockets and took out a penlight, small notebook, and pencil as he joined Cowan on the porch.

"Guys?"

Barker turned and looked at me.

"It's pretty rough in there."

He gave a tight nod and stretched his shoulders again.

I watched them move slowly through the door, taking pictures, bending to the ground, studying the door frame, in no hurry to get to the body. It wasn't going anywhere, and the first evidence trail walk was important, told them things I would have missed. Cowan kept up a running commentary that served no purpose except to focus him. Several minutes later I heard one of them say "Holy shit," but couldn't tell whether it was Barker or Cowan. I hoped it was Cowan's stomach turning. Divorced indeed, like about five times.

Within twenty minutes the porch and driveway had filled with uniforms and plainclothes. There was the occasional flash of light as Watson and Kirk with CSD, Crime Scene Division, took the requisite pictures.

I was sitting in the driver's side of Jeannette's maroon Toyota with the door open when Sergeant Mosher arrived.

"Your hat, Jeffries."

"Yes, sir." Always with the hat thing. I've never figured out how a hat makes you a better cop, but the brass sure seemed to like them.

"Anything in there?"

I assumed he meant the car and not the house. "Couple of Rolling Stones tapes and one of Beausoleil. Two romance novels and a photography book checked out," I flipped to the back, "five days ago from Goodwood Library."

"Set 'em aside for the detectives. Inventory the car while you're at it."

"Yes, sir." I hated inventorying cars. I hated anything that involved a lot of paperwork. Hell, I really hated doing anything that someone else told me I had to do.

There wasn't much more of interest in Jeannette's car. Some gum, two movie stubs from a week past, loose change. A couple of rolls of film CSD would get developed; no telling where your leads could come from. A pay stub from a refinery over in Plaquemine. The car was registered in her name. Unfortunately, no signed note that said "I killed Jeannette." Not that I expected any such thing, but it was amazing what perps could overlook in the panic of their crime. One of my favorite cases was solved in five minutes after the victim took us to the alley behind the building where she'd been raped, and there was the asshole's ID lying on the ground. I still enjoyed the memory of his face when I held up his driver's license and said, "Missing anything?"

Tires crunched on the drive, and I looked up to see Tracy Skinner's unit pull in. She was built like a Jeep—all squat rectangles, with an unruly mess of red curls that bobby pins couldn't keep in place—and one of the first women in the department to make sergeant.

I got out of Jeannette's car and went to meet her, pulling the surgical gloves off as I walked.

"Better get your hat, Sarah," she said. "Lieutenant's on his way."

I nodded, then jerked my head back toward the house. "Somebody tortured the hell out of her."

She sighed and pulled her hat down more tightly over her forehead. "Some days I can handle this shit better than others. Today's not one of them." She readjusted her gun belt. "Any kids?"

"Not that I can tell."

"There's one small kindness."

"She didn't die quickly."

"Been dead long?"

"At least twenty-four hours, I'd say. But the scene's fresh. No sign of a cleanup. CSD might be able to lift some prints." This was hopeful thinking on my part. There's another thing TV has screwed up for law enforcement, making civilians think lifting prints is like peeling the wrapping off a popsicle.

"Where's Mosher?"

"Just inside. He gave me that look," I said.

Tracy's lips twitched, and she rested her hands on her gun belt. "What'd you do?"

"Entered through an open window."

"Open? Or closed but unlocked?"

"Closed but unlocked. There were flies. I could smell it."

Her jaw jutted forward, and she pursed her lips. "Shit."

We both looked at the ground. I couldn't exactly disagree with her, but I subscribed to the belief that the sign of a good cop is one who has as many complaints as commendations in the personnel file. If you're doing your job, you're going to be pissing off some people. No doubt Tracy was thinking about the same incident I was, the burglary I'd worked last fall over on Jefferson Highway. That time there was somebody inside. Two somebodies, both very much alive. The apartment manager saw a man entering through a window and called the police; she was adamant that a woman lived there alone. Turned out the apartment manager was right, she just didn't have all the facts: the woman who lived there had a boyfriend who was enacting some sexual fantasy they both harbored. They were not happy when I came busting into her bedroom hollering, "Police!" The Lieutenant like to fried my ass over that one, but Tracy and Mosher did some dancing overtime for me, and all I got was a letter in my file suggesting I consider other alternatives in the future. I liked holding on to that word *consider*; it held a vastly different meaning than *use*.

"Look," I put a hand out to stop Tracy as she started up the drive. "I think the group should do this one."

She stared up at the house then off to the trees on both sides of the house before she looked back at the road. "There's an old woman down the street asking what's going on."

"That'll be the complainant. She called it in."

"We don't need nosy neighbors."

"Yeah. I'll take care of it."

For all the action going on at Jeannette's house, I couldn't hear a thing except mockingbirds, cardinals, and the occasional squirrel chatter up in the trees on the walk back to the complainant's house. A barely there breeze kept the leaves whispering, a soothing barrier between where I'd come from and where I was headed. I stopped about halfway and turned around to look in the direction of Jeannette's house. Couldn't see a thing either. I wondered what it looked like at night. No streetlights to worry about this far out from town.

The sun had hit its full stride, and by the time I reached the complainant's rutted driveway, I'd worked up a good sweat. I cursed, for the bazillionth time, our Chief's move last year to blue, wool-blend uniforms. The previous black-and-gray polyester-knit uniforms weren't as stylish, but they weren't wool. Wool in Louisiana. Even cops in backwater towns like Amite and Breaux Bridge didn't wear wool-blend uniforms. And the brass wondered why they were having such a hard time persuading officers to wear their bulletproof vests. I'd like to see one of them work a wreck on Interstate 10 in the middle of a July day wearing a hat, bulletproof vest, fifteen pounds of gun belt around their waist and those goddamn wool-blend uniforms. Throw in the first day of menstrual cramps for good measure, and the average man would faint after five minutes.

The neighbor woman stood up from the folding chair she'd placed in the middle of her driveway near the road when she saw me round the corner. I hated this part of my job almost as much as I hated paperwork and listening to the Lieutenant. I always felt inadequate.

"You bringin' bad news, ain't you?" she said.

"Yes, ma'am." I figured she was the type who would prefer straightforward. "I'm sorry. Jeannette's dead."

Her whole body sagged, like all the bones in her shoulders, arms, and knees had dissolved, and for a second I thought she might collapse. I took a step forward, my hand coming up to catch her, but she pulled herself upright, turning her head slightly away from me, her chin tucked into her shoulder, lips curled over her teeth in a tight line. I reached out, lightly touched her shoulder, and felt it flinch.

She stepped away. "Yup," she said. "That sumabitch."

"The husband?"

"Yup."

"Last time he was here was three nights ago, Friday night?"

"That sumabitch," she said, still working her lips together. I took this to be a yes and decided I liked this woman. She must have been a hell of a teacher. I was never any good at math, but I'll bet she would've whipped me into line.

"You hear his truck leave, Mrs. Whitehead?" I took a small brown spiral notebook out of my shirt pocket and flipped it open.

"I ain't married. Doris is good enough for me." Her tone was terse and unyielding.

I blinked once, tried to get my mouth around calling her Doris, and settled for a "Yes, ma'am."

She gave a short laugh that carried little humor and shook her head. I stood there for a few minutes, the sun beating hard on the back of my neck, watching her stare at the ground. Finally, I said, "His truck? Did you hear it leave?"

She looked up at me as though I were slowly coming back into focus. "I can't recollect for sure. My window units get noisy. But his rig was gone by six Saturday morning when I came down for the paper."

"And the last time you saw Jeannette was Thursday?"

"Thursday evening, right around supper time, 'bout six or so. She dropped off a book she'd gotten at the library, one on insects for my garden. I didn't ask for it, she just brought it." Doris Whitehead finally sat back down in her chair. "That's the type of person she was."

"She sounds like a good woman."

Doris Whitehead glared up at me, and for a moment I felt like a fifth-grader who'd messed up on long division. Again.

"She was a ninny for not leaving him. I told her a passel of times, but she wouldn't listen. Said he didn't mean it, said he was sweet most the time. I never saw no sweet in that man."

"He beat her frequently?"

"Yup." Lips curled back over her teeth into a tight slash.

"Police ever been out here?"

"Once. Last winter. I called y'all out, but you didn't do nuthin' about it," she said. I cursed inwardly when my eyes shifted, almost on their own accord, from hers.

"It would have been up to Jeannette," I said softly.

"She was a nice woman, and he was no good," she said somewhat fiercely. "She helped me out around here, regular like. Climbed up to the roof and cleaned my gutters this spring, held the stakes two weeks ago when I tied up my tomato plants. Liked to sing a lot. That rock-and-roll stuff. Don't know any of the names, but I'd hear her sometimes at night. She didn't sing when he was home." Doris Whitehead's hands kept gripping her skirt and bunching it into her fists.

"She got any family you know of?"

She paused, looked off toward Jeannette's house. "A mother over in Slidell. Last name of Richardson. But they weren't close."

I studied her profile. There was something she wasn't telling me, something she was holding back. It could simply be shock or grief, perhaps regret. Still, if I'd learned anything over the years working this job, it was that everyone had their secrets, a part of themselves they rarely, if ever, showed anyone else. We all told lies, to others, to ourselves. None of us were who we seemed. And that was as much a fact as the dead body in the house next door.

I heard a car go by, then a second later the crunch of tires on shell, and decided not to probe any further. "I'm sorry, ma'am. Truly I am. The detectives will be over here in a bit. I'll let them know what you told me, but they'll be working the case, so they'll want to talk to you. See if you can think of anything else that might be relevant. Never know what might help."

"He's got a fellow he hangs around some with. Never met him. Ralph, Roger, Robert, Ray, Ronald—something like that starting with an *R*. Lives in Denham Springs, Greenwell Springs, one of them Springs towns. Jeannette didn't like him much."

I nodded, jotted it down in my notebook. "We'll start trying to track Vince down today."

"Sumabitch better not come back round here," she muttered.

Something in her tone made me look at her hard. "You own a gun, ma'am?"

"Yup."

"Ever used it?"

"Killed a moccasin out back two springs ago."

We stared at each for at least five seconds with her chin getting higher the longer our eyes held the other's gaze. And I knew, even as I spoke my next words, that Doris Whitehead would do exactly what she wanted and nothing less.

"You best give us a call you see any sign of him, understand?" I gave her my toughest voice and underscored it with looping my thumbs through my gun belt. I could have been talking to a tree for the effect it had on her.

"Lemme ask you sumpthin before you go," she said.

"Ma'am?"

"How d'you do this?"

"Ma'am?"

She rubbed her hand up against her ear, like when she'd told me about the flies. "All this with the dead bodies and guns and no-good sumabitches. How d'you do it?"

I stared at her. A number of images came to mind—my boyfriend's hands, a fifth of bourbon, women standing in a circle, the backboard on a tennis court—as I groped for something to say. None seemed right to share without an explanation, and I wasn't up to explaining anything, so I settled for what I tried for most.

"Gently," I said.

She nodded slowly and shifted in her chair. "That's sumpthin." For the first time since I'd met her, her lips relaxed.

"Ma'am." I turned away, wishing for once I was wearing my hat so I could tip it at her. She'd had that kind of effect on me.

It was only a little past 8:00 in the morning, and already it had been much too long of a day. Somewhere, children shifted restlessly in their desks trying to focus on the intricacies of long division, people settled into work without fear of injury or loss of life, teenagers started the delicate nonverbal dance of desire, babies swooshed into this world tasting their first hungry breath of the same air their parents breathed, fish darted hard against the current in search of food, and some sumabitch somewhere had Jeannette's blood soaked into his pores.

I could have cried, but it wasn't in my job description.

Watson and Kirk were packing up the CSD van, and both the ambulance and the assistant coroner had arrived. So had the Lieutenant. I stopped at my unit and retrieved my hat, fitted the back down over the hunk of hair I had bobby-pinned up into a bun, then pulled the brim firmly down on my forehead, and tucked the stray strands up under the hard plastic band. The edges of a headache came on immediately.

"Sarah," Kirk called out as I walked up. Kirk went by the nickname of Fat Baby, which I'd never figured out as he was skinny as a nightstick. Maybe it was his nearly bald head, much larger than the rest of his body, or the frequent jovial expression on his face. He was madly in love with his wife of ten years, and they had about six kids with another one on the way.

"Hey," I said. "Y'all find anything useful?" I liked both of them, as I did most of the CSD cops, even though I thought they spent way too much time drinking coffee at the Denny's on Acadian. Most uniforms viewed them as odd ducks, but I figured anyone who worked every god-awful crime scene in the city—Watson was up over eight hundred murders—needed to be odd simply to survive.

"Too much, and never enough." Watson sighed. His black-rimmed glasses perched precariously on his nose, and his thick, wavy hair was past regulation length. "He beat the hell out of her back and legs with that racquet before he used it elsewhere. Bruising along the margins of most of the wounds, so probably the perp used multiple objects. Cigarette burns on her buttocks. Strangulation attempts. White lines indicate two rings missing, one off the ring finger."

"Find the missing finger?"

Watson tugged at one side of his mustache. "Kitchen sink. The disposal. Sick bastard."

My stomach squirmed. "Any prints?"

"A partial-palm bloodstain transfer on the wall and a thumbprint on the racquet. One bloodstain transfer on the floor near her body, a boot looks like, squared-off toe," Kirk said. "Bunch of others throughout the house, probably nothing we can use. We'll see what Fingerprint can do with it, put a rush on it through AFIS, and we'll have an answer by tomorrow if the perp's prints are in system. God, I love high-tech law enforcement." He grinned like a happy Labrador.

"Any surprises?"

Watson choked off a snarled laugh. "Besides the tennis racquet?"

"And the mutilation? Sure rockets this one up to the top-ten list of scenes I've worked," Kirk said. "Definitely a crime of passion, someone who knew her. Lot of simmering rage. I've seen torture before, but never like this. Cowan's going to try to track down the husband through the trucking company."

"Think it's the husband?" I asked.

"Bet my pension on it." Kirk slammed the back door on the van. "Sometimes this job makes me want to puke."

"By the way, your boy radioed us. He's headed out this way," Watson said.

"Dubois?"

"Dubois, she asks, all innocent like." Kirk tossed an exposed film roll up into the air and caught it with his other hand.

I rolled my eyes at them.

"When you gonna leave that boy and come give me some sugar?" Watson poked me in the ribs with his index finger.

"When you leave your wife," I said, tapping him on the arm. This had been a running conversation between us for years. I had a hunch he was half serious. Sometimes, I thought, so was I.

Inside the house, the paramedics, Barker, and the assistant coroner were crowded into the bedroom doing the bagging routine: Jeannette's hands were wrapped in paper bags; each piece of torn, stained clothing on the floor was placed in a plastic bag and tagged as to the contents; her body was being readied to slide into a white body bag. Cowan was on his hands and knees looking under the kitchen sink, still muttering to himself in a gee-whiz, golly tone; the assistant DA watched him silently. In the living room, the Lieutenant was trying to look as if he belonged. Tracy and Mosher stood in a corner near the front door, their thumbs looped inside their gun belts.

"Officer Jeffries," the Lieutenant growled through a toothpick he was rolling between his teeth. I steeled myself. I despised the man. He was an overweight bully intimidated by intelligence. Especially female intelligence. He was every negative stereotype of a cop come to life.

"Sir?"

"You called this in?"

"I did."

"And you came in this window?"

"Yes sir. Smelled it from outside."

"The one with the screen still on it?"

"And all the flies," I said. "It was loose. Came off when I jiggled it."

"When you jiggled it. That so?" The Lieutenant shifted his considerable bulk to his other foot and took the toothpick out of his mouth and pointed it at me. "You think I'm stupid, Officer Jeffries?"

"No sir." Yes sir, dumb as dirt. I did exactly what six of us standing outside this house would have done. One or six, didn't make any difference.

"And those scratch marks on the screen?"

"I don't know, sir. It just came off when I was checking the window. The window was unlocked; I announced myself and entered the house."

"You announced yourself?"

"Yes sir."

We stared at each other for a second or two. And then I smiled at him. Sweetly. Big mistake.

"You have an attitude problem, you know that, Officer Jeffries?"

"Yes sir."

Barker walked in from the back bedroom, stripping off blood- and body-fluid-stained surgical gloves. "Nice job, Jeffries. No contamination that we can tell. Got lucky with some fingernail scrapings. Anything from the woman next door?"

"Nice job, my ass," the Lieutenant muttered, his doughy face set in a scowl.

I handed Barker a piece of paper with Doris Whitehead's name, address, and phone number. "She's expecting you. You find the papers from Metairie Trucking on the desk in the other bedroom?"

"Along with the letter." Barker glanced at the Lieutenant then me. "We got a problem here?"

"No problem," said Mosher.

"Nope." Tracy unfolded her arms, tried to catch my eye.

"What letter?" I said.

The Lieutenant's scowl deepened farther into folds of flesh. He could have easily won best in show for ugliest shar-pei.

Barker gestured toward the window. "I would have dropped the screen too, Lue."

The Lieutenant grunted.

"Yep." Tracy grasped the back of my arm, fingers digging deep, and pushed me toward the door. "She'll write this all up in her report. Everything you saw and did and why, right, Sarah?"

I nodded all the way out the door.

"You sure push it," Tracy said once we hit the driveway.

"He's an asshole."

"He's also the Lieutenant. I can't keep covering your butt when you leave it wide open. Write yourself a good report, hear me? Now put yourself 10-8 and get back out there."

"Gotta pee first."

She smiled. "After that."

"What you think?"

Tracy took off her hat and brushed back her hair. A thin red line marked her forehead. "Whoever did it should be hung by his balls and fried over a long slow fire."

"We can call the group on it?"

"I don't know, Sarah."

"What do you mean?"

"Something about this one doesn't feel right."

"How so?"

"Just doesn't. Maybe we can do it somewhere else, up the levee."

"Here," I said firmly. "This is where it happened; it needs to be here."

Tracy shook her head. "All this shit with Darcy; the perp's still loose. Maybe we should lay low for a while."

"For crissakes, Tracy, the perp's not coming back here."

"Everybody's jumpy."

"That's not a good enough reason."

She toed her boot into the ground. "Lemme think about it. Old woman next door going to be a problem?"

"Nah, she's got window units. Can't really hear much over there, see anything either. But she's got a gun. Claimed she'd shoot the husband if he came back."

"She said that?"

I shrugged. "More or less."

"I don't know." Her fingers worried the snap on her speed loaders.

I watched her, debating how far I could push, wondering how much of this was really about Darcy. Tracy was tough and no-nonsense 95 percent of the time, but she also had an indecisive streak I'd seen surface occasionally, and it always spooked me. I couldn't stand fence-sitters. Make a decision and live with the consequences was my motto.

I pulled my hat off, tucked it under my arm, and rubbed my temple with the edge of my wrist. "She deserves it."

"They all deserve it, Sarah." The wrinkles around her mouth and eyes deepened. "I'll call you tonight."

I nodded, but I'd already made up my mind. Alone, or with others, I was coming back here.

I drove up the road a ways, in the opposite direction of Doris White-head's house. The next house sat about five hundred yards away and across the street, hidden by three huge magnolia trees with limbs that almost touched the ground. A wide empty lot bordered the under-growth north of her house. Unlike the suburbs, the houses here weren't stacked one against the other with no room for breathing or privacy.

I was almost to River Road when I saw Ricky Dubois's black Jeep turn the corner and head my way. I pulled onto the dirt shoulder and waited. Ricky was a photographer for *The Advocate* and a sweet mix of lighthearted and serious—extra emphasis on the lighthearted. He'd majored in philosophy at LSU, something he claimed was redundant because he was Cajun. He also cheated at tennis.

"Hey you," he said, grinning back at me. "Rough morning?"

"Kind of." I reached my hand out the window and laced my fingers through his. He had the largest hands of any man I'd ever known. And the smallest feet.

"Kind of?"

"Let's see, the Lieutenant jumped all over my ass, I've only had three cups of coffee, one cigarette, I need to pee, and," I checked my watch, "I still have five hours left on shift."

"Poor baby. You want a lollipop?" He reached into his pocket and pulled out a purple Tootsie Pop. My favorite.

"That's not going to work."

"Boiled shrimp for dinner?"

I tugged at his hand.

"Massage?"

"That's cheating."

"You gonna tell me about it?"

"Nope." I removed my hand and pulled up the Velcro flap of my pocket for a cigarette. I smelled Old Spice on my fingers. "Ask Watson and Kirk." Watson and Kirk were Ricky's closest friends. I had a hunch that Ricky harbored a secret desire to become a crime scene investigator but hadn't quite admitted it to himself yet. He quivered like a hound dog whenever he arrived on a scene and started taking pictures.

"Damn," he said, rubbing the bridge of his nose.

"Yep."

"Where you headed now?"

"Back out there." I leaned my head against the headrest and watched the sunlight catch the little bit of black still left in his curls. He was only twenty-six, nearly five years my junior, but going gray in a decidedly sexy way. "Write up my report."

"Coffee later then?"

"After you talk with Watson and Kirk."

He laughed, but it wasn't a happy one. "You're a mystery, *cher*."

"No, I'm not. Just a few basic rules, is all." We'd had this talk before, dozens of times. Other cops told Ricky about their cases, even though officially no one was supposed to talk to the press except the PIO, so he figured I should too. But I didn't want anyone accusing me of handing Ricky info just because we were sleeping together.

"This is a stupid one."

"Makes sense to me."

"Only you."

I looked at him. "Does this mean no shrimp for dinner?"

"2D-76." The dispatcher's voice cut through the radio chatter. "I'm holding. You available yet?"

"So much for peeing, he's holding," I said to Ricky. "Something special probably, like that loose-snake-in-the-house call last month. Or maybe," I grinned with mock enthusiasm, "a wreck. On the bridge."

He sighed and put the Jeep into gear. "Lemme go before they load up the body. I assume you can confirm there is a body?"

I nodded. "One."

"Dead?"

I cut my eyes at him. Nodded slowly.

"That earns you this and nothing more." He tossed the Tootsie Pop through my open window. "Later."

"2D-76," I responded to HQ dispatch. "Put me 10-8. Whatcha got?"

"2D-76, got a 35 on the Mississippi River Bridge. Can you copy?"

Lovely. A suspicious person. On the bridge. I hated the bridge. I hated heights. Could be an idiot jogger. Could be a suicide attempt in the making. Could be a figment of some motorist's imagination. Then again, maybe it was that sumabitch Vince.

Of course it wasn't. There wasn't anyone there once I got up on the bridge. I delayed clearing myself from the call and took the exit ramp into Port Allen then cut back up across the bridge, watching the ribbons of water below and the sun bounce off the white dome of the LSU Assembly Center to the south and the tall, tapered-at-the-top monolith to the north that was the State Capitol, fondly referred to as Huey's Penis by most of us female cops.

I stopped at a convenience store just east of the river to use their bathroom, grumbling as I unsnapped the four keepers holding my gun belt to my pant's belt, slid them out and stuffed them in my pockets, unhooked my gun belt—heavy and awkward with gun, holster, flashlight, portable radio, speed loaders, two handcuff cases, and a key ring—and put it on the floor by my feet, unbuckled my pants' belt, unzipped my pants, and finally, thank you God, peed. Then I had to put it all back on again. And male cops wondered why it took us so long to use the bathroom.

I put myself 10-8 as I walked out the door, and the dispatcher immediately said he was holding, could I copy. I sighed. It was going to be one of those days.

We get it drilled into our heads early on never to use the term *routine patrol* because in just one second everything can change. Nothing is routine. You start thinking "routine," that's when you get hurt. But the truth is, most days are routine—a series of never-ending calls that you fill out the paperwork on. The truth is, most of police work is boring.

The rest of the shift passed in a blur of calls—a few thefts, a loose dog, three traffic accidents, a disorderly person who turned out to have a warrant for fraud, an unknown disturbance that remained unknown because no one ever came to the door, and a quick run through four different supermarket parking lots netting five tickets for parking in a handicapped zone to keep Sergeant Mosher happy and off my ass.

I managed to write up my report on Jeannette in between calls, propping my clipboard up against the steering wheel, carefully detailing everything I did and saw, except using my pocketknife on the screen and not announcing myself. By the end of shift I wanted a strong drink, a cold shower, and a hot bubble bath, preferably all at the same time.

Gwen was already in the precinct, sitting in one of the old school desks that always struck me as incongruous for the setting, signing a stack of reports. Her out-of-the-box blonde hair was mashed down from hours under a police hat and way too much hairspray. My own probably didn't look much better.

"Motherfuckers, Sarah; they're all motherfuckers."

I nodded and threw my reports into Mosher's in-box, all signed. Davy, thank God, had already left. I think I would have throttled him. Something funny, indeed.

Gwen shifted in the small desk. "Stopped this gal hauling ass down Florida Boulevard. Claimed she didn't know how fast she was going because she had her baby's picture up in front of the 'speedthermometer.' Speedthermometer! Jesus!" Her laugh sounded like a burro with hiccups.

I barely smiled, busied myself with checking in my portable radio and shotgun, conscious she was studying me.

"Tell me about it, girl." She got up from the desk, swiveling her hips to avoid catching her holster on the arm of the chair. "I'll buy you a so-dee pop."

Under all her gruffness, Gwen was a mother hen; she relished fussing over me and covering my ass when I needed it. Which I had upon occasion. Nothing serious—backing my unit into a ditch when I was miles outside my assigned patrol zone; firing my weapon at a fleeing burglary suspect whom I had no chance in hell of hitting, but I was pissed he'd run; calling in sick when Ricky persuaded me a day in bed together was infinitely more interesting than work; drinking a little too close to shift time. Gwen hadn't flinched. She'd gotten two other units to help push mine out of the ditch; she'd convinced the sole witness to my shooting three rounds into the air that no shots had ever been fired; she told the Lieutenant she'd checked on me earlier that day, and boy was I sick; she loaded me up on coffee and suggested none too mildly that I stick to drinking after shift, not before. Her loyalty was fierce despite her rough edges.

We leaned up against my unit out on the back lot and watched the evening shift leave for their tour of duty as I quickly filled her in on the basics of Jeannette's demise. Despite the increased humidity from the usual afternoon threat of clouds hovering to the south, I welcomed the heat. It took me out of my brain.

"That's a sick motherfucker. Gotta be the husband." Gwen methodically worked her thumb down each knuckle of her right hand until it popped.

"Most likely. Too much anger, too much passion to it."

"Unless it's some wacko serial killer."

"I wouldn't bet on it. Facts don't add up. They usually dump the bodies somewhere else." I kicked at the gravel. "And they aren't that sloppy." Time to polish my Red Wing boots. Again. The Lieutenant liked his officers spit-shined.

"Not always. That's all we need, some sicko scumbag torturing women."

"Well, we got it. One woman at least. And I'm betting on the husband."

"You don't think she was a hooker, do you? We've got that guy been raping and killing hookers off North Airline."

"Jeannette was not a hooker." I finished my soda and tossed it through the open window of my unit.

"You never know about these women, Sarah."

"Gwen."

"Come on, she could've been."

I raised an eyebrow.

She snorted, the one that meant "You're such a fuckin mama," and shook her head. "All right, all right," she said. "Ms. Jeannette was not a hooker."

"I want the group to do this one," I said, expecting her usual grumbles. Gwen figured it was an exercise in futility, called it "touchy-feely shit we shouldn't be dredging up." Said it made more sense to go light a candle at St. Joseph's.

Gwen started in on the knuckles of her left hand. "Talk to Tracy about it?"

"Yep."

"And?"

"She's got the heejies about it for some reason."

"Can't discount those. Remember that call over on North Street?"

"This is different. We aren't the target. The woman's already dead." I pushed my lower back harder against my unit, relieving some of the pressure from the gun belt digging down on my hipbones and into my kidneys.

"You aren't going to do anything foolish, are you, girl?"

"I'm just going back there."

A couple of uniforms came out the back door carrying shotguns. We watched them stow the shotguns in the crevice between the unit's seat and floor, slip their five-cell flashlights into the gap between the prisoner screen and the inside roof, pull rain gear out of the trunk. I looked up at the sky. The afternoon storm was about to hit.

Gwen leaned up against me, bumped my shoulder. "I'm with you, you know."

"I know." The smile I gave her was only my second real smile of the day. "I know."

I lived in an area of town that had no real name, no clearly defined neighborhood. It was on the wrong side of Government Street to be considered the Garden District—an eclectic collection of mansions, bungalows, and renovated shotgun houses—and on the wrong side of

Acadian to be part of the upwardly mobile Capitol Heights area. My garage apartment sat back from the road, a huge live oak full of ball moss sheltering one side, in the middle of a cluster of short streets inhabited mostly by older widows. With the exception of the Medi-Vac helicopters flying in and out of the BRG Hospital four blocks away, it was quiet.

I'd been here nearly three years, and despite Gwen's occasional attempts to get me to buy my own place ("a woman over thirty should own her own house, Sarah") and Ricky's recent less-than-subtle hints that we should live together ("I'm over here most every night anyway"), I had no intention of leaving. I didn't want the responsibility of owning, and I liked picking and choosing the time I spent with Ricky. I felt safe here, safer than any of the apartments and duplexes I'd lived in during my ten years as a cop. There was only one access point: a massive, solid-wood door on the ground floor with three locks. A second solid-wood door at the top of the stairs with two locks. And anyone who wanted to come through the windows either had to throw an extension ladder up against a wall or possess Spiderman-like qualities.

I passed my landlady's tiny stucco house and pulled up to the garage. As I got out of my unit, I heard the familiar whir and click of the electric shuffler my landlady and her friends used for their Monday-afternoon bridge game. The game was less about bridge and more about the gin and tonics and neighborhood gossip that flowed faster and deeper than the Mississippi. I'd sat in on a couple of hands at their invitation soon after I moved here and quickly determined those old ladies could run circles around me—and drink me under the table.

They yoo-hooed and waved at me to join them on the sun porch, but I smiled and shook my head. Upstairs, I let my shoulders slump, tossed my keys on the couch, started unzipping and unsnapping, letting the edges of my cop persona start to dissipate as I ditched my gun belt—blessed relief of the absence of weight—stripped to underpants and camisole, walked to the bathroom, pulled the bobby pins out of my hair, combed it back with a wet brush, filled the sink up with cold water, and submerged my face in it.

I wandered aimlessly around the apartment, trying to figure out what to do next. I hated day shift; the hours stretched out in front of you. At least on evening and dog shifts there was work and there was sleep, with a few hours for play crammed in and no energy left for much of anything else.

Eventually, I fixed a bourbon straight up and sat out on the porch off my kitchen and tried not to think. I briefly considered going out to City Park and blasting the hell out of the backboard as I so often did after day shift, but the sight of my racquet made my stomach quiver. When the afternoon shower hit with a vengeance, I made a second drink and carried it to the bath, where I soaked for a long time, dozing.

Later that evening Ricky and I sat at an old table from my parents' house and peeled shrimp, dipping them in the aioli he'd made, talking mostly about the former governor's latest shenanigans, which were considerable; about the mayor's attempts to keep Catfish Town financially feasible. Ricky teased me about my insistence on deveining each shrimp before I ate it. He'd taken off his shirt and shoes, and I watched the muscles bunch and relax in his arms and down his chest, eyed the thin tuft of dark hair that trailed below the waistband on his jeans. For the first time that day I felt soft.

The storm had cleared out and a light breeze smelling of wet grass came in through the windows. Ricky's massive Rhodesian Ridgeback sprawled on the floor snoring, her head resting on my foot. She was a beautiful grayish-tan dog named, for reasons Ricky could never explain, Peacock. She didn't have an arrogant, showy bone in her body. He frequently accused me of loving the dog more than him.

"That would be an affirmative," I'd reply. I didn't much care for cats, but dogs I had a soft spot for. They trusted so implicitly and loved unconditionally, the only creatures that had those characteristics as far as I could determine, besides babies. The only time I'd ever teared up at a scene was on a burglary off Barber Street where the perp had shot and killed the complainant's two gorgeous German shepherds, which had been gated off in the kitchen. The guy stood there, shaking his head, and said, "Why'd they have to kill my dogs, man?" I'd had no answer to that one.

"You hear about the letter they found?" Ricky asked.

"Who?" I said, still staring at Peacock, wondering what she was dreaming about with all those nose twitches.

"The one that woman wrote."

I tensed slightly, remembering Barker's earlier comment about a letter. "From today?"

He nodded.

"Her name was Jeannette," I said softly. "What about the letter?"

"Jeannette." He nodded again, got up, washed his hands, then pulled a sheaf of oversized colored photographs out of his backpack, sifted through them, and handed me one.

"They found this letter in a desk drawer with a bunch of other stuff," he said.

I stared at the photograph. Two pages of narrow, spiral notebook paper were barely readable. They lay on top of other papers and two paperback books, one of which I could just make out the title of: *Night of the Assassin.*

"How'd you get this?" I said.

"Kirk. I went down to HQ while they developed the stuff." He started peeling shrimp again.

I looked at him. "Why?"

"I thought it was interesting."

"Did you?" I turned the photograph sideways. Her handwriting was painfully childish: big curvy letters, tiny circles over the *i*'s, fat loops, self-consciously styled *e*'s and *a*'s, spelling and grammar errors. I started with what she'd numbered page (2); only four lines were visible: . . . *if it was going to ruin our marriage. For the past two weeks I have been home waiting on you and you are still* . . .

Page (4) lay crosswise over page (2). I turned the photograph upside down and continued reading: . . . *after a hard days work and* _talk_ *to me about nothing in particular but everything in general. I would like a husband that doesn't put that much important on sex. I want a husband that I can sit down and express my likes and dislikes, my fears, and my disappointments with true understanding not just be listening because I'm telling. I would like to do the same with you. Honey I sorry this letter is so long. I have a lot on my mind. I want this marriage to work because.* . .

I put the picture to one side, took a sip of white wine, and methodically peeled another shrimp, deveined it, dipped it carefully in the aioli so it was completely covered, then put it in my mouth and chewed thoughtfully.

"Interesting, huh?" Ricky was careless as he peeled and often had to spit out pieces of shell still clinging to the shrimp, which he did now, grinning at me as he wiped his face with the back of his hand. Peacock groaned and stretched, licking my bare foot once before she returned to her dreams.

"What we think is that she wrote that letter and gave it to him, her husband. The whole thing reads like that. Mentions him hitting her and stuff too. It was dated a week ago." Ricky chewed noisily as he talked, drank from his Abita Turbodog with enthusiasm. "He got pissed, went back out on the road, thought about it awhile, stewing away, came back, she tried to talk to him, and he started torturing her, figured he'd show her who was boss, and eventually he just went too far and killed her."

"Is that so?"

Ricky stopped, a shrimp halfway to his mouth. "What'd I say?"

I took a deep breath and was about to launch into a withering attack when the phone rang.

Ricky laughed and bit into the shrimp. "Saved by the bell, *cher*."

"Fuck you," I said as I went back to the bedroom, picked up the phone.

Tracy spoke quickly. "I'm not thrilled about doing this."

"Tracy—"

"Save it. We'll do this one. Tomorrow night, eleven-thirty. Park on the levee, across from the T-intersection. We'll go on to her place in two cars, park beyond her house."

"I'll call Gwen," I said.

"No talking about this at work tomorrow, okay?"

"Thank you."

"We're in and out, ten minutes tops, understand?"

"Thank you," I said again, but she'd hung up. I punched in Gwen's number, and told her the plan.

"We're not going in the fuckin' house, right?" she asked.

"Do we ever?"

"Done. Pick you up?"

"You're on the way. I'll swing by and get you."

"Ricky over there?"

"Yeah."

"Plant a big wet juicy one on him for me."

"Oh, please."

Her burro hiccup laugh blasted out of the earpiece as I hung up. I turned around and jumped to see Ricky's outline standing in the doorway, backlit from the kitchen.

"Girls' night out?"

"How long you been standing there?" I spoke sharply, still pissed at his enthusiasm over Jeannette's crime scene.

He walked over, put his arms around my waist. "Long enough to know you're deserting me for a bunch of women tomorrow night."

I stood stiffly under his touch. "Gwen and I are going out for drinks with a few others after they get off shift."

"I'll be here, if you want."

"We'll be back really late."

"Trying to get rid of me, *cher?*" Just an undertone of teasing to his voice.

Yes, no, I thought. It was unsettling sometimes to realize how much he cared.

"About earlier, I was insensitive." He kissed my hair, rubbed his hands up my back. "That woman, Jeannette, she got to you today, didn't she?"

I nodded into his chest, fighting the urge to sink into his warmth, trying to hold on to the more familiar feeling of irritation. He trailed his tongue down to the place where neck becomes shoulder and bit lightly. He lingered there, kissing and licking and nibbling until I gave in, moaned, brought my hands up, and pulled him hard against me, losing myself in the firm curves of his body, his smell, the taste of his flesh, remembering that this was why I stayed with him.

We undressed each other quickly and collapsed onto the bed, me saying, "Hurry, hurry," and him saying, "Slow down, *cher,* slowly, hush," as his fingers and lips traveled over my body. Peacock lumbered onto the bed, licking bare flesh, taking up most of the available space, and we tumbled to the floor, me on top of Ricky, and I didn't think for a long, long time.

Much later, when Ricky was sleeping soundly, still on the floor, and Peacock was snoring crosswise on the bed, I slipped into Ricky's shirt and went to the kitchen porch, lit a cigarette, and watched the sky, too bright from the city's lights even at this time of night to see many stars, watching the nearly full moon bob in between the leaves of a tulip tree, thinking about Jeannette and her longing to be heard, her desire for a deeper connection, how being lonely in a relationship was the worst kind of lonely, those silly romance novels in her car, her impish grin in the picture on her dresser, her mangled, tortured body. I imagined what it must have been like for her, what she was thinking as he came at her with the pliers, the cigarette, the tennis racquet, what he might have said to her—and what he didn't. Round and round until I pulled the wastebasket over and threw up, dry heaves wracking my body as the tears finally came. I sat against the wall and sobbed. Peacock appeared and leaned heavily against me, licking my face, her breath stale and doggy, trying to catch each tear. By the time I'd finished, my cheeks and nose and chin were sticky from her tongue. I wiped my face on Ricky's shirt, lit another cigarette, and contemplated all the ways I'd like to torture that sumabitch Vince Durham.

Gwen was in a full-out snit when I picked her up the next night. Seemed her husband, Joe, was not pleased she was going out with the girls, thought she should transfer out of uniform so she could work a straight day shift, didn't care for the chicken casserole and mirlitons she'd fixed for dinner. He thought she might have gained a little weight.

I nodded and said "uh-huh" at the appropriate times as Gwen vented. I was used to it. The job was hard on marriages.

Ask any cop why he or she became a cop and half of them will say, with a wry grin, it seemed like a good idea at the time; the other half will say they knew someone on the force—and it seemed like a good idea at the time. Only a handful will claim they'd always wanted to be a cop; those are the ones to watch out for. The job often eats them alive, or they eat up the job.

Gwen had started as a civilian in Traffic Records, a common entry point for women back then. Her brother had been a cop for a short time; now he ran a service station off Jefferson and made good money.

I'd dreamed of being a veterinarian. My daddy'd had a small piece of land in east Texas that didn't yield much—he was always fixing somebody's car or tractor or refrigerator to pay the bills. After my mother died from ovarian cancer when I was eleven, he'd laid out our choices: stay and probably go under, or move and have a fighting chance. We drew up a list of pros and cons, weighed our options, and faced the facts: the farm would have to go. We moved to Port Arthur so Daddy could work on a shrimp boat. He keeled over from a heart attack my freshman year at LSU. I hung in for two more years, but the science classes were hard, and, to be honest, I'd discovered my body and was more interested in sex than in studying.

I worked retail jobs for a couple of years, but I was bored, restless. Then a boyfriend, a parish deputy with a good smile and even better hands, whom I'd been dating for several months, suggested I try the police department or the sheriff's office; even the State Police, he said, were hiring.

"People shooting at you? I don't think so," I'd told him.

He'd laughed. "Nah, not as a cop, honey, as a dispatcher or working in Records. It's decent pay, good benefits."

On a lark, I took the civil service exam and scored surprisingly high. When there was an opening, I joined the city police as a dispatcher, working rotating shifts. I liked both the simplicity and complexity of the job, matching up units with calls as if I were working some enormous chessboard. I was also very good at it.

I broke up with the deputy, but his comment stayed with me. Why had he laughed at the notion of me as a cop? The longer I worked in the subterranean level of the Governmental Building where Communications was housed, the more I realized I wanted to be out there, on the streets, not just sitting behind some desk. I wanted to work the source, not function as an intermediary.

I pulled myself away from my thoughts when Gwen snorted.

"What?" I said.

"You've said barely a word since I got in this car," Gwen said. "Something bugging you?" She'd pulled her hair into a loose ponytail and wasn't wearing her wedding ring. But her face was made up for an evening out, her diamond studs were in, and her perfume was suffocating. I rolled both our windows down farther.

I glanced at her quickly and smiled. "Nope."

"You're not saying much."

"You've been doing all the talking," I pointed out.

"And what've I been saying?"

I shrugged sheepishly. "I was thinking about when we joined the department."

"What the hell for?"

"Wandering mind."

"Girl." She shook her head and popped two knuckles on her right hand. "This shit isn't good for you."

"Thinking?"

She snorted. "That too. I meant going out and praying over dead people you don't know."

"Fuck you." I lingered on the vowels, grinned at her to take the sting out. "I don't pray."

She grinned back. "Right."

We were quiet as I drove down Dalrymple, the university lakes shimmering off to our left despite the cloud cover.

"Remember Letticia Baldin?" I said.

"Who?" Gwen lit a menthol cigarette and hung her arm out the car window.

"The little girl in Tigerland last winter."

"That was a fucking mess," Gwen said, rubbing a thumb across her brow. "Jesus. You're on a roll. What's eating at you?"

You, partly, I thought, and realized that was more than half true, and it made me sad. Gwen had never done wrong by me. If anything, I owed her. But there was a place inside me that was restless, raw, crowded, and had been for some time. I couldn't put my finger on the cause. Find the cause, you correct the problem. I sighed, shifted in my seat. We passed by the sorority and fraternity houses, crossed Highland, swung around the Indian Mounds. Gwen popped more knuckles, took deep drags on her cigarette.

We'd just driven past the tiger's cage, LSU's real live mascot pacing somewhere in its concrete cave, when she said, "How the hell do you remember their names?" and for a second I thought she meant the tiger.

I glanced over at her. "How the hell can't you?"

"I remember the motherfuckers who do it. The rest is as much of a blur as I can make it. James Duncan."

I nodded. "The stepdad."

"That felt good, catching him." She pitched her cigarette.

"Gwen!"

"What?" Her tone was just as testy as mine.

I pointed at the ashtray, and she scowled, gazed out the window. I wondered if she really didn't remember Letticia Baldin's name. We'd worked it together, brought the group out two nights later to the parking lot that faced her first-floor apartment.

Letticia Baldin had been a vivacious nine-year-old with poor vision, dyslexia, and an aptitude for art. She'd been the oldest of five children and frequently ran the household, or attempted to. Her mother was a drunk, her stepdad a crack addict. Her mother, in a moment of lucidity, had thrown James Duncan out several weeks before. He came back to the apartment one night, strung out and looking to steal something he could sell to support his habit. He thought everyone was gone, but Letticia was there, sleeping in the front bedroom. We knew from his statement that she stood up to him, told him to get out. We knew from the crime scene that she fought and fought hard. He beat her, stabbed her multiple times with a pocketknife, tried to strangle her with his hands. He hit her so hard on the chest with a hammer that her heart was bruised from its impact with her spine. Still she fought: she clawed him, broke two ribs, and left three bite marks in his arm and upper back. Finally he took an electrical cord, stood on her body, and pulled it tight around her neck until she stopped kicking and breathing.

"You know, I worry about you," Gwen said as we turned onto River Road.

"You back on that again?"

"You work this shit over too much."

"Nah."

"Yeah you do."

"No, I do not."

"You're doing it right now. I can see it in your face, girl."

"Gwen."

She gave a small strangled laugh. "You know what I do out there? I pray we catch whatever pissant fucker did it and hope we don't get caught ourselves."

"Then why do you do it?"

She looked at me like I was stupid. "Because you ask me. The more important question is why *you* do it."

I shrugged.

"Like beating a dead corpse," she muttered, then did her burro's hiccup laugh. "Sick pun, huh?"

I bit back a reply as she pointed, said, "Look, they're up there."

We drove up the dirt road that led to the top of the levee. Four cars were pulled off in the grass. Tracy, Cathy, and Angie leaned up against one car. Marge and Beth, partners out of Plank Road Precinct, leaned against another, a study in contrasts: Marge was wide and solid with dark wavy hair and thick features; Beth was tiny, delicate almost—the gun on her hip was almost bigger than her forearm and gave her an unbalanced look—her blondish-white hair was cropped as short as a man's. Like Gwen and me, everyone wore jeans, sneakers, and dark sleeveless tops or T-shirts. All of us had been on the job for seven years or more except Angie, whom I didn't know well but thought had too quick a smile. The others I liked and trusted: Beth for her steadiness and practicality, Marge for her grittiness and humor, Cathy for her decency and integrity.

Tracy walked up looking tired. Somehow she always looked diminished in civilian clothes, more middle-aged too. "Marge and Beth will ride with you; the rest will come with me. No lights once we hit the road."

"Anyone else coming?" Gwen asked.

"They're working or couldn't make it."

"Smart move," Gwen muttered as Beth and Marge climbed into the backseat. "What's new, ladies?"

"Cathy thinks her husband's drinking again," Beth said.

"Yeah," I said, "I heard." Cathy's husband, Ray, worked in Auto Theft and could be a morose jerk.

"Really?" Gwen leaned forward and studied Cathy through the windshield. "You never said anything."

"Knowing Ray, it's possible," Marge said.

"You think?" Beth said.

Marge nodded. "Good detective, though."

"They make a strange couple," Beth said.

"He's an arrogant fucker," Gwen said.

Angie passed in front of our car, raised a hand in greeting. She looked as if she were promenading down sorority row: her steps bouncy, arms swinging, whistling an unrecognizable tune.

"She's different, isn't she," Beth said, more comment than question.

I grunted.

"She's young," Marge said.

"I heard she fucks like a rabbit—" Gwen began.

"Gwen," I warned.

"What? What's with your Gwen thing tonight?" She snorted, her "dickhead" snort. In the rearview mirror, I saw Beth and Marge exchange quick glances.

"Nothing," I said.

We rode with the windows down, the warm, humid air barely moving over our skin, the faint light from the moon guiding my way and throwing jagged patterns across the road as I drove slowly past Doris Whitehead's dark house with the window units going full blast, past Jeannette's quiet, empty house, and pulled off on the shoulder, then cut the engine.

Tracy motioned for me to the lead the way, and I checked quickly to make sure my gun was snug in its belt holster; the others were doing the same. We never went anywhere without our guns: the supermarket, bars, out for dinner, running errands. Sometimes it was in a purse, sometimes tucked under clothing. There was no downtime really, except in the sanctuary of your own home.

I cut on my five-cell flashlight to orient myself then shut it off and once again traversed the length of Jeannette's empty driveway— her car gone, impounded for evidence—feeling a moment of déjà vu as I heard our footsteps crunching louder than I liked on the shell driveway. We moved as quietly as we could, stopping often to listen before moving on. I always loved this moment, it seemed magical to me, when your eyes slowly adjusted to the dark and you realized you could see more than you thought, when you became a part of the night instead of fighting against it.

"It is fucking spooky out here," Gwen whispered. I stifled another "Gwen." She always said this. It was her way of saying, "I'd rather be somewhere doing something else."

Still, she had a point. It was always a little unsettling returning to the scene of a crime, middle of the night or not. Something lingered, took on subtle vibrations that thickened the air: this way violence was, here be the shadow of terror.

Don't be silly, I chided, shaking myself back into the moment.

The moon flitted in and out behind the clouds. Other than the sounds of our breathing and our footsteps, the silence was unnatural and heavy, the humidity smothering, a thick blanket you couldn't take off. Sweat trickled down my neck and back, gathered at the edges of my hair.

Technically we weren't supposed to be here. No one was supposed to enter a crime scene until the Homicide detectives took the tape down. So we were always careful to stand only on the boundaries of the taped-off area, careful to leave no trace of our presence. And we never entered a structure. Then again, we were the law, and we could go pretty much where we damned well pleased. Still, how would we explain our presence here? We hardly talked about it among ourselves.

If we were ever caught, at the very least there'd be lots of questions. And the department *was* overly cautious these days, toeing the inside of the official line since Steve Darcy's shooting. We could be transferred to desk jobs, deemed unstable. Or too emotional. Wacko women, Wiccans, spiritual mumbo-jumbo, supernatural raising of the dead: who knew what other cops would think. Especially the men. How do you explain the need to honor a woman who has been brutally murdered, to remember her for who she was, to give at least some weight to the life she lived and fought to keep, to say, "We remember you, we will always remember you and what you went through."

Beth cut off a sneeze, whispered, "Allergies, sorry."

I led them to the rear of Jeannette's house, under the shadow of a large pecan tree and several hackberries, so we faced the window of her bedroom. We stood in a tight circle, our shoulders just touching. I tucked my flashlight in a back pocket and folded my arms, suddenly wishing I were here alone. It seemed terribly important, urgent even, that they feel the nuances of her life, not just see her as another murdered woman.

"Well?" Tracy pushed a hunk of hair off her brow, gestured at me to begin. I shut my eyes, trying to find the path that would bring her to life for them.

I traveled back to the moment I stood over Jeannette's body, opened my eyes, and spoke in a low voice about what I knew of her life, the letter she'd written Vince, what he'd done to her. Marge and Beth swore several times under their breath; Tracy sighed repeatedly. Angie and Cathy kept their eyes closed, Cathy frowning slightly. Only Gwen looked at me as I spoke, her gaze steady, her earlier comment hovering at the edges of her blue eyes: *You know, I worry about you.* I'm okay, I wanted to tell her, really truly. It's just a blip, a bump; I'll get over it.

A slight rustle off to our right made us pause, listening. Angie put her hand on her gun.

"Critters," I whispered.

"Five minutes," Tracy said, her voice clipped but soft. "Then we're out of here."

I stared at Jeannette's house, thought about her singing rock-and-roll songs when Vince wasn't home. I remembered the Rolling Stones tape in her car, and a line floated up: *you can't always get what you wa-ant.* I thought about Gwen's bad pun—beating a dead corpse. Is that what we were doing? Was this all just some egoic salve, an exercise in futility? Fact: A dead body. Fact: There was nothing we could do to change that. Fact: We were alive, and she wasn't.

The moon came out from behind a cloud and reflected off her bedroom window. She would have seen that moon at night, lying there in bed next to her silent husband—him done for the moment with her body—her yearning for more rising up in her throat, making her bones scream. Did she long to leave, I wondered, just to get the hell out of there, or did she really believe she could make it work, that Vince would see her, hear her?

I readjusted my gaze. Something wasn't right.

I must have made a sound, because Gwen looked over at me, and her face changed expressions fast. The second she whispered my name, half question, half alarm to her voice, I thought I saw movement beyond the window, a darker blur in the shadows of the interior, and it dawned on me that the blinds were up, not down as Barker and Cowan would have left them, not down, my mind quickly registered, as they'd been on all the other windows we'd passed by on our way back here.

Now everyone else was looking at me too and following my gaze to the window.

"Blinds are up," I whispered. "Should be down." I bent my knees, my hand on my gun as I quickly looked to the right, just inside the edge of the window. Looking directly at objects in the dark doesn't work; the mind plays tricks and vision blurs. As I shifted my eyes, trying to look without looking, Tracy was already on the move. "Something's in there," she hissed.

Icy-hot beetles scurried through my body.

"Motherfuck." Gwen tugged at my arm. I shook her off, my throat and mouth dry and tight, ran quietly toward the window in a crouch, Marge and Beth flanking me on either side. Gwen swore again, but I knew from the sound of her footsteps she was right behind me.

We stood on either side of the window, our sides pressed up against the wood, guns out and pointed upward in both hands, speaking in urgent whispers, using hand signals. Tracy stood behind an oak tree, where she could see us and the south side of the house.

"Cover the front," Marge said.

"Cathy and Angie have it," Tracy said.

Beth and I did a quick glance in the window at the same time, pulled back and shook our heads.

"Sarah." Gwen had her hand on my back, both pressing to let me know she was there and tugging to get me to move back.

If that *was* Vince in there, if our too-tense nerves hadn't imagined movement, what would we do with him? Get to a phone. We needed to get to a phone and get units out here. I took a step back.

Beth had just ducked under the window toward us, and I'd taken several more steps backward, following Gwen's hand now bunched around my T-shirt, pulling me, when several sounds came in quick succession: a soft thud inside the house, the squeak of a screen door, and just behind those noises, the distinct crisp sound of a shell being racked into a shotgun from the north side of the house.

There was a tangled rush of movement: Marge followed Tracy around the south side as I edged to the north corner, Gwen's gun inches from my shoulder. Beth was just behind us, her funny allergy wheeze squeaking rapidly.

Gwen and I looked at each other, nodded, and we stepped out, Beth at Gwen's shoulder, around the corner, saw the figures coming down the kitchen steps, moved quickly into a wide stance with knees slightly bent, arms outstretched, guns pointed at what I now saw were two men.

"GET 'EM UP, MOTHERFUCKERS," Gwen yelled, me right on her heels with a thick, deep "FREEZE, POLICE," trying to see their hands in the patchy moonlight. Empty, I thought, the hands look empty, but they were moving in and out of the shadows, those hands, they kept moving even as the men attached to the hands froze, heads turning slowly toward my voice, when a gun went off, twice, my ears slapped hard with the sound, and the first man, the one farthest from the house, pitched forward and collapsed onto the dirt.

The other man—thin, short, heavily bearded—threw his empty hands into the air. "What the fuck you doing?" he said, backing up several steps, even as I was running, all of us running, Gwen and Beth beside me, Marge and Tracy from the other side of the house, running toward the men.

Gwen reached down to the man on the ground. Two large gaping exit holes gushed blood from his back. "Gun, he had a gun."

"I heard a shotgun being racked," Beth said, and Tracy said, "Me too."

"Don't move, don't think of moving," I hissed at the living man, his eyes round and white, his breathing rapid, a half snarl quivering brave around his lips.

Marge and Tracy knelt beside Gwen. "Where is it?" Gwen kept saying. She felt under his body, patted the ground beside him.

Tracy touched a hand to his neck. "No pulse." No movement either. This man had died quick and hard.

"SHIT, he had a gun; I saw a gun." Gwen's voice was soft but emphatic, anger and fear all mixed together in a way I'd never heard before. Panic, I realized. I was hearing panic in Gwen Stewart's voice. My stomach twisted.

"It could've traveled some when he fell," Marge said, and she and Tracy started making wider circles. Beth pulled the flashlight out of my back pocket and joined them. Cathy stood off to one side, her hands resting on her waist, watching Gwen.

I pulled out my badge and held it up in front of the man's face. "Name?" He wore black jeans, a dark red T-shirt, and a baseball cap.

"You women all cops?" His voice was both incredulous and sarcastic.

"What is your name?"

"Vince."

"Vince." I felt a rush of elation and smiled, my not-at-all-sweet smile. "Pleased to meet you. And who's this here?"

"Roger. What the hell you shoot him for?"

"He had a gun."

"Ain't neither one of us had a gun, you stupid bitch." The look on his face was contemptuous. A pit opened wider in my stomach.

"Motherfucked," Gwen muttered and heaved the dead man over, started patting him down, her movements jerky.

"Freeze!" Marge said suddenly, and I looked, saw her and Tracy and Beth with guns pointed toward the trees. The flashlight illuminated Doris Whitehead, stepping out from behind an oak tree, shotgun pointed at the ground.

Oh, sweet Jesus. "Not the woman," I yelled. "She's okay."

Vince shifted, whispered, "Goddamn nosy old cooze," and I looked over at him. "Uh-uh," I said. "Steady there."

Out of the corner of my eye, I saw Marge take the shotgun from Doris Whitehead's hands. She gave a tight-lipped smile to Marge, who carefully opened the shotgun and ejected the round.

"That explains the shotgun," Tracy said, and Gwen swore again. I found it hard to breathe. Vince cut off a chuckle when I looked at him.

"Officer Jeffries," Doris Whitehead said. "This is that sumabitch

I told you about." The satisfaction in her voice was tight and grim.

"You know this woman?" Marge asked.

"Name's Doris Whitehead. Lives next door," I said.

"I get my hands on you—" Vince growled. His hands began to drop, and he shuffled forward.

That's all it took. I never said a word. I just tackled him low at the knees, letting my shoulders carry us to the ground, my weight and fury hold his squirming body down, my hands moving quickly over his upper body, checking for weapons, him yelping and panting as he fought until Beth came around and pressed her knees against the flesh near his collarbone, digging in so hard he grimaced, swearing at him not to move, not even to think of moving, telling him to shut up. I straddled him, pulled out a wallet, a screwdriver, a wad of cash, two rings, pliers, a pack of cigarettes, and a hefty set of keys from his pockets. Beth kicked each object out of his reach as I tossed it. I checked his groin, squeezing his balls hard enough to get a squealed "oomph" out of him, ran my hands around his waistband, down his legs, the backs of his knees, inside his socks, three fingers inside his workman's boots. I looked at Beth, said, "That's it." She nodded, her allergy wheeze rattling like a fan, but she didn't ease up the pressure on his collarbone.

I sat back, resting on his knees, and looked at him. His hands dug into the ground. His baseball cap had come off during our struggle, revealing a rapidly receding hairline, dark hair trimmed close to his scalp. He was wiry, his nose thin and creased at the tip, his large black eyes defiant and close set, but he was also scared. I could feel the tremble in his limbs, smell the fear on his breath. Good, I thought, get a little taste of what Jeannette experienced.

When I looked back up, they were all watching me, except Gwen, who was still looking for the gun I was pretty sure she'd never find. "I'm fucked," she said, her voice terse.

"I believe we all are," Cathy said.

"Where's Angie?" Marge said.

"Split," Cathy replied, and when I curled my lip, she said calmly, "Like we should have done."

"We are in a world of shit here," Tracy said, so matter-of-factly that my heart skittered and stopped momentarily. The earlier rush of anger curdled with glee dissolved; I settled back into my body, felt my muscles and bones, breathed deeply, and took it all in: what we'd walked into, what Gwen had done, who we had, and my throat snapped closed.

Gwen muttered, "Fuck all."

Vince sneered, gave a half-laugh that stopped abruptly when Beth pressed down harder on the pressure points beside his collarbone.

Rage burned out of my pores again, at Vince, at Gwen, at the situation in which we found ourselves. And I knew, I just knew that's what he'd done—laugh—as he came at Jeannette. I picked up the pliers I'd tossed on the ground, held them up in front of his face. "Is this what you used on her?" My voice sounded coarse and unfamiliar.

It took effort, but he dredged up another sneer. "On who?"

The urge to beat his face into a bloody pulp drummed so hard in my hands I felt light-headed. Beth clamped a hand over his mouth. "Bite me and you'll regret it." Then she looked at me. "Well?"

"They're gonna do to us what they did to Steve Darcy," Tracy said, her voice thin.

"Ladies, I'm out of here. Sorry," Cathy said, and she turned, walked back toward the road.

We watched her silently until Beth sneezed, cleared her throat, said, "We need a plan."

Gwen had stopped looking for the gun and was sitting back on her ankles, staring stone-faced at the ground, one hand rubbing hard against her thigh.

Marge's wide body moved gracefully toward me; she dropped a bandanna and her cuffs onto the ground beside my feet. "Gag him and cuff him. Then we talk."

"What, you were expecting this?" I said. Marge hesitated but said nothing, returned to standing by Doris Whitehead, who still had a look of rough amusement to her mouth. A piece of me wanted to stand up and follow Cathy down the driveway.

I stuffed the bandanna in his mouth, tied the ends at the back of his head. I took some small pleasure in making sure the gag was tight. He watched me, his eyes full of imploded fury. Gwen had gone motionless. I said her name.

"What?" Her eyes were blank and heavy. Perspiration had smeared her makeup into a grotesque mask.

"It's okay," I said, wanting to mean it.

"The fuck it is," she spit back, the anger deep in every line of her body.

Beth and I rolled Vince. She stood, keeping a tennis shoe placed firmly on the crack of his butt while I cuffed him hard enough to make him grunt. He wasn't wearing a wedding ring. I straightened up, kept one foot on his right ankle, pressing hard on the bone, knowing it had to hurt. I had no idea what to do next. Normally we'd read him his rights, cart him off to a unit, and transport him to downtown booking. I looked at the body again and shuddered slightly. Fact: We had a dead unarmed man. Fact: We had a murder suspect. Fact: We were fucked.

Marge said, "Here," and she unbuckled her belt, slipped it off, reached down and grabbed Vince by one arm, pulled him up, walked him over to the railing by the kitchen door, threaded her belt several times through the cuffs and the railing, pulled it tight and tied a knot. "Move and we kill you and no one's the wiser," she said. I shot her a startled glance. She motioned impatiently for the rest of us to join her over by the tree line. Gwen moved as if her joints weren't quite in unison.

"We kill you?" Tracy said.

"It's an option." Marge rubbed the toe of her tennis shoe against the ground.

"No way," I said quickly. Marge glanced up briefly without moving her head, her toe still moving across the ground. Doris White-head smiled, her lips tight against her teeth. "Then what?" Marge said, one thick hand cutting through the air to the dead man's body before returning to rest on her thigh.

"Do we even know for sure this guy did it?" Beth said softly.

"He did it," Doris Whitehead said.

"Cowan and Barker are getting a warrant," I said, quickly outlining my conversation with Kirk earlier in the day outside Headquarters. The bloody fingerprints at Jeannette's house had come back a match to Vince Durham. He had a long record that included aggravated battery. An old girlfriend had filed a restraining order against him, and he'd spent three months in jail for beating the hell out of her with a hot iron. The trucking company said they hadn't heard from him in four days, that his rig was parked on the company lot. Barker and Cowan were getting a search warrant for it—and Vince—in the morning.

"But there's no warrant yet?" Beth asked.

I shook my head. "Not that I know."

"What about this other guy?" Tracy said.

"He had a gun," Gwen said again, but listlessly this time.

"A friend, Roger somebody," I said. "Only prints inside were Vince's and Jeannette's."

"Doesn't mean he didn't help him," Gwen said.

"Reality check, Gwen," Marge said. "There was no weapon in his hand."

Gwen's face shifted into ugliness, and she stepped up to Marge. "I saw a gun, goddamnit." Then she whirled, lunging toward me. "This is your goddamn fault with all your goddamn motherfuckin' weepies over some woman stupid enough to stay with a motherfucker like him."

I looked at her, stunned, protest caught in my throat. Then I hauled off and slapped her, hard.

"Whoa, whoa, whoa," Tracy reached out and gripped Gwen's arm, pulled her back several steps.

For less than a second Gwen looked like a four-year-old. "Damn," she whispered. When her face smoothed back into a hard mask, I turned away. My hand tingled and throbbed.

Beth put a hand on my shoulder, said, "It's not Sarah's fault. We didn't have to come. Anyone of us could have shot him. It was dark, hard to see." Beth's forehead crimped into deep lines beaded with perspiration.

"Yeah, try telling that to IA," Marge said.

"We need to make some decisions and make them quick." We followed Tracy's gaze toward Vince, who was struggling against the belt, his body twisting one way then the other, his feet trying to find leverage.

"We can't hang around here," Beth said.

"What do we do with the body?" Marge said. "And him?" She tilted her head back toward Vince.

"I thought he had a gun." Gwen spoke to the ground, her fingers pinching the seam along her jeans. Her cheek was mottled where I'd hit her.

I looked at Doris Whitehead, who stared back with a preternatural calm, then at Vince, then down at the body, and finally at Gwen. I imagined our positions reversed. My stomach flipped once, then curled up in a fist.

"Okay," I said, and they all looked at me. "The three of you take Gwen back to the cars. Leave. Ms. Whitehead here will call the police, tell them an off-duty police officer needs help, she's got a murder suspect."

Gwen was shaking her head even before I finished. "Uh-uh. Don't be a fuckin' martyr. You aren't taking the fall for me."

"Won't work," Marge said. "He'll tell them there were others. How do we explain there's no gun?"

"Anybody got a throw down?" I asked.

They all shook their heads.

"We could get one," I said.

"Where?" Beth rubbed her nose with a finger.

"There's no time," Tracy said.

"No." Gwen's hands were jammed deep in her back pockets. "My fuckup, my call. I'll stay."

"They'll tag you," Tracy said softly. "There's no way you can cover this. You'll go down. We'll all go down for this."

Gwen turned away, slammed her hand against a sapling hard enough to snap it forward.

I stood with my hands on my hips, looking at Vince, looking at the body. Work the facts, I kept thinking, just work the facts and weigh your options. But all I came up with was a big fat zero and the fervent desire to be somewhere else.

"Can I make a suggestion?" Doris Whitehead spoke slowly, calmly. She stared at some spot beyond our heads, and for a second, I saw the schoolteacher in her. "It'd been simpler if you girls hadn't showed up—"

"Talk about begging the fuckin' obvious," Gwen said.

"—I'd have taken care of it, killed him, and that'd been it."

"And you'd have gone to jail," I said.

She put her hands out, palms up. "I'm an old woman, he scared me, I knew he'd killed Jeannette. Who's gonna convict me?" Her lips pulled back over her teeth in a half-smile. "Maybe he even had a gun. We can all tell a few little lies." She finally looked at me, her eyes dark, probing. "I still could."

"Good God," I said.

"Maybe—"

"No," I said, speaking as clearly and carefully as I could. "No more killing out here tonight. Not an option, understand?" Marge busied herself brushing invisible dirt off her pants, but said "Okay" without meeting my gaze. I looked at Beth who quickly said, "Agreed." Tracy nodded slowly. Gwen avoided my eyes.

"Gwen?"

"Y'all just leave, and I'll handle it," she said.

I looked at her profile, her shoulders hunched slightly forward, and I knew exactly what she'd do. The realization made me woozy. "No," I said, my voice soft.

"We all stay or none of us stays," Beth said firmly, and Marge and Tracy nodded.

Gwen made a funny noise, but sob or cough, I couldn't tell.

Doris Whitehead drew in a breath, pulled her shoulders back, and spoke briskly. "All right then. Here's what I'm proposin'. You need time to think, and I've got a place to do the thinkin'. We take him out to my fishing camp off the Pearl River. 'Bout eighty miles from here. Used to be my husband's, but he's gone, and it's mine now. No one passin' by regular like to hear us, or him. Need a boat to get out there. Give you girls the time you need." Before I could open my mouth she'd anticipated me. "Coupla you come with me, to make sure, you know," she hesitated, her smile almost coy, "it's all on the up and up."

I squinted, befuddled by her logic. "We can't transport him some- place else. That's kidnapping. It's illegal."

Marge's chuckle was short and not humorous. "What do you call this?"

Gwen gave a funny strangled laugh. "Fucked?"

"And how is this going to help us?" I said, still trying to get my mind around the concept of taking Vince somewhere else.

"Give us time to think when we aren't panicked." Marge looked at Vince as she spoke.

They had a point. We couldn't stay here, and I wasn't letting Vince go.

Tracy cleared her throat. "It might work. Temporarily."

"Buy us some time," Beth said.

"What about the body?" Marge said.

"Take it with us?" Beth said.

My mind had latched on to the "temporarily" and was churning as fast as my stomach now. "We leave it here. Gwen, that your issued gun or a personal one?"

"Personal," she said.

"Good. Registered?"

"No."

"Even better." I held out my hand. "Give it here. We'll dump it in the river."

"I'm not giving you my gun."

Beth wiped the back of her hand against her nose. "Pretty isolated up there in places, swampy and all. We could dump the body there too."

"No," Tracy said. "Sarah's right. We don't need to transport a body and a murder suspect. Leave him here, take the gun."

She and Marge exchanged glances, and Marge said, "Okay, then."

"Are y'all out of your fuckin' minds?" Gwen said. "Shoot him, here, now, if you're going to do that."

"No," I said. "We'll figure something out."

"Well," Doris Whitehead said, "lemme go get my car ready." She sounded as if we were off on a field trip.

I stared dully at her figure as she disappeared down the driveway, blinked, then tried to gather myself up to do what needed to be done. I would have given anything at that moment to turn back time. Way back, beyond police work and college and high school. Back to the womb, I thought, or dancing across the kitchen floor to the crooning of Marty Robbins, my feet on top of Daddy's shoes, or up in his arms, waltzing through air thick with the possibility that my life could always be like this—safe, loved, beautiful, simple—back when *conse-*

quences was a foreign concept, a word I couldn't even pronounce much less need to understand.

I drove with the window down, letting the wind tear at my face and whip my hair into a tangle, as we headed east down Interstate 12, hovering just below the speed limit, toward the I-59 cutoff north that would take us to Pearl River. The taillights of Doris Whitehead's old Buick in front of us flickered, and I worried about some overly zealous state trooper stopping her. Or us. Gwen sat silently in the passenger seat beside me. Vince was in the trunk, cuffed, gagged, his legs tied tight with rope Marge had retrieved from her car along with an extra set of handcuffs. We'd all shook our heads, amazed, as she hauled the stuff from her car. "You must've been a hell of a Girl Scout," Tracy said, and briefly, for the first time that night, we laughed. Even Gwen's burro hiccup laugh surfaced momentarily.

Tracy, Beth, and Marge had stayed behind at Jeannette's to clean up the scene, removing all traces of our presence the best they could, including Gwen's bullet cartridges. They'd promised me repeatedly they'd leave Roger's body exactly where he'd fallen. I imagined Cowan and Barker working that scene, Kirk and Watson collecting evidence and taking pictures, Ricky there as well. My stomach twisted another notch.

I glanced at the dash clock: 12:05. Just over thirty minutes since we'd parked on the levee. I wondered whether Doris Whitehead's camp was on the Louisiana or Mississippi side of Pearl River. Kidnappers transporting across state lines.

I chain-smoked cigarettes and watched the thick line of trees whiz by—dark, jagged blurs against the midnight blue of the sky— the tires humming and thump-clicking over patches in the highway. I watched the green and white signs approach and disappear: Denham Springs, Satsuma, Hammond, Covington, Abita Springs. I barely registered my favorite sign: Baptist Pumpkin Center.

We'd just pulled onto I-59 when Gwen cleared her throat. "I fucked up." The dashboard lights partly illuminated her face.

"Yeah. Well."

We were quiet for a minute, then I said, "I shouldn't have hit you."

"I would've." She snorted, her "fuckin' mama" snort. "Sarah Jeffries losing control. Really a fuckin' watershed moment, huh?"

Doris Whitehead pulled out into the left lane, and I followed her, passing a slow-moving Datsun with a missing license plate.

"I could've sworn he had a gun," she said.

"I know."

"Did you see it?"

I shook my head. "No."

"Shit."

A car passed us. Then another. "I'm sorry you have to pull this alone," she said.

I shrugged.

We'd decided I'd pull the first watch with Doris and Vince. Tracy, Marge, and Beth had day shift; they'd head up to the camp as soon as they got off shift. Gwen and I were off Wednesdays and Thursdays, but Gwen had her husband, Joe, to deal with.

"Joe going to think it's weird you driving my car home?" I asked.

"Probably won't even notice."

"Tell him I had too much to drink, that you dropped me off at my apartment."

"It's my fuckup; I should be doing this."

I tried to imagine her and Doris Whitehead baby-sitting Vince. And then we'd have two dead bodies to worry about. "It's okay."

Gwen thumped her head against the windowpane. "You're the only one without complications."

She was right. That was my life in a nutshell. Not complicated. I went to work, I came home. But there was Ricky. I tried to remember. We'd had dinner together, was it only six hours ago? He'd fixed pasta with oysters and andouille sausage while I put together a salad, cutting avocados in long strips. We'd walked Peacock over to Baton Rouge High and let her chase squirrels, came back holding hands, watching the clouds blend into dusk, put Peacock on the back porch and made love, long and unhurried, on the living room floor. He'd left at 10:30, kissed me on the nose, said, "Have fun, *cher*. Talk with you tomorrow."

"Ricky's not at the apartment," I said.

Gwen sighed. "I'll tell Joe I'm going to see my sister in Metairie and get back up here in the morning as soon as I can."

"Okay," I said.

She shifted in her seat. "Don't decide anything until I get there."

Irritation pushed up vicious and alive, hard under my skin. Decide? Decide what? I wanted to yell. But I didn't say anything except, "Okay."

We pulled into a tiny, dark marina way off the main road just after 1:30. On the Louisiana side, I noted with grim relief. It wasn't really a marina, more like a dock with some boats tied up and a broken-down shack near the water's edge. The mosquitoes were thick and hungry. Gwen helped us load Vince, a shotgun, and two sacks of groceries and clothes into a small boat. He struggled only a little bit until Doris Whitehead slapped him hard across the face and Gwen muttered something into his ear. I looked away.

Gwen put her hands on my shoulders, pulled me into a rough hug as we stood by my car. "Thank you," she whispered into my ear. I stepped away first.

"Give me your gun." I held out my hand.

She hesitated, then pulled it out, emptied the bullets into her palm, and handed me the gun.

"And the bullets."

"That was a good gun." She dropped them into my hand. "I wouldn't have shot if I hadn't thought he'd had a gun."

"I know."

"I'll be back by noon, one at the latest."

I touched her once on the shoulder, then turned to Doris Whitehead, who'd been sitting in the boat quietly, waiting on us, and said, "We're all set."

Doris Whitehead turned on the engine, and we pulled away from the dock. I sat crossways in my seat, between Doris and Vince, and watched Gwen's figure, barely distinguishable from the trees, until a bend in the river hid her from view.

I'd never been on a river this dark and remote at night. I could see the outlines of small buildings occasionally along the shore, but there didn't seem to be anyone around or in them. The moon kept playing hide-and-seek between the clouds, and I heard splashing, fish

I supposed, or perhaps alligators, once the flapping of some great bird off to the side; otherwise, it was quiet. About five minutes out, I slid Gwen's gun out of my back pocket and held it over the edge of the boat, the water warm to the touch. I let the tug of the water pull it out of my hand.

I looked at the back of Vince's head, his hands clenched tight in the cuffs. He squirmed some, but mostly he seemed to be waiting, his body one tense line, the breath coming through his nose in a soft, rapid wheeze.

Doris Whitehead moved the boat through increasingly smaller channels with confidence, and I was impressed at her adeptness doing this in the dark. Gwen and the others would never find their way out here. Doris Whitehead would have to go back to the marina midday and wait.

After about twenty minutes we pulled up to a dock that ran parallel to the shore for a considerable distance with a short, six- or seven-foot protrusion out into the water from the middle of it. Doris Whitehead cut the engine and tied us off to a narrow metal pole on the shorter dock, beside four rungs that led to the top. She gestured for me to get out first. I bent down and untied Vince's legs, then quickly went up the rungs. Doris Whitehead pulled Vince to his feet. "Nothing funny, boy, there's gators and moccasins all around. And I feed 'em regular like when I'm out here, so they'll be ready to chomp hearin' the engine," she said.

He looked at the rungs and then up at me, the bandanna in his mouth stretching his cheek muscles into wide commas. I motioned to him, reached down, and grabbed him by the shoulders as Doris Whitehead kept a hand on his back, and we guided him up onto the dock.

When Doris Whitehead joined us, he balked, tried to say something. I hesitated, then reached to untie the bandanna. "Don't," Doris Whitehead said, but I ignored her, told him if he yelled no one would hear him and the bandanna wouldn't come off again, and then pulled the cloth out of his mouth. He coughed several times, licked his lips, shifted his jaw back and forth. "Fuckin' bitches," he growled, and I reached up with the bandanna, but he pulled his head away, said, "Gotta piss."

Doris Whitehead and I looked at each other.

"I'm not undoing these handcuffs," I said.

"And I'm not gonna hold his thing," she said. "Let him do it in his pants."

"No." I reached forward and unbuckled his pants, his eyes boring into mine, a slight smirk on his face. "I'm going to take you to the edge there, hold on to you, and you can do your business." The smirk disappeared. I pulled his pants down around his ankles, then his underpants, dark green briefs. His penis was small and a bluish dusty rose, his balls shrunk up and shriveled in a mass of dark hair. A fetid odor drifted up off him. I turned him around, walked him to the edge, put one hand on the link between the handcuffs and the other on his shoulder. "You try anything, and I push you in," I said. He squatted a little, his legs trembling, and we stood there until he'd finished.

He'd dribbled some on himself, and I stared at the dark patch between his legs, his penis dangling loose and damp against his skin. When I looked up at him, he must have seen something in my face because whatever he'd started to say he bit back, and his jaw tightened, his eyes shifted away from mine. I jerked his pants up, turning my head away as I did, buckled his belt, and grabbed him by the arm. "Let's go," I said to Doris Whitehead, and pushed Vince in front of me as we followed her up the dock and onto a dirt path that led several yards back into the dark woods.

Her cabin was larger than I'd expected, cleaner too. A good-sized bedroom led off the main room that functioned as living room, kitchen, and dining room. Three big armchairs and an old navy blue couch were crammed up against two walls, a table, refrigerator, and stove against the third. There were no pictures, no knickknacks. Doris Whitehead lit a kerosene lamp and then led us into the bedroom, where I had her hold the shotgun on Vince as I uncuffed him. He rubbed his wrists slowly, stretched his shoulders forward, his eyes following me carefully as I gestured for him to get on the bed. "What the fuck you bitches think you're gonna do with me?" he said, but there was more fear in his voice now than anger, and I gestured again. He hesitated. I shoved him slightly, enough so he stumbled back and sat down heavily, the bedsprings squeaking. I cuffed his right wrist and attached it to the bed frame, then used the other set of cuffs on his left hand. Tied his feet back up again, replaced the bandanna, and propped the pillow up under his head so he could breathe more easily.

"I'll make us some coffee," Doris Whitehead said. She took the lamp back into the main room, and put it on the kitchen counter along with the shotgun.

Vince diminished to a gray outline with darker shadows cast by the angles of his body. He seemed not quite human—a black mirage, except for his eyes and the hard red slash of the bandanna.

"I find it fascinating, really, that you've never mentioned her. Your wife," I said softly. He blinked once, pulled his right hand hard against the cuffs. "Never asked us a damn thing about why we were at your house." I kept my face still, expressionless. "Curious, isn't it?"

He muttered something into the bandanna, but I turned my back and left, keeping the bedroom door open, and moved an armchair so I had a direct view in. I could just see his outline on the bed.

"Black okay?" Doris Whitehead said, and I nodded.

While the water heated, she busied herself emptying the grocery sacks, putting food up into the cupboards and into the refrigerator, opening the shade partway over the kitchen sink. I watched Vince, and I watched her. She wore olive-colored cargo pants and a maroon T-shirt, the material stretched out tight across her breasts and the rolls of fat beneath. Her face looked like a Rottweiler's, massive with jagged eyebrows, but watchful and steady too, the folds of flesh under her chin jiggling slightly. Not a pretty woman, I thought, probably never was. Needed a better haircut, something more flattering, less harsh. Looked home done.

When she moved to pull back the drapes on the far wall, I said, "No." She stiffened a minute, then said, "Of course," and closed them.

She turned on the ceiling fan overhead and then a large floor fan that rattled at the far end of every turn. I got up and turned it off, looked back at Doris Whitehead, who watched me stone-faced, and said, "Too noisy. I need to be able to hear him."

"It'll get hot in here by midday," she said.

"Then it'll get hot," I replied, and settled back into the chair and studied Vince's dusky outline again until bile rose up into my throat, abrupt and corrosive. I stood, said in a thick voice, "I'm stepping outside for a minute."

I knelt on the dock at the edge opposite from the side Vince had used, waiting to throw up. Nothing came but acid coating my mouth. I spit and waited some more. I wanted to howl, just tear the sky open. But I kept taking deep breaths, and the nausea eventually passed. I looked at my hands, flexed my wrists. Water lapped softly against the wood, and I stuck a few fingers in; it was body temperature and smelled slightly metallic under the fish and wet clay odors. Then I remembered the alligators and jerked my fingers out.

The sky was huge. Away from the city, I could actually see the stars, a whole blanket of them playing peekaboo behind gauzy clouds. I lit a cigarette, studied the smoke wafting up through the air. There was no way on earth, I realized, I could kill Vince Durham or be a party to killing him. And there was no way on earth I could let him go. Those were two facts I could not reconcile.

After a while I returned to the house, stopped in the doorway of the bedroom, Vince's eyes watching me. I looked away first, came back to the chair, and picked up the mug of coffee Doris Whitehead had placed on the floor beside it. She'd settled in the chair on the far wall, the shotgun within grabbing distance. The light from the kerosene lamp made her face softer, less grim.

I blew on the coffee, took a sip. The taste of chicory was so strong I struggled to swallow the first mouthful without wincing. "Thank you," I said, and meant it, the bitterness running through my body, clearing out the numbness I'd felt since Gwen fired her gun. I slipped my gun out of its holster and tucked it in my lap, shifted my hips more comfortably into the chair.

Doris Whitehead cleared her throat, rubbed a thumb against her chin as though she were playing with a stray hair. "It's different for you, isn't it?"

"Ma'am?" I looked at her over the edge of my cup.

"From them other women. Some of 'em believe and some of 'em don't so much, but you feel it more strongly, don't you?"

"I'm not following you."

"What you told me after you found her, that you do it gently. That's not the way it is at all for you, is it?"

I stared at her openmouthed.

She smiled a little, settled back farther into her chair, put one foot up on a small stool. "I've been watching you, thinking about all you said the other day, how kind you were to Jeannette, to me, and I figure you're leaning up against some mighty big doors inside, trying to keep 'em closed." She took a sip of her coffee. "But you ain't having much luck, are you?"

"Well, I think under the circumstances—" I started, my voice indignant.

She waved a hand across her face. "Nah, before, way before this. I can see it, right under your skin. Not like that friend of yours that shot the other fellow."

"Gwen's a good cop—"

"But you didn't shoot him. She did. Now you're wondering what to do with him, ain't you?"

I took another swallow of coffee, tapped a finger against the rim of the mug.

"Not married, are you?"

I shook my head slightly, watching her warily.

She nodded, satisfied, but satisfied as to whether she'd gotten it right or satisfied I wasn't married, I couldn't tell. "Boyfriend?"

I thought of Ricky's teasing smile, his hands moving quietly down my belly, between my legs. "Kind of," I said, surprised to hear my response, surprised to realize that this was exactly how I thought of Ricky. Indefinite. Lovely in the moment, but not permanent. Just a kind of, something in between work and sleep. An antidote, like all my boyfriends had been. I'd just never admitted it to myself before. I fought back the sudden burn of tears.

She smiled at her feet. "Betcha got him confused half the time."

I gripped my cup tighter. "I think everything is rather confusing right now, don't you?" I spoke slowly, enunciating each syllable, like I did when talking to prisoners, explaining why they should tell me the truth about what had happened. I gave her the look too, the one that said, Let's cut through all the bullshit. Sometimes this worked; sometimes it didn't.

Doris Whitehead's face ran through a lineup of emotions: blank, amused, grim, and finally something like acceptance floated up. "You like stories?"

"Ma'am?" I thought of my mother reading me *Bambi* and *Peter Pan*, then starting the *Black Stallion* series, a chapter each night, until I became impatient and learned to read on my own. I wished I hadn't been in such a hurry now; I'd have liked more memories of her voice.

Doris Whitehead rubbed her hand hard against her ear. "I'm gonna tell you a story. Help pass the time. And we got lots of time together, you and me. And a course with him." She smiled her tight-lipped smile, lips stretched across gums, and jerked her head toward the bedroom. "But this isn't for him, it's for you. Want some more coffee?"

She stood up and moved past me to the kitchen, taking my cup with her. I tucked my gun into the back of my jeans and went into the bedroom, checked the ropes around Vince's legs, the gag in his mouth. His eyes were hard and tight. I couldn't resist patting him on the head. His arms jerked hard against the cuffs, and he muttered something through the gag. "Good boy," I whispered, unsettled at the equal mixture of venom and sadness I felt.

Doris Whitehead handed me my cup, full and hot. She leaned her head against the back of the chair, the skin under her chin almost taut, and started speaking slowly to the ceiling, so soft I had to concentrate to hear.

"Grew up in New Iberia, married just out a high school to a boy I'd known since I was three. Carl was a decent man. Didn't talk much, but then we didn't put much weight on talking back in those days. Surviving, that's what we focused on. We worked hard, both of us. Lived with his parents for the first five years. I worked in a grocery store for a while, him working construction. When we'd enough saved, cutting corners here and there, putting a little bit away each month regular like, we bought the house in Baton Rouge. Didn't look like that then, needed lots of fixing up. More opportunities, we figured, in a big city. We had dreams, see. Nothing big, just poor-people dreams. He kept working construction, following the jobs, and I worked in one a them plants across the river. Just like Jeannette."

She stopped for a minute, took a sip of coffee, her eyes fixed on the far wall. "I started taking some classes during the day at the university, working night shifts, until I got my teacher's certificate, started teaching math at the elementary school over in Brusly." She smiled faintly. "Always liked math. Wrong answers and right answers. No in between."

I nodded, thinking about my fondness for facts in the territory of gray that was my job, when the one big fact I was having a hard time accepting, or knowing what to do with, shifted in the bed, and there was a thud, the bedsprings squeaking loudly. I went to the door, then came back and sat down. "He's fine," I said.

"He's a sumabitch," she said.

"Yes."

We were both quiet a minute before she started talking again. "We worked hard all our life, regular like, and never seemed to get ahead. Always bought thirdhand cars, shopped at the thrifty store, cut coupons. This camp, this was our dream. We both loved to fish, loved the river, loved the solitude. Sometimes it was almost enough, you know, having this place? Nothing here when we bought it. Built this whole thing together, Carl and me, with our own two hands. Never had no children, something wrong with one of us, but we never bothered to find out which of us it was. No reason to, I figured. But long hard days, scrimping and saving regular like. Took care of his parents until they died. What I'm trying to say," she finally looked at me, and goose bumps popped up on my arms, "is for thirty-two years we lived paycheck to paycheck, and I worried how we were gonna end our days. You understand?"

I nodded.

She tucked her head back and looked at the wall again. "Three years ago I happened to open an envelope from the bank." She went quiet again, and I started calculating the age she'd gotten married, years she'd been married, added the three years ago to come up with a rough total, and looked at her in disbelief. This woman I'd thought to be in her midsixties was at least a decade younger.

"Don't know why I done that," Doris Whitehead continued. "Not on that day with that envelope. Must a been fate, or," she sputtered out a laugh, "the Lord decided I needed to wake up. Some angel watchin' over me, or the devil pullin' me up by my panties. Never been able to figure out which. Carl always handled the money, paid the bills, told me how much we had to live on for the month, handed over my allowance. That's the way he was, said money was the man's business and the home was the woman's, even though I'd worked all my life and the last half of it with numbers. I just gave him my paycheck every month. I was a ninny." She twisted her mouth up into a pout and blew a lip fart, the noise and gesture so unexpected I jumped a little and lukewarm coffee sloshed onto my leg.

"It was an accounting of our money," Doris Whitehead said. "There was over a quarter million dollars in our savings account. Three hundred and forty-two thousand dollars." She whispered the words as if she was seeing that statement all over again. "The man I'd slept with, seen naked and sick, the man I'd fed every night, the man I'd believed in every single day of my life, regular like, believed him that we were on the edge of poverty. He'd been sockin' away money from his jobs, telling me he was making less than he was. The sumabitch."

"My God," I said. "I'm so sorry."

She looked at me, her eyes tight. "Yeah, that's what he said. I'm so sorry, Doris. I didn't realize I'd put that much aside, Doris. Please forgive me, Doris."

"What was he going to do with all that money?"

"I didn't bother to ask. What was the point? I woke up right quick then and there and divorced him, quit my job, and took half of what was in that savings account, along with the house and this camp and told him I never wanted to see his sorry ass again."

"My God," I said again, all the pieces falling into place. "No wonder you don't think much of men."

She came out of her chair so quickly that my hand went to my gun. "Damn it all, it don't have nothin' to do with men. Don't fall into that trap, missy. None of what I been telling you has a damn thing to do with men, who they are, or who they aren't. It's to do with women. Hear me? With us. You and me and Jeannette and your friend doing all that shooting. All of us. Every woman that breathes on this earth and them that don't anymore as well. It's to do with knowing ourselves, not fooling ourselves, knowing what we're capable of. Who we are in here," she thumped on her chest, "and up here," she said, tapping her temple. "Sheesh. You ain't heard a word I said." And she stomped out into the kitchen, slamming the pot hard against the stove and striking a match. The burner let out a loud whoosh.

After a minute I got up and checked on Vince, who seemed to have dozed off, a faint snore coming from low in his throat, his fingers twitching. I told Doris Whitehead I was going to smoke a cigarette, but she just stared at the pan, waiting for the water to boil.

I walked down to the dock and squatted on my heels, pulled the smoke deep into my lungs. Exhaustion swept in like one of those fierce, sudden Louisiana afternoon thunderstorms, and I tried to remember when I'd slept last, really slept. Sunday night. Seven solid hours with Ricky's arm wrapped over my side, one hand barely cupping my breast before the alarm went off at 5:15 A.M. and I got up, headed to work, found Jeannette's body.

Fact: What we had done was wrong. Panic of the moment, true; protecting our own, true. But we should have stayed, accepted the consequences: Gwen losing her job, the rest of us suspended probably. If it had been just me, I'd take him back, admit to all of it. But I couldn't make that decision for the others; I couldn't make that decision for Gwen. All I could do was hold firm to what I knew for sure: no more killing. The question was, could I live with letting him go?

The muscles in my thighs started to ache. I laid my gun on the dock and stretched out, pulled my T-shirt out of my jeans, enjoying the taste of air on my skin. My fingers trailed across my belly, pulled up the slight pooch of flesh. I ran two fingers up under my last rib, following that upside-down smile to the middle point, then walked them up my sternum. I heard my mother's voice again: *The itsy-bitsy spider went up the water spout.* . . . I pulled my hand out and let my fingers keep walking up alongside my heart to the dip where my neck began, pressing against my larynx, along the curve of my jaw, my other hand coming up to walk in the opposite direction, both hands moving now, fingers walking, walking, along the side of my ears, down into the hollow of my eyes, following the ridge of bone, pressing hard, the tips of my fingers feeling the spongy-firm orbs resting deep in their sockets, back up and above my eyes, walking across my eyebrows, down along my nose, feeling the contours of my skull, imagining the flesh eaten away, here under all this flesh the steady bone, pulling down hard against the skin, fingers pressing deep in a slow slide, out across my cheeks, smoothing it all away.

When I went back in, Vince was still sleeping and Doris Whitehead seemed to have relaxed out of her anger. She sat staring at her coffee cup, told me there was more if I wanted it. When I said I needed to pee and asked if there was an outhouse somewhere round back, she chuckled and pointed to a door off to my left that I'd barely registered.

I opened the door, flipped on the light, and stood there, frozen in midbreath. It was a small room, painted robin egg's blue, a big window of glass blocks taking up one wall without curtains or blinds. On the other wall, the wall facing me, hung a black-and-white photograph of a naked woman, her back to the camera, standing in a field, high grass brushing her calves. Her dark hair was pulled back up off her neck, just a few loose strands caressing her shoulder blades.

I heard Doris Whitehead's footsteps and then her voice just behind me. "Sumpthin else, ain't it. That's Jeannette's."

I looked back at her quickly. "Her picture?"

"Her picture, she took it. Her room, she painted it. Her body. That's Jeannette." She smiled at me gently and patted me on the back. "Go on. Use it, and then I'll tell you."

I closed the door slowly and stayed in there a long time, staring at the photograph, following the curves of her body, those muscular calves, the vulnerability of her neck, the narrow shoulders. I ached to see all of her, the living, breathing Jeannette: that funny mole swimming between her eyebrows, the angle of her cheeks, the texture of her pores, her collarbone, breasts, the V between her legs, the shape of her knees. But all I could do was imagine, remembering the picture of her on the dresser, her body on the floor. Was her expression shy, giddy, solemn, interior, mischievous? What had she been thinking right at that moment? I reached out a finger, touched the glass lightly, right at the nape of her neck. And for a second, just a second, I felt her there in that room with me, soft breath on my own neck, and I flinched, shut off the light, and left.

Doris Whitehead had a bottle of whiskey sitting by her feet. She offered me some, but I shook my head no, tilting my head toward the bedroom. Not when I'm on duty, I almost said, and winced at the absurdity.

"Tell me," I said.

Jeannette dreamed of being a photographer, Doris Whitehead told me, but she flunked out of LSU after a year, unable to pass the basic classes. Mostly she was self-taught. She worked at a refinery to pay the bills. When she met Vince—at a bar in Port Allen, Doris Whitehead said with distaste—and fell in love, he promised her she'd be able to try school again. But that never materialized, Vince always having one reason or another why it couldn't work just yet. Still, she persisted, taking rolls of film down to Southern Camera off Government Street where one of the salesmen befriended her and got them professionally developed on the cheap.

"Vince didn't like that," Doris Whitehead said.

"The salesman?"

"Everything. He was a controlling sumabitch."

I glanced toward the bedroom, Vince's faint snore just discernable over the wisp of the ceiling fan overhead. I wondered what his dreams were, so twisted up and blocked that he couldn't let Jeannette pursue her own. What tiny terrors chased a man so hard that he'd torture the woman he claimed to love?

"She started coming out here with me about a year ago," Doris

Whitehead continued. "She loved the solitude like me, liked takin' pictures of the water, sunrises, trees. Simple stuff. She kept tellin' me we could really fix this place up, wanted to try with one room, so 'bout three months ago, I told her go ahead. Do the bathroom. Figured if I didn't like it, I wouldn't have to look at it all that often."

"And did you?"

"Like it?" Deep lines appeared around her mouth and eyes. "I loved it," she whispered. "She always had a way of makin' me see things in a new way. See the beauty in things, in people. That was Jeannette." Her eyes went distant. "I loved her like she was my own daughter." She laughed gruffly. "Not that she didn't have her faults. She could be stubborn. Bad with money, petty sometimes. Often," Doris Whitehead stopped, searching for words, "dense. She was sim-pleminded, not real smart, you know, far too trustin', but she could see, my God could she see, things you and I wouldn't, in everything and everyone."

"Except for Vince," I pointed out.

She seemed to fold into herself then, deflate. "Yup. Him she was blind to. Never could figure that out."

We sat there quietly for a while. It was warm, and, despite all the coffee, my eyelids kept drooping. Once I was so close to the edge of sleep that I jolted upright, reaching for my gun. I looked at my watch: 3:23.

"Go on, get a few winks. I'm wide awake. I'll watch him," Doris Whitehead said.

"Not if you keep drinking that whiskey."

She smiled, got up and tucked the bottle in a cabinet, came back and put the shotgun across her knees.

I scooched my chair around closer to the bedroom. "I'm just going to rest my eyes," I said, and closed them to one last view of Vince's body, listening to her steady breath, Vince's jagged snoring, the ceiling fan, and underneath all that, the rustle of trees and occasional splash of water. *Can I let him go?* The thought swirled around like a twig caught in an eddy, twitching this way and that.

Despite my best intentions, I drifted off to sleep.

*   *   *

I dreamed the usual dream, the recurring one.

A gun, pointing at me. I never see the person holding the gun. Just the hand and the gun. Terror so raw I can taste it, my limbs heavy and dense, my throat constricting, breathing quick and shallow. Pulling my own gun up slowly, too slowly, out of my holster, like my arm is concrete, so very slowly the gun comes up. My index finger thick on the trigger, absent of bone and muscle; I can't pull the trigger, and then, with great effort, I do, the hammer flying forward, but my gun dry-fires, no bullet comes out, and the other gun, the one pointed at me, fires. Slow motion the bullet comes toward me, mind screaming at the body to move, but the body doesn't respond. The bullet enters my chest, hard heavy whoosh of pain, air gone from my lungs; I'm thrown backward with the impact. A cold white light grows from that place, rippling through the pond of my body, my limbs going cold, dissolving, and then it's dim, I'm floating in a milky grayness.

Usually the dream ends there, and I wake, disoriented, the residual taste of death and terror in my mouth. But this time I keep bobbing along in the sea of gray, a sense of aching loss and regret but a kind of acceptance too, when the scene shifts abruptly and I'm in a precinct, one I've never seen before, but there are the usual battered desks and chairs, the institutional green on the walls, filing cabinets with cockeyed drawers, the floor pitted and gritty, everything not quite clean, not quite new, an undertone of sweat and cigarettes and stale coffee, a hint of mildew, cops moving about and talking, noise like a distant beehive.

I'm standing in front of a one-way mirror, facing a lineup room. There are people behind me, but I can't see them.

Six females walk into the lineup room, right to left. They are a mixture of young and old, tall and short, black and white, children and adults. I'm confused; you don't mix age and race and height like that, not for a lineup. They turn and face me. I gasp. A black woman is missing half her face; a young girl's face is bloated blue and purple; an elderly woman has empty eye sockets and a torn ear; a teenager's arms and legs have deep gashes and burns.

"They're dead," I say. "These women are all dead."

"Yes," a voice says behind me, one I don't recognize. I try to turn my head to see him, but can't. "Which one?" he says.

"Which one what?"

"Which one did it?"

"None of them did anything!" My voice is shrill with indignation.

"Next," the voice yells, and the females turn, shuffle out the door on the left. Six more females enter from the right. They turn and face me. Bile chokes my throat. I want to run screaming from the room. But my feet won't move. My body won't respond.

"Which one?" the voice says again.

Letticia Baldin is dressed in pink shorts and a blue T-shirt; she's chewing gum and having a hard time standing still, all wiggly energy and curiosity. The skeleton woman, Val, cuts her eyes up at the ceiling, a smile dancing around her mouth; her hands tap lightly against her thighs. Jeannette. Jeannette in her hiking boots, the Guatemalan shirt and khaki shorts, her hair pulled high on top of her head, looking straight at me, calm and steady, that mole between her eyebrows catching the light. Gwen looks pissed. Doris Whitehead looks grim. And me, this mirror image of me in the other room is red-eyed, my hair in disarray, my fists clenched tightly. I am looking at myself about to burst out of my skin.

My stomach rearranges itself into a throbbing braided knot. "You've mixed the dead with the living," I whisper.

"What's the difference?" says the voice.

And then my body does respond. I turn, launch myself at the voice, rabid with fury, but midleap I am hurtled toward consciousness. I fight it, fight to stay there, to understand, to finally understand.

But it's too late.

I opened my eyes, disoriented, dry-mouthed, my heart thudding hard in my ears, my neck sore. Weak light filtered through the kitchen window. Early dawn. Doris Whitehead's chair was empty. I squinted toward the bedroom, then stumbled forward, gun in hand, to the bedroom doorway, saw the rope and one set of cuffs lying there on the bed, but the other set of cuffs and the gag and Vince gone. I moved quicker, dread coming up from my stomach along with disbelief that I hadn't heard them leave, to the front door, threw it open, and a great whoosh of relief came out of my lungs.

I could just see them through the trees and overgrowth out on the dock, Vince facing the water, his pants down around his legs, Doris Whitehead pointing her shotgun at his feet. He just needed to piss again. I sagged against the door frame, giggled weakly. Poor Vince, having that woman pull his pants down, eye his privates. I could only imagine what she'd said to him, the look she'd given him.

Vince turned around, and I saw his hands move, out in front of him, and Doris Whitehead said something. I frowned, looked down, and saw the cuffs glinting on the dock beside Marge's red bandanna, looked back up quickly as Doris Whitehead's shotgun came level to his chest, and I knew.

I pushed off running, hard, my legs stretching long, the fierce "NO!" I wailed, deep and hollow, drowned out by the KA-BOOM of the shotgun. Still I kept running, branches slapping at my face, tearing at my clothes, kept screaming "NO!" as I cleared the trees, thinking even as I ran that somehow I could stop this—the blotched red hole appearing in Vince's chest, his legs buckling, his slow tumble back into the water, Doris Whitehead turning to look at me, a grim, knowing stare. Running faster, my shoes hitting the deck, each thud of my foot traveling up my legs, the sick realization that this was what she'd always intended if she had her chance. And I gave it to her. She knew I couldn't, wouldn't, do anything once it was done.

I stopped at the edge of the dock and looked down into the thrashing palette of water—white, green, pink, brown, red—Doris Whitehead's quiet, satisfied voice coming from a great distance through the roaring in my ears, "Gators'll get him. Won't be anything left for us to worry about."

I looked up, away from the wet, choked screams below me, tears clouding my eyes. Fingers of light stretched out and danced on the water as the sun crested the trees. A figure appeared, hovering just at the water's edge on the far bank. It was Jeannette. She was bathed in light, her face serene. And in that instant before she vanished, she looked right at me, her eyes shining, but whether from sorrow or joy, pity or compassion, I can never say.

WHERE I COME FROM

When I left, I drove for days: east until the taste of salt was heavy on my skin, north up the coast avoiding large cities, then a hard left through the twisted hills of West Virginia, following the dash compass west/northwest. When I slept, which wasn't often or for long, I parked in campgrounds or church parking lots; never at rest stops. Sometimes I drove all night and well into the morning and then found a cheap, local motel for a shower and a real bed until nightfall came again. I wore the same clothes for days, rarely turned on the radio, ate raw vegetables and fruit and crackers, drank gallons of water and coffee. When I hit the far shoulders of Idaho, I circled back south, down through the blistered red of Utah into New Mexico.

I drove aimlessly for hours, well below the speed limit, following two-laners with little traffic, passing through dusty, anonymous towns separated by long, uninhabited stretches, until whatever had propelled me this far left me wrung dry inside, unable to muster the energy to continue.

I didn't know what I was looking for until I saw it: a small, hand-lettered rental sign resting against a POPULATION 986 welcome marker. The town was a clump of adobe and stone—tired buildings squatting close to the ground on sagging foundations—with a small plaza and two traffic lights.

I found the house on a pitted, faded street on the far outskirts of town. It was a perfect square set back from the road, with weathered wood once painted some shade of gray and an old metal roof the color of rotten apples. Twisted, stunted trees reached toward the wide front porch, half hiding the sun.

My flesh seemed absent of bone or muscle as I walked up to the front door and found it unlocked. Inside, one large, worn-looking room was broken only by a half-wall between the kitchen and another large area with a closet of a bathroom and a door that led out back. Behind the house, open rocky spaces crept up small, uneven hills, and high grasses—bleached brown and burnt yellow—rippled in the hesitant, late-afternoon breeze; a large stand of what looked like cottonwood trees hunkered in the distance. I stood there a long time, both dazed and comforted by the harsh bleakness, by the near absence of green. It seemed as good a place as any.

The FOR RENT sign directed me across the street and two houses down. An elderly Mexican woman opened the door. I'd never seen so many wrinkles or eyes so black. Two huge braids, more silver than black, wrapped her head twice around. Her chin looked like a swollen knuckle; her ears were small and as translucent as a new-born's. She stared at me a long, painful moment after I asked about the possibility of a month-to-month lease. At first I thought she didn't understand English, but then she smiled, nodding, revealing three missing front teeth, two on the bottom and one on the top.

"No, no," she said in a thick accent. "*Docientos por un mes.* Two hundred, one month. *Si?* Stay long you want."

I paid three months rent in advance. She shook her head as she took the money, her whole manner signaling displeasure.

"*Quieres mucho,*" she said. "In you, *el miedo tiene hambre,*" and walked barefoot beside me back to the rent house, leaning into me and gripping my arm with surprising strength. My knowledge of Spanish was dismal; I'd studied French long ago in high school and picked up the Cajun patois. But I knew that *mucho* meant much. The rest of what she'd said was a mystery. Much what, I wondered. I wanted nothing but a shower and sleep.

"*El aire 'tá bueno.* Air good," she kept repeating. "*Los arboles recuerdan las memorias.* Trees . . ." she brought her cupped hands together, "remember. *Si?*"

I wasn't sure what she meant about the trees, which I was grateful stirred no memories for me, but after ushering me into the house with a short gesture and handing me a small silver key, she turned and made her way slowly back across the street, talking in Spanish, one hand cutting a graceful arc in the air. For days afterward, I felt the heat of her energy.

I unloaded the car, opened the windows, turned on the ceiling fans, then drove back into town and found what passed for a Goodwill in the main square and bought fold-out furniture—couch, table, chair—a cast-iron skillet, an old library lamp, and some silverware from a listless woman who was content to let me tell her the price marked on each item.

A man with narrow hips and a lean, deeply lined face was unloading an oven from his pickup out in the parking lot, and after he watched me maneuver the table and chair into my car and then stand, stumped by the couch, said, "Want some help?"

"No, thanks." I didn't bother looking at him.

"Don't think it'll fit on your roof." There was an undertone of laughter, but when I turned to him, his face was expressionless. His nose was small and sharp; a dimple rested on his chin, almost like an afterthought. "It's no problem, really."

I hesitated. He grinned lopsidedly around the toothpick he twirled in his mouth and said, "I'm not the biting kind."

"No?"

He gestured back toward the store with a tilt of his head. "They don't deliver."

"No. I don't suppose they do." I looked at the couch, thought maybe I should try hunting for a futon, but this didn't look like a town that would even know the word. Maybe a mattress? It was hot, and I was tired.

"Thank you," I finally said, the air sucking all life from my words. He tossed his toothpick, and we lifted the couch into the truck bed. I gave him my address, which made him start and turn to stare at me, his pale green eyes hidden deep in a tanned squint.

"Well, you must be something," he said. His brown hair was cut short, with the faintest touches of white at the edges.

I raised an eyebrow halfway.

"Place's been empty nearly two years," he said. "She's turned down the last three people who tried to rent it."

I shrugged, avoided his gaze. As I pulled out of the parking lot, he stood at the back of his truck, watching me.

The heat was sharp and relentless, and I was acutely aware of my own tired smell. I'd been in the same sleeveless white T-shirt and jeans for three days. The thin line where my watch used to rest was sunburned. Looking down at my arms, hands clenched on the steering wheel, I thought it seemed remarkable they were a part of me, these strange clumps of flesh, and I was unsettled by the momentary feeling that I was separate from my body, that it was merely a shell.

Back at the house, an ash gray cat crouched in the middle of the room. It stretched out its front paws in greeting, then huddled up again, purring.

"Aye," said the man behind me, "you got yourself one a Tommy's cats." When his face relaxed out of the sun, tiny sugar lines appeared around his eyes. He was younger than I'd initially thought, maybe in his early forties.

"How'd it get in?" I demanded, checking the back door, then moving swiftly past the row of windows across the near wall looking for openings.

"Tommy's cats have their ways. They're always welcome here-abouts." He stomped his boots on the wood floor. "Still solid, no ter-mites. Clean too."

"Well, how do I take this back?" I asked.

The man looked at me. "What?"

"The cat? I don't want it. I don't do cats."

"You don't do—" The man gave a low chuckle. "You're a funny one."

I moved toward the cat, put out a leg to sweep it encouragingly toward the door, but it arched its back, hissing, and swiped a paw at my hiking boot.

"Jesus!" I stepped back as it resettled into its crouch, staring, tail twitching with short snaps. I looked back at the man.

He shrugged. "Squatter's rights."

The cat didn't move out of its tense crouch as we brought in the rest of the furniture.

"Where to?" the man asked, tilting his head toward the couch just inside the front door. Even wearing jeans and a button-down shirt with the cuffs rolled back, he'd barely broken a sweat. Hair bleached gold from the sun ran up forearms corded tight with muscle. He smelled faintly of manure and something medicinal.

"It's fine, leave it," I said. "You've done enough, thank you."

"Pick your spot," he said firmly. "Then I'll leave."

We looked at each other. I was struck by how at ease he seemed, how his presence filled the room, and this perception made me edgy. His hand rested on the arm of the couch, waiting.

I nodded toward the far wall, then bent to move boxes, bulging garbage bags, a loose tarp, and sleeping bag out of the way. I liked that he didn't offer to help. After I pushed everything to one side, we put the couch against the inside wall. I wanted to face the windows when I woke.

I held the screen door open for him, but when I turned around, he'd slid the toe of his boot up underneath the tarp. He looked at the shotgun and bulletproof vest, the revolver still in its holster, then dropped the tarp back down.

The guns weren't loaded—at least those weren't—so I let the screen door bang closed, walked down the steps and out into the yard. It was cooler out here; the sky had softened to a bruised apricot. Seconds later the screen door banged again, and I heard his boot steps. His faint shadow passed me first, headed toward the pickup.

"Hey," I said. "Is there any work to be had around here?"

He looked at the house briefly, then back at me, one boot resting on the running board. "What can you do?" he said, his smile more tease than genuine.

I didn't answer.

He shrugged one shoulder, got in the truck, and put it in gear.

The truck was rolling slightly when he leaned out the window. "They're looking for a driver at the UPS next town over. You look like you could handle it, if you're interested. It's either that or a waitress job at Maria's back on the square. Take your pick." Metal screeched as the truck bottom scraped the dip between driveway and road. He didn't wave or acknowledge me again as he drove off.

Next door, two Mexican children hung on the fence, their toes curled over the bottom rail. Their straight hair was long and even darker than their wide, round eyes. I thought one might be a boy, but I wasn't sure. I held their gaze, each of us measuring the other, when the yard behind them wavered into a flicker of light and shadow, and I saw water churning, heard babble, white noise connected to nothing. And then the smaller of the two children waved, a slight wrist movement from a hand held stiffly upright at the chest, and I returned, a gentle slide back into my body. I nodded briefly in acknowledgment.

That night I fell asleep under the watchful gaze of the ash gray cat, her body hunched tightly against the floor near my bed. Thunder rolled in the distance. I kept waiting for the edgy panic of nightfall, for the muscle memory of where I came from, yet I woke only once, to rain drumming hard on the roof and the slight sweet smell of pine. I slept again, dreaming of many disembodied hands dancing in trees, mother-of-pearl fingers playing a trill against one another only to separate and dance and swoop again through rustling golden leaves.

The place I had come to seemed governed by heat, a transparent, shimmering blanket of hot that smothered the lungs. This world seemed to go quiet between noon and four. Even the birds' chatter hushed, though I frequently saw hawks soaring open-winged across the cloudless sky, lazily riding the air currents. Nut brown beetles buzzed along the ground, their hard-shell bodies making futile attempts against screens and glass, falling back with a dull thonk. Dogs dug shallow pits in the dirt under porches or at the base of trees and lay panting, not bothering to raise their heads when anyone came near. Only their eyes moved; occasionally a tail thumped.

The paperwork to apply for the UPS job was minimal, and I

passed the physical easily. It was a temporary job, which was fine with me. Three months, they told me, maybe five; the regular fellow had tripped and shattered an arm and wrist. I endured a week's on-the-job training from a burly Mexican whose gestures were impatient and words were curt. The training basically involved a set of rules— always run to and from the truck, don't accept food or drink from customers, smile at everyone, complete and turn in all paperwork at the end of the day, wear your back brace. I started work two days later.

The branch I worked for was in the largest town UPS serviced in the tricounty area, with thirty-five hundred people, a one-screen movie theater, and a Wal-Mart. Two and a half hours north/northwest, according to my map, was a city of 250,000. I asked for a route that would take me in the opposite direction. The fellow in charge politely told me that this wasn't the sort of place where you could make such requests and reminded me that I was filling in for someone else and that his was the route I was getting, which ran south, mostly farm roads and blue highways.

I made a mental note to talk as little as possible, get in, do my job, and get out. I wondered how long the information on my application would take to make the rounds of coffee shops and barber chairs, then decided it didn't matter. I didn't plan on staying long.

I liked the job. I could wear shorts; no hats required. I enjoyed the preciseness and simplicity: you picked up packages, you dropped off packages, you filled out paperwork. There were no surprises—except for a few growling dogs—no partners, no one to be responsible for, and no supervisors per se. Just me and my truck and the landscape. Cars were sporadic, and once I got out of town, which took about three minutes, they were practically nonexistent. I had the roads to myself. I liked to go fast, changing gears hard on the hills, letting the air sweep in through the open side doors of my brown panel truck, drying the sweat that had formed in layers all over my body. I imagined my skin presented a modern geological specimen, each stop adding another layer of sweat that dried crusty as I got the truck up over forty again.

After the first day on my route, I located a barbershop and told the grinning old Mexican what I wanted. He tsk-tsked as my straight reddish-blond locks fell, but I couldn't be bothered with braiding or bobby pins anymore. I was bemused to discover my hair curled, wispy flips this way and that, without the weight.

The customers on my route were mainly Anglos and Mexicans, a few native Indians. I deliberately ignored many of the UPS rules: I got to know the regulars, enjoyed the few minutes of idle chatter, usually about the heat or the contents of the package I'd delivered, and I was offered enough iced tea or water that I didn't need my water jug. I liked that they were all generally happy to see me. I even started picking up some Spanish words: *hola* and *qué pasa*, *gracias*, *de nada*, and *cómo se dice*. I enjoyed the way they felt in my mouth, the indulgent smiles the natives gave me as they corrected my pronunciation or repeated a word several times until I could control the vowels. I was an utter failure at rolling my *r*'s.

I started at 8:00 in the morning and finished anywhere between 5:00 and 6:00 in the evening. It was physically hard work—the heat and the wind through the truck and the constant rattling over less-than-serviceable roads wore me down so that by quitting time both my brain and body were numb, and the promise of the cool pleasure of the shower became a single-minded purpose.

Back at the house, I'd lean against the shower wall under the sharp needles of water, raking my fingernails hard across my flesh, scraping up grayish pills of dried sweat and dead skin to find the new underneath, wondering how long before all six layers were born of this place, finally downing half a beer in a single swallow before the second half went as rinse for what was left of my hair.

The damn cat, as I taken to calling her—and she was a her—relaxed out of her crouch and took to lying on her side purring, watching me, tail flicking irregularly at some imagined slight. Any attempt to move her from her spot resulted in the same arched hissing threat of the first day. I'd discovered where she came in, a hole under the house by the hot-water heater in the closet. I waited until she left the house one evening, hunting out back for prairie dogs or chipmunks or birds, and then boarded up the hole. An hour later, she let forth an ungodly screech that did not stop. I endured ten minutes of her protest then pried loose the board. She slipped swiftly up and out into the room where she furiously licked her fur.

I was defeated and not a little admiring of her tenacity. She didn't demand much of me, only access to the house. I became accustomed to the purr and the watchful gaze, and after the first week she joined me on the porch after my shower, where she lapped milk, I drank beer and smoked cigarettes, and we watched the sky turn from apricot to lilac to ragged strips of plum before night fell for good and stars danced out across the world like rain scattered on a mountain lake.

The street came alive as the sun began to drop and people migrated outside to porches or lawn chairs set up in the shade of juniper, pine, and oak trees. Unasked, the two Mexican children from next door came over the second week, shyly approaching my porch. They stood at the bottom of the stairs, smiling at me, until I smiled back. It seemed impolite to snub them, and I soon looked forward to their nightly visit.

One of them was a boy, I'd discovered; Isael was seven and his sister, Luisa, was five. They talked, and I listened. Their chatter wove the darkening strands of night into a cocoon of suspended time that was soothing. The ash gray cat let them scratch under her neck, something she'd refused me the couple of times I'd tried. They named her Luz, which they said meant light.

"She is not so dark as the other *gatos*," Luisa explained, "*y cuando* the sun hits, the fur is like hot light, so we call her Luz, *si?*"

I looked at the cat, splayed out across the wood, her purr a deep rumble of fading thunder, and thought she was still a damn cat, but I told Luisa that Luz was a grand name, and she giggled, stuffing her fist into her mouth.

Isael and Luisa brought me lizards, grasshoppers, beetles, and lightning bugs and showed off their latest scratches and bruises. I bought a hummingbird feeder, and we tried to imitate the Rufous hummingbirds' noisy trill and laughed at the pugnacious antics of the males fighting for territory. Isael taught me the names of some of the plants: yucca and agave, ocotilla and creosote, mesquite and prickly pear. And the Mexican evening primrose, which was my favorite; it bloomed only once, for just an evening, the long, delicate petals a startling spot of color. Luisa and Isael played with my water hose, making dark whorls in the dirt, writing their names in my front yard, until their mother chased them in for the night.

Eva Posidas, my landlady, had sent several dishes over by way of her granddaughter, Marisela, the mother of Luisa and Isael—pork and corn tamales, black beans cooked long and low with bits of meat and green chiles and some other unknown green substance, corn and chile enchiladas with a spicy red sauce. Marisela brought me home-made tortillas and something that resembled grits. She told me her husband, Jose, the father of Luisa and Isael, would help me with any-thing that needed fixing on the house. "*Abuelita* said we are to watch over you, Sarita," she told me, her words only slightly accented. I told Marisela that the house was fine, and I was pretty self-sufficient. She laughed in consternation at this comment, her lips moving like butterfly wings.

Luisa and Isael liked to tell me stories about their family. They told me their great-grandmother, Eva Posidas, had grown up in a small village in Mexico and come here many years ago with her par-ents and eight siblings. They told me she could be fierce, their *abuelita*, "as angry as the prickly pear," Isael said.

"But not to us." Luisa ran her fingers the wrong way across the damn cat's fur. "Just to the people who make her insides itch."

"Or if she forgets something," Isael said. "She doesn't like forget-ting, and she forgets a lot."

Luisa reached over and pinched Isael. "You aren't supposed to say bad things about people."

"Eh, eh, no pinching," I said. Isael scowled at Luisa. "Tell me more about your grandmother's family." I rubbed his knee where Luisa's fingers had dug in.

"They were the first ones here, *guelita*'s family," he said slowly, still scowling at Luisa. "They built much of what you see. My great *tío* built your house with his own hands. They named this town for a special tree that lives in the woods near Moon Mountain. *Guelita* says it's a healing tree, there are many of them, and she has found many good plants there."

"*Guelita?*"

Luisa pointed toward Eva Posidas's house. "Grandmother. *Guelita*."

"I thought '*abuelita*' was grandmother."

"It is. They both are," Luisa explained.

"Ah." I nodded as if I understood. "And where is Moon Mountain?"

Isael waved his hand toward the west. "Out there. I've been twice. I even heard it sing once."

"The mountain?"

Isael looked at me strangely. "Sometimes, Sarita, you are funny when I don't think you mean to be funny."

I lowered my head slightly and grinned at him in mock horror. "No one's ever told me that before, Isael."

"That's bad?"

"No," I reassured him. "It's funny."

He paused for a moment, clearly trying to determine how it was funny, before he said, "The tree. They are the ones who sing."

"Really? What did the trees sing?"

Isael shook his head slowly. "They don't have words, just," he shrugged one shoulder, "singing. You have to believe though, to hear it sing."

"*Guelita* taught us," Luisa said. "She's a *curandera*."

"I see. And what does a *curandera* do?"

"She makes all the pains go away," Luisa explained. "She cracks an egg over your head and," she slapped her hands together, "it's gone. I'm going to be one when I grow up. *Guelita* said so."

"But you must want them to go away, *el dolor*," Isael said. "You must ask for the help."

"Ah." I nodded thoughtfully, trying to keep my expression serious.

I liked their myths and stories, and I liked their names—Luisa, Isael, Eva Posidas, Marisela, Jose—they tasted like liquid chocolate on my tongue. I liked the easy way they accepted me into the neighborhood, never asking questions about who I was or where I'd come from. Everyone seemed remarkably accepting and friendly, nodding or raising a hand when I passed by, and I soon came to recognize their figures and faces. Half the town was related in some way. Mostly it was a quiet place with people living simple lives—no tragedies, no crime—although dirt bikes and off-road vehicles sometimes raced along the trails behind my house, and music boomed from radios in cars driven by teenagers late on a Friday or Saturday night. Occasionally there was a fight, but mostly with words. Isael told me I needed to watch out for snakes and bears when I went out walking in the evening.

Across the street, under a stand of tall, toothpick pine trees, lived an elderly man, who, as far as I could tell, rarely left the worn bench on the front lawn, and a woman of uncertain age who was either wife or daughter, perhaps a sister. She too brought me food—cornbread and some kind of tasteless, overcooked beans with tomatoes. She hadn't said much after handing me the food with a quick, hesitant smile. "Let me know if he bothers you." She gestured vaguely back across the street. "He can get noisy at times."

I couldn't imagine how the old man would bother me. He simply sat. His bald head was covered with copper freckles, some the size of pennies. Light blue eyes hid beneath great bushy eyebrows that seemed more like caricatures than features. The only part of him that moved occasionally was his head or his hands readjusting themselves on the cane he clasped firmly in front of him. Frequently he stared at me. At first it was unnerving when I sat out on the porch, until I decided he wasn't really seeing me. I took to waving at him when I left in the morning and when I came back at night. I never got a response: perhaps I imagined his eyes widening or a look of puzzlement crossing his face, but his stoicism became a challenge. Luisa and Isael said he talked to angels.

"Do you believe in angels?" Isael asked.

"Sure," I said.

Luisa frowned and tapped me on the knee. "You need to believe more."

"I'll work on it," I whispered to her, if only to wipe the lines of concern from her brow.

I saw the man in the pickup truck several times around town, and we always nodded in acknowledgment. His truck was parked in front of Eva Posidas's house frequently. Luisa and Isael told me he was their mother's cousin, Enrique, and that he caught coyotes, mule deer, squirrels, and bears.

"Sometimes," Luisa said in a breathy whisper, her sticky body sprawled across my knee, "even rats!"

"Once, a cougar," Isael said proudly.

"For eating?" I asked, which they thought was very funny.

"For the government," Isael said.

It was several weeks before I learned from Marisela that he worked for the county as an animal control officer. When I asked her how he got into that kind of work, she grew unusually solemn and said, "We all have a gift; that is his."

"Animals?"

"Lost things," she said.

"Cougars and rats and bears get lost?" I asked.

"Everything gets lost sooner or later," she said, and changed the subject.

When I started thinking about his hands, or the easy way he'd chuckled, or the fine, sugar lines around his eyes that begged to be touched, I drank more beer or chased Luisa and Isael around the yard with a stream of water from the hose.

Mostly there was little energy for thinking, and I was content to let each day unfold.

I had quickly taken to sleeping with the windows open, enjoying the soft, barely cool, night breezes that lulled me to a deep sleep, only to waken frequently at two or three in the morning with that same heart-stopping abruptness that had sent me fleeing weeks ago. Each time I reached forward for the voice, longing yet fearing the timbre of the whisper, but here the room was silent and empty, save for the rustle of the trees and the sense that something had just left.

Unable to fall back asleep, I'd get in the car, glide out the driveway and down the street with my lights off, then hit the gas and lights simultaneously, roaming back roads at high speeds, the green glow of the dashboard comforting, letting the wind and the hum of the tires drown out any vestige of where I'd come from—of other nights of cruising, of guns and terse commands, the squeal of tires, feet pounding the pavement; a man falling backward into water, hands outstretched; dried, burning eyes and the stink of exhaust and stale cigarettes; flies on a door; the refineries burning late at night, coughing up cloudy belches of orange flames; coffee- and adrenaline-fed highs; black roads snaking past buildings looming like great metal beasts; pink halogen lights promising a false dawn for hours.

Some nights, I screamed, letting my voice and the wind and the tearing pain in my throat obliterate vision, smell, thought. Some nights I played with the seduction of letting the tires take me off the road into warm blackness, just letting go and succumbing to whatever was chasing me.

Once, just as daylight broke, I crested a hill and slammed my brakes on at the sight of a city laid out in front of me like an enormous turtle of lights. The ungodly power of all I'd done swept over me in a cold, shuddering rush, and I pressed my head hard against the steering wheel. When I looked up, hands were descending, the same translucent hands I'd dreamed my first night in this land—five, eight of them, floating and dancing down around my car with a fan of light growing from behind.

I don't remember getting home. My next conscious moment was standing in the doorway of the house, the ash gray cat staring at me unblinkingly as the sun crested the trees, with the sense that once again, something had just left.

If I'd known where to go, I would have fled again.

Early one evening, two months after I'd arrived, when the sun was still visible and bright in the sky, and Penny Face, as I'd come to call the old man across the street, and I were having our nightly staring match, a light brown unit cruised slowly down the street and stopped in front of my house. The ash gray cat stopped cleaning herself, frozen in a twisted, one-leg-in-the-air pose. I was jolted but not surprised. Sooner or later, I knew, this was bound to happen. I'd been hoping for later. But wary anticipation is never preparation for the actuality. A chunk of my old life had found me, and the rush of anger was tremendous. Until that moment, I hadn't allowed myself to admit I was truly hiding.

The sheriff's deputy unfolded himself from the car, put on his hat, rechecked the slip of paper in his hand, then started toward the porch. I could feel the eyes of the neighborhood follow me as I stubbed out my cigarette and went down the steps to meet him.

I knew what he'd do before he did it, so I let him maneuver me so that he stood facing the street but with a view of my front door. I told him yes, my name was Sarah Jeffries.

"Anyone else live here?"

"The cat." I gestured toward the damn cat, back in her crouch, tail flicking. He didn't find this amusing.

"Some folks are worried about you. Asked me to give you this number to call," he said. He looked like a typical cop. From the hash marks on his sleeve, I knew he'd been doing this awhile.

"Some folks," I said.

"Well, this person here." He handed me the slip of paper with Gwen Stewart's name on it. I could see the outline of his bulletproof vest under his shirt, bulking out his chest into an unnatural rectangle.

"And what will you tell her?"

"Ma'am?"

"I'm assuming you'll be contacting her," I said. I matched his lack of expression with one of my own.

"We'll send an acknowledgment that we found you, that you were contacted."

"I see." I looked down at the ground, then back up at him. "Social Security number?"

"Excuse me?"

I recognized his attitude, slightly withdrawn, slightly disdainful, that by-product of power and authority. I wouldn't have been happy with this sort of assignment either. Crap calls, we used to call them.

"How she tracked me. Social Security number? I haven't been using my credit cards. Or through the reference check?"

"I wouldn't know about that, ma'am. I was just asked to give you the message." His hands moved to rest lightly on his gun belt. I recognized that maneuver too.

"I doubt that. The po-lice," I drawled carefully, "don't deliver messages to average citizens, except in case of death or emergency." I handed the slip of paper back to him. "And that's what I am, Corporal. An average citizen. And this is no emergency. Tell her I received the message. Tell her I'm fine and I'm sorry. But she's not to contact me again. Tell her that. I know there must be a harassment law here. Cop or not, I'll file. Tell her I said that, too."

The deputy looked at me, his lips tight, eyes invisible behind sunglasses. I knew what he was thinking—or close to it. Troublesome woman was one possibility. Pain in the ass was another; bitch the most likely. Maybe even lesbian. It was an easy classification for the job; any number of variations could be plugged in. He'd go back out there, tell his buddies about this fucking uptight ex-cop he'd talked to; they'd all shake their heads, exchange stories about other trouble-some women they'd known, and chalk it up to someone who couldn't take the heat. I could read it all in an instant.

I had to give him credit though; he did just what I would have done. He turned around, laid the note on the bottom step, and put a rock on top of it. Then he walked past me without a word, back to his unit. I stood facing the house as I heard him drive away.

The neighborhood was quiet except for a few dogs barking, the trees rustling in that same strange hesitant breeze that always crept up with the first gesture of night. I continued facing the house until a small shadow reached out and met mine. I knelt down and smiled at Luisa.

"Sarita, you are in trouble?" she whispered, little lines deep in her forehead.

"Hardly," I said.

"The police came one time and took Henry away after Veronica and the baby died." She twirled her hair against her lips, her voice so low I had to lean closer.

"Who's Henry?" I asked gently. I reached out a hand to stop the twirling motion.

"*Enrique,*" she said, as though it were obvious, and pointed back across the street.

Isael appeared at Luisa's shoulder. "You are in trouble?" His round face was smooth with a grown-up seriousness.

I sighed. "No, he was mistaken, that's all. It's okay."

"Police are trouble," Isael insisted.

"Sometimes," I said.

I stood, half pivoting toward the street, and looked up. Everyone was watching me, including the man in the pickup truck.

"Henry?" I asked Luisa, and she nodded.

Henry leaned against the bed of his truck, arms dangling down over the side. When our eyes met, he straightened up, looked as though he might walk across the street, and so I did the only thing I could think to do—I waved, a big sweeping wave, walked through the house and out the back door, where I sat watching the rocks until even they blended into the blanket of night.

The envelope came two weeks later. No return address and no signature on the folded spiral notebook paper, but I recognized the handwriting; I'd seen enough of it over the years. It was printed in the sloping all caps style that was Gwen's trademark. She didn't start with a salutation—just short and to the point. "*HAND AND FOREARM FOUND 17 MILES DOWN PEARL RIVER. CORONER SAYS ALLIGATORS. NO OTHER EVIDENCE. CASE CLOSED ON ALL OF THEM. WHAT THE FUCK ARE YOU DOING? COME HOME.*"

Home. I stared at that word for a long time.

Three days later I went to Esai's Hardware Store one town over and bought a shovel, some duct tape and a large brown tarp. I pulled out of the driveway a little after 2:00 A.M., the street folded up and silent, and drove south for thirty minutes, until I came to an old dirt road I knew from my route. A few unpaved driveways branched off from it early on. I cut my headlights and continued on for several miles, the sense of a road growing fainter, until it dead-ended at the base of a hill that wanted to be a mountain. I got out, put the tarp on the ground, moving slowly, deliberately. The Ithaca pump shotgun first, then the four-inch .38 Smith and Wesson, then the three-inch .357 Magnum. Each unloaded and placed on the tarp. Then the five-cell flashlight, bulletproof vest, precinct pins, and name plate. I studied my badge for a long time, holding it in the palm of my hand, before I placed it carefully on the tarp as well. The bullets I dropped into a separate plastic bag, which I tucked into the back pocket of my jeans. I secured the tarp many times over with the duct tape.

The trees seemed more silver and black than green; pine needles shifted restlessly. An owl hooted off in the distance. The scars and puckers of the moon, high in the night sky, were visible and distinct. It smelled clean here, just a slight husky scent of leaves and earth. My eyes adjusted quickly to the dark, and I walked easily into the woods about five hundred yards, carrying the shovel and tarp. It was awkward to rest both against my left shoulder as I wove and ducked between tree limbs.

The ground was a bit harder than I'd expected, but I dug steadily. A film of perspiration soon covered my body, and my breathing came deep from my lungs. It felt good to move my muscles this way, to work in the dark, to excavate the hole and watch the pile of dirt grow. Once I stopped and listened for a long time to a rustling nearby, remembering Isael's comments about bears at night, about Henry catching a cougar. When the rustling moved away, I stood there a bit longer, waiting for my heart to slow to a normal rhythm, pushing all thoughts of choices, fate, and the allure of what-ifs from my mind.

I dug two holes, a small one for the bullets, about fifty feet away from the larger and much deeper one where I placed the tarp. I sat on the lip of the hole, smoking a cigarette, and watched the shadow patterns from the trees dance across the ground until there was nothing left of my cigarette. Then I refilled the holes quickly, tapping down the dirt with my hiking boots, spreading the compost of pine needles and leaves back over the broken ground. I found several large rocks and placed them on top of the larger hole, worked them down into the dirt a bit.

When I was done, my hands throbbed. A blister had popped up on the thumb of my right hand and two more on my palm. Red dirt clung to my boots, jeans, arms, shirt. I stood there for a minute, staring at the ground, then looked up to the sky, through the trees and said, "There."

No response but the slight whistle of the wind and my own thudding heart.

Fall approached timidly. The nights got cooler and the breeze shifted somewhat; there was a different smell in the air that I couldn't quite pin down. Laughter and music in the neighborhood was louder, dirt bikes raced more frequently up behind my house, and dogs wandered freely, no longer panting except from joy or exuberance. Penny Face wore a tattered green sweatshirt after the sun disappeared; his wife-mother-sister brought it out and tugged it none too gently over his head. The damn cat was gone for long stretches at night; I'd wake to see her eyes glinting at me in the darkness from the far corner of my bed. She'd started sleeping there, never curled up or sprawled out, but hunched over, ready to flee at my first movement.

Isael and Luisa still visited every night. Isael had some respect for personal space, but Luisa loved to drape parts of her body, or all of her body, on me. She reminded me of a dog I'd been fond of, a massive Rhodesian Ridgeback named Peacock, except Luisa wasn't as big and she didn't have a propensity for licking. She did, however, like to put her lips as close to my face as possible and whisper, sometimes questions, sometimes comments, sometimes simply nonsense babbling.

"*Por qué*, Sarita," she asked one evening, "*¿estas tan triste?*" Her fingers traveled across my arm like tiny lizards. The sun had just dipped below the trees, and Isael sat near us, rolling marbles against my front door, watching the damn cat watch the marbles.

"*Triste?*" I could tell from her expression that I'd mangled the word only slightly.

"Sad."

"Good heavens, what gave you that idea?" I poked her in the ribs, which usually instigated a wild tickling game. But she veered the middle part of her body away like a wayward river and stuck a finger, caked with dirt and damn cat hair I noted, into my cheek, hard enough for me to say, "Ow!" in mock pain.

"From here." And then she poked a finger in my other cheek. "And here." My forehead. "Here." And then my lips. "Here too, the upside-down smile."

I gave her a big, exaggerated smile. "I'm happy. See? Right-side-up smile." I sank into a real grin, enjoying the stretch of my face muscles.

The damn cat finally pounced on a marble, and it went flying off the porch, the cat tumbling after it.

"That's not what the trees say." She rested her arms and upper body on my thighs.

"Trees shmees. I don't know what tree you've been talking to, but he's off his bark." I poked her again in the ribs.

She gave a short yelp and screwed her face up in mock disgust. "Trees don't bark!"

"*Guelita* says the trees know everything, and that you are sad."

Isael spoke each word as though it was a perfectly round pebble he was handing me. "That is why you have the guns, to keep away the sadness."

I sighed and rolled my neck to the left then the right. Hocus pocus and the trees again. But Isael was the opposite from his sister in many ways, more contained, more serious, more watchful; I'd learned it was best to answer him directly. "I'm not sad," I said. "And guns make sadness, more often than not. They don't keep it away."

"You were *la policía?*"

I nodded. "I used to be, in a place a long, long way from here."

"What was it called?" Luisa asked.

"Lousyana."

"Lousyana?!" She sputtered with laugher. "What kind of name is that?"

"And the guns made you sad?" Isael watched me carefully.

"Sometimes."

"Poppa uses his gun to kill deer."

"That's different," I said. "It's so you can eat, yes?"

"Were you scared?" Luisa's voice was hushed and tiny. "When you carried the guns and were *un policía?*"

I looked at them, their two hard bodies smooth and dirty and unscarred, their eyes big and steady with interest. "No," I lied.

That night, the hands visited me again in my dreams. This time there were more of them floating and swooping through the trees, a giddy dance of celebration among golden leaves. Pale blue ribbons wove through the fingers and palms, twirling gently over and over. And hovering over them were several pairs of eyes, deep brown eyes with just the faintest hints of white around the edges. The eyes seemed kind, patient. A low-pitched moan started, then rose up in octave and strength; the sound was a cross between keening and singing, and it seemed to follow the movement of the hands, growing louder and louder until I was conscious and realized the sound was external to my dream.

I opened my eyes, sat up in bed, and for a moment thought I saw movement high in the far corner by the back door. I blinked, and the shuffling spots disappeared, a trick of the moonlight and dark, but the wail continued to rise and fall. It came from outside. And it was real.

Penny Face was howling. He stood in front of his bench, one side of his body leaning heavily against the cane in his left hand, his right hand moving as though he was brushing aside cobwebs. His head arched back, the skin against his neck almost taut; he threw long ago-nized vowels up to the night sky.

I slipped on jeans and a T-shirt and crossed the street, wincing as my feet caught the edges of rocks and pinecones. The anguish in his voice filled every cavity inside my head with tiny, hammering fists as I drew closer. His mother-wife-sister stood behind him, her palm hov-ering against his waist; a too-girlish nightgown in lavender and pink swallowed her body and puddled about her feet. She looked so dis-tressed I momentarily felt more concern for her. When he paused to take in another bellyful of air, the noise like a distant hum of an air-plane's engine as his lungs filled, she said, "I'm sorry. He just goes off sometimes." Her face was like crumpled tissue, all deep folds and crisscrossed lines.

"How do we stop him?" I asked, but before she could answer he let loose again. I shivered at the urge I felt to join him, the sheer ecstasy of being inside the howl.

And then others surrounded us, hands reaching out to Penny Face: on his arms and shoulders and back and chest. Marisela and her husband, Jose; Eva Posidas, her face wreathed in quiet intensity, braids hanging loose over her ample breasts whispering gentle words in Spanish; two men I recognized from the neighborhood, both of them slight yet muscular in the manner of men who work their bod-ies hard; a wasted slip of a girl from four houses down along with her mother; and Henry beside me, that husky scent of manure drifting off the hard lines of his body, mingling with the smell of the pine trees. All of them, palms flat on Penny Face's body.

I didn't join them; I watched and listened, felt time stop, swal-lowed inside the sound. Eventually his howls grew less urgent until he subsided completely into a hoarse, shallow panting, his eyes closed, his body slumped sideways, barely standing.

Eva Posidas looked at me, said, "No worries, Sarita," then said something else in Spanish before she took one of Penny Face's arms.

Jose took his other arm, and they led him into the house, his mother-wife-sister following slowly behind them, her nightgown dragging in the dirt. The others quickly dispersed, their footsteps scraping softly into silence.

"Sweet suffering Jesus," I whispered, my head still full of his voice.

"It doesn't happen too often." A man's gentle twang came from behind me, and I pivoted to my left in a jerky, abrupt motion.

"Whoa!" Henry said, one palm out in front of him. "Uncle."

I relaxed my fist, lowered my hands to my thighs.

"You're a jumpy one." He too was barefoot, bare-chested as well. Several scars snaked up his belly, one down his upper right arm. There wasn't an ounce of fat on him that I could tell. He grinned. "Like your hair short."

I stopped my hand midshoulder before it could touch my hair. "And you like to make pronouncements."

He cocked his head sideways, his mouth open slightly, the lines around his eyes folding inward. "Aye, I suppose I do. Doña Eva has accused me of that before." He stuck his hands deep into the pockets of his jeans and rolled backward slightly on the balls of his feet. "Here's another one, though, an easy one, if I may. That tough shell doesn't suit you."

"You don't know a damn thing about me," I said.

He gave a deep chuckle. "No great mystery to observation."

"Where do you—"

"Hang on." He took several steps backward, his eyes crinkled up at the corners. "Are you always this defensive?"

I don't know why Doris Whitehead's sly smile came to mind then, but it did. I tucked my hands up under my armpits. "Are you always this familiar?"

"Excuse me?"

"Like you're supposed to know me, that you have the right to analyze me."

He stared at me thoughtfully. It took all my willpower to hold his gaze before he spoke. "Perhaps I owe you an apology then. This is a small town. We're used to looking out for one another."

"I'm not like him." I gestured back toward Penny Face's house. "I don't need looking after."

"We all need looking after, Sarah Jeffries." His half-smile was so unexpectedly compassionate, his look so wistful and piercing, that I felt the quick burn of tears.

"Oh, go to hell." I turned and strode back across the street, seething with the idiocy of it all—unnerved that he knew my full name, with our conversation, my attraction to him, Penny Face and his howls, this town, my life.

The ash gray cat, crouched in the open doorway of my house, pulled her upper body slightly away and hissed as I came up the steps. I thumped my foot on the floor as I opened the screen door; she skittered inside. I slammed the door, and we both retreated to our corners, glaring.

"What is your damn problem," I said. I sat on the bed crosslegged, lit a cigarette, and watched her, her shoulder and hipbones sharp, long edges. She was prickly, independent, mercurial. Not a lovable bone in her body.

I stretched out on the bed, closed my eyes, and tried to think about nothing, but Henry's half-smile hovered around every corner. Doris Whitehead's comment floated up from what seemed years ago: *Betcha got him confused half the time.*

Fuck you, Doris. I shoved back hard against the memories, put my fingers in my ears, squeezed my eyes tight, hummed fiercely in the back of my throat to erase the sight of Gwen's stupefied look when I told her I was turning in my two weeks' notice; Ricky's quiet, "I figured it'd come to this sooner or later, *cher*, you leaving me"; Doris Whitehead's grim, "Won't be anything left for us to worry about"; the soft whisper of my name that had woken me every night since Vince had died.

I hummed louder, white spots dancing in front of my eyes, and suddenly there was Penny Face's howl echoing faintly under my own noise, like the edges of a tune you can't quite remember. I stopped abruptly. Was this the talking to angels that Isael and Luisa had mentioned? If so, it was not a happy conversation. Perhaps the old man had it right after all, that angels looked down on us not in compassion, not raising their voices in glory or grace or even redemption, but in despair, keening at our hateful ways, our guilty, tattered souls.

At the end of September, the fellow I'd been hired to replace was cleared to return to work. I figured I was looking at another week or two of employment at the most when my supervisor called me into the office. But he surprised me, offering to extend my temporary position through the holidays. I didn't hesitate. Eva Posidas patted my cheek when I asked about renting the house for another three to four months. "It's the way it must be, *m'ija*."

Perhaps it was the cooler weather, perhaps it was accepting I'd be here awhile longer, but I had a sudden burst of energy that manifested itself in a desire to clean. I'd never been one to spend much time worrying about sparkling counters, clean floors, layers of dust, streaked windows, or grimy buildup. Now, suddenly, I wanted this house clean. I woke up early on a Saturday morning, drove to the local grocery, and bought a mop, pail, broom, sponge, stiff-bristled brush, plastic gloves, and a whole slew of cleaning products.

I'd just drawn a pail of hot water when Eva Posidas appeared at my door holding a handful of rosemary. "The smell, *es bonito, si?*" She raised a fistful to my nose. "This you," she crushed and rolled several leaves in her palms, "and put on *ventanas*." She scattered some across a windowsill. "Cleans it all out."

"*Bueno. Gracias*, Doña Eva," I said, wondering what "it" the rosemary would clean out.

She stood in the middle of the room, one hand folded against her waist, and looked around carefully. I watched her warily. She made me uncomfortable, as if she was one step ahead of me, although ahead of what, I wasn't sure. For a moment, I saw her resemblance to Isael. "You fix this up. *Pinta*. Paint, that's the word? Something pretty. Do what you like."

There is a beauty in the simplicity of cleaning; you focus on exactly what is in front of you. As with most anything, there is a correct way to proceed, a way that minimizes the effort and maximizes the outcome. Like cleaning your gun or preparing your uniform. Buy the best tools and clean more frequently than you think is needed.

Change out your bullets every three months. Use a toothbrush, real bristles. Don't buy the cheap gun-cleaning kits. Splurge on good gun oil and find a cloth diaper. Wipe the dirt off your shoes with an old T-shirt—never paper towels—apply saddle soap with a cotton rag, then black polish mixed with your own saliva, then use a good, soft brush to bring each shoe to a full shine. Clip the loose threads on your uniform; iron the trouser and sleeve creases sharp. Use Brasso—just a touch or it will turn green—for jacket buttons and badge, name plate, sharpshooter and precinct pins. Do it right, and you lose track of time; you lose track of yourself. You are the task and nothing more.

That weekend, I was the task. Every inch of the house fell under the onslaught of my heavy-duty sponge: the walls, the ceiling, the window and door frames, the wood floors, every faucet and fixture and light. I cleaned the windows with newspaper, which I vaguely remembered my mother doing long ago. I worked late into the night, and when I finished on Sunday, I felt a satisfaction that made me grin. I took a long, hot bath and slept hard: no whisper, no waking in panic, no dreams. The ash gray cat reappeared on Monday morning as I was getting ready to leave for work. She stepped gingerly across the floor, her nose sniffing the ground with every step, her tail flat out behind her.

"Careful," I told her. "I might get it into my head to give you a bath."

The following Friday, with Marisela's permission, I took Isael and Luisa to Esai's Hardware Store to help me choose paint. We selected a light yellow for the walls and soft white for the trim. With some persuasion from Luisa, I bought a small can of tomato red for the one wall in the kitchen because, as Luisa said, "Kitchens should be happy places, and red is happy." I stayed up late that night taping the floorboards and window trim, using a ladder Jose had lent me, and slept hard again until first light.

Luisa and Isael showed up at 7:00, ready to help. By 8:00, Luisa was bored and spattered with yellow; by 9:00, Isael had wandered off. By noon, I'd finished three walls and my wrists and shoulders ached.

I heated up my frying pan, dry, and cooked three tortillas, one at a time, until they puffed up tiny brown spots, flipped them once, and added asadero cheese and thin slices of green chiles. Rolled them up, slapped them on a plate, grabbed a beer from the refrigerator, and went out to the back stoop where I sat and ate, cheese dribbling down my chin, the beer cutting the heat from the chiles. The damn cat wandered up from wherever she'd been hiding and studiously licked the plate clean.

It was a glorious day—crisp and bright, not a cloud in the sky—and I was happy in my sense of accomplishment and exhaustion. I lay back against the concrete and let the sun cook me into a dreamy daze. Only the rough whine of dirt bikes up behind my house and a lawn mower puttering somewhere down the block prevented me from falling completely asleep.

I don't know what snapped me back. But suddenly I was in my body, conscious of my skin, alert, heart rate thumping a bit quicker from a small jolt of adrenaline. I sat up quickly, eyes blinking against the rush of sunlight. And then I was on my feet, throat tightening, knowing something was wrong even before I could process the information.

Isael cleared the small hill behind my house, head down, legs churning. He looked up, saw me, opened his mouth, and I was running toward him even as my name came in three short gasps of air from his mouth.

I met him halfway. The panic on his face, the smears of blood and dirt on his hands and shirt, settled the dread deeper in my stomach.

"Luisa," he said. "Hurt."

"Show me."

She was in a ravine the next hill over, just off a trail. Her head lay wedged between two rocks; one leg rested on a clump of grass at an impossible angle.

"The boys on the dirt bikes," Isael said, his voice thin and quavering. "They knocked her over."

"Was she conscious at all? Awake? Moving?" My fingers searched for a pulse. None.

He shook his head. "We weren't supposed to be here." His voice was choked with suppressed sobs.

She wasn't breathing either. I ran my fingers quickly over her body: a good gash where the bone had broken through her leg, a deeper wound on the back of her head, but how deep or big, I couldn't say because I wasn't going to move her head if I could help it. At least the blood wasn't pooling; that was a good sign. Unless the weight of her head was holding in the blood.

"Okay." I turned to Isael and gripped his upper arm hard until his eyes focused on mine. "Not your fault. Understand?" He nodded slowly, sniffling back tears. "Good. Now go get help, have them call the police, an ambulance. Bring them back here."

"Mamma and Poppa are gone."

"Go to your *guelita*'s, a neighbor's. Use the phone yourself if you have to. 911. You know the address, yes? Understand?"

He nodded more quickly, turned, and ran.

I pulled three large rocks out of the way, bruising my knuckles and tearing a fingernail, and knelt down beside Luisa. The leg wasn't bleeding much; neither was her head from what I could tell. I moved her head only slightly to arch the neck, wincing as I did, hoping I wasn't causing any more damage, praying I wasn't condemning her to a life of paralysis. If she lived.

I pinched her nostrils closed and lowered my mouth to hers, then remembered to check inside first: a two-fingered swipe and no obstructions. I hesitated. Was it five breaths and two compressions or two breaths and five compressions? I searched back through muscle memory.

Two short, gentle breaths, careful not to overexpand her small lungs. Then locating the sternum, lacing my hands together one on top of the other, heel of my palm firm against her chest, and five shallow but sharp compressions.

I lost track of time. Two breaths, five compressions. The sun beat hot against my back and legs; my arms and hands were slippery, and sweat dripped down my forehead and neck. Smaller rocks dug into my knees each time I shifted from mouth to chest. Her body was so tiny. I'd never done CPR on a child. I'd never worked on someone I knew; the bodies I'd worked on had been strangers, victims of violence or car accidents, one time an allergic reaction to multiple yellow jacket stings. And there had been others around to help me, others who knew more than I did. I knew so little. Two breaths, five compressions. I'd never really noticed the freckles on her chin before, the tiny scar under her left ear, the way one eyebrow grew straight across and the other arched. Such a small chest. My back hurt, my arms ached, my wrists throbbed, there was a cramp in my thigh. It was hot, dusty, dirty, and she wasn't breathing, her heart wasn't beating. Two breaths, five compressions.

I heard movement behind me, feet digging in the dirt for traction, but I didn't stop.

"Sarah." It was Henry. "What can I do?"

"You know CPR?"

"Yes."

"Compressions? I'll breathe."

His hands appeared on her chest, and I counted: one, two, three, four, five. Then I breathed: one, two.

"They're coming?" I asked as I watched his hands work. Briefly I looked up, checked his face, relaxed slightly.

"Yes."

"Isael?"

"With Doña Eva, waiting for the police and ambulance."

I don't know how long we worked like that in tandem, silent, watching her face, his hands, her chest before we heard the sirens, voices, and footsteps approaching.

Henry pulled me up and away from her as the paramedics and police surrounded us, his hands firm on my shoulders. I stepped away from him, watched the paramedics' faces. I recognized the sheriff's deputy who'd come by my house weeks ago, and we nodded at each other—short, impersonal nods. I gave them what little details I knew as they worked, watching Luisa's head carefully for a rush of blood that never came as they applied the neck brace and bagged her, as they moved her to the portable stretcher. What could I tell them that they couldn't see for themselves?

Stumbling back down the hill, following the stretcher, I felt like three separate beings: there was the physical body—hands still feeling the rhythm of the compressions, the echo of her mouth under mine, the ache of most every muscle, my stomach hollow and burning and familiar; there was the detached, professional cataloguing details and assessing the situation; and there was this other me, deep inside, howling.

The hospital—a squat, rectangular, brown hunk of brick slapped down in the middle of nothing—was twenty miles away. They'd gotten Luisa's heart beating in the ambulance. Marisela and Jose arrived soon after we did, their faces clamped tight against their fear, and disappeared into the critical care room. The rest of us, family and neighbors, crowded into a cold, dingy room with green linoleum and hard chairs. We waited. Some talked, and some, like me, stared quietly at a wall or counted the ceiling tiles. Isael kept looking at me, quick, darting glances. Eva Posidas sat stoically, hands clasped in her lap, murmuring in Spanish. Henry paced methodically around the circumference of the room. And I kept wondering if I'd made a horrible mistake, if I'd misunderstood. Was I supposed to have been watching Luisa and Isael? Had their parents left because they thought the children were at my house, painting, and I was watching them?

When Isael left to use the bathroom, Henry stopped, standing over me, and said, "Thank you."

I stared at him, stunned. "I was supposed to be watching them," I whispered.

Eva Posidas clicked her tongue. "*Los niños estaban conmígo. Permití que ellos jugaran afuera. Nada es su culpa. Ella tiene nuestras gracias por encontrar a Luisa.*" She patted my knee once then knitted her fingers together again and pressed them into her lap.

I looked at Henry.

"She's upset, the English goes. She says it wasn't your fault," he said. "They were supposed to be with her, she let them play outside. She appreciates what you did for Luisa."

"I didn't do much," I mumbled through the heat of anger toward the old woman for her carelessness and her stoicism.

His index finger touched my arm. "You were there. You kept her alive."

"Such that it is," I said, rubbing the palm of my hand along the spot he'd touched.

Eva Posidas made a small whiffy sound and moved one hand

through the air before it settled back into her lap. "*A Sarita se la está comiendo el temor y ella no puede encontrar en símisma el perdón y tener esperanza. Ella piensa que entiende mucho, pero ella sabe poco. Ella nunca vivirá bien hasta que entienda que nadie lo puede tener todo o lo entiende todo. Ella piensa que es fuerte, pero ella es débil. Sólo al abrazar nuestra debilidad podemos ser fuertes.*"

I'd looked at Henry as soon as I heard my name. "What did she say?"

He watched Isael approach us from the hallway. "You give up too easily and you try too hard."

"Jesus! Who do you people think you are?" But I said it softly, for now Isael was in front of us, his eyes checking my face again. I gave him a tired smile. "It's okay, Isael. Promise." He nodded, but I knew he didn't believe me. I didn't blame him. I didn't believe me either.

I sat there, my body aching and restless, thinking about Eva Posidas's long rush of words and Henry's short translation: you give up too easily and you try too hard. What did that mean? It was a paradox, unsolvable. And what else had Doña Eva said that Henry hadn't translated?

Just when I thought I couldn't spend one more minute in that room, Jose came down the hall, his hands jammed deep into his pockets. Isael ran to him, and he pulled the boy into a tight hug before he stood and told us that Luisa was alive.

Her heart was beating, but she couldn't breathe on her own; an EEG showed brain activity; although the wound to her head itself was not deep, there was a great deal of swelling around the brain; she was in a coma; StarFlight would take her to a major trauma center in Las Cruses later that evening. There was hope, Jose said; we all needed to pray.

I slipped out as everyone gathered around him. The sun was disorienting; I'd expected it to be dark outside.

The street where I lived was deserted except for Penny Face sitting on his bench, staring at nothing. I got out of my car and walked across the street, pulled toward him despite myself. His eyes seemed to track me as I approached, but it was a trick of the light and shadows. There was no comprehension, no intelligence, no one at home inside those eyes. I squatted down on my heels in front of him. Saliva had crusted in one corner of his mouth, and his body odor reminded me of a mixture of wet river mud and cockroach-infested apartments I'd worked calls in.

"What do you know, Penny Face?" I said softly. "What's chasing you?"

He just stared at me, those blue watery eyes with nothing in them.

"Luisa, you know her? The little girl across the street? She was hurt today. Badly. She says you talk to angels. I think you see something else, don't you?" I tapped him on the shin.

A hot flush ran through me, and I stumbled to my feet and stepped back as briefly, quicker than a finger snap, Penny Face was present, here, seeing me, a mind processing information, and then, even quicker, so quick I thought I might have imagined it, his lips turned up slightly into some semblance of smile, a horrible, familiar smile. And then he was gone, blank again, the wind rustling the leaves on the ground, and my stomach clenched tighter than steel.

I crossed back over to my house, trying to quell the tremble in my body, the dryness in my mouth. The empty plate that had held my lunch still sat on the back stoop of my house; the back door was still open. The ash gray cat had disappeared. My stomach twisted and turned. I stood for a minute looking up at the quiet hills beyond my house, taking deep breaths before I put the dish in the sink, opened the can of red paint, stirred it, and started painting the half wall in the kitchen. It was unabashedly red.

I'd just finished the first coat and sat down on the porch with a cigarette and beer, looking everywhere but at Penny Face, when Henry pulled into my driveway. He got out of his truck and walked slowly up the sidewalk.

"Want a beer?" I asked, lifting mine toward him. "There's more in the fridge."

He shook his head. "I don't drink."

"Really. You look like a drinking man."

He reached out and wiped a finger across my cheek and held it out to me.

"Smoke. Burns my eyes." I used the heels of both hands to wipe my cheeks and jaw dry.

"Uh-huh. Should quit smoking then." He reached out a hand. His palm was large and deeply lined, the fingers long and narrow with little hair on the knuckles. His nails were clipped close; one had a fading black spot that covered half the nail bed.

"What?"

"Let's go for a drive."

"Right." I didn't move.

"I'm not the biting kind."

"I've heard that one before."

"Trust your instincts." He smiled slightly.

I thought of Luisa's comment about the police taking him away, about a woman and baby dying. "Where to?"

"Something I want to show you."

I shook my head at the ground. "Henry." After a minute I looked up at him standing there steadily, waiting. I looked at the lines around his eyes and mouth, the slight stubble starting to sprout on his chin and cheeks, his hand still hovering in front of my face. I took his hand, warm and dry and firm, and let him pull me to my feet. "Let me close up the house." I went inside, closed the back door, put a flannel shirt on over my tank top and jeans, laced up my hiking boots, then took a box down from the closet shelf and tucked the one gun I hadn't been able to bury, a .38 Chief's Special, in a small belt holster, into my waistband. I buttoned the shirt up partway and went back onto the front porch, locked the front door. Henry was in his truck, the engine running. I slid into the passenger seat and fastened my seat belt. "Okay," I said, feeling as if I had a foot in two worlds—the past and the present—and neither of those worlds willing to let me be. "Show me what you want to show me."

When he brought the truck to a stop thirty minutes later, I didn't move. My stomach was a hot coil.

"The locals call it Moon Mountain." Henry pointed toward the hill that wanted to be a mountain. "The back side is scarred and puckered, just like the moon. Not much grows there." He got out of the truck and looked at me. "Coming?"

I hesitated.

"What are you scared of?"

"I'm not scared."

"You brought a gun." He pointed toward my waist. "Most people carry them because it makes them feel big or they're scared."

I shifted forward and sideways in my seat. "Guns have never made me feel big. And I'm not scared. I'm in the woods with a man I don't really know. I'd say it was prudent."

He shrugged, grabbed a bottle of water and shoved it in his back pocket, and slammed the truck door closed.

I followed him into the woods, relaxing slightly when he took a path that ran perpendicular to where I'd buried the tarp. We hiked steadily for twenty minutes on a trail that cut up sharply through mostly pine trees. The sun had dipped well below the tree line, and the air was much cooler here. I kept my eyes on his back and his hands, tucked my elbow against my waist several times. My body ached, my stomach burned, and my breath came in short, hard gasps by the time we rounded a bend and came down into a small clearing.

My stomach flipped once, and I took in a deep breath. We were surrounded by tall, slender trees. Sunlight filtered through golden leaves that danced and fluttered, like thousands of pale butterflies, but with a soft clattering noise. The trunks were a light gray, almost white, with mottled darker patches. I reached forward and touched one; it was both cool and warm.

"*Populus tremuloides,*" Henry said. "The common name is quaking aspen, but everyone just calls them aspens. They're more common in the northern part of the state. This is the only stand in the county. The elevation is high enough and cool enough for them to thrive."

I looked up through the branches. "Seems more like dancing than quaking."

"Quaking isn't necessarily negative, is it? You can quake with joy as much as you can from fear."

When I looked over at him, he was smiling at me, that compassionate half-smile, the tiny sugar lines folded up near his eyes. And his eyes, full and tender, seeing me. Too much there, in his eyes, for me to stand. Tears close to the surface burned again, as quick and as hard as the bile roiling in my stomach. I turned away, trying to bite back the waves of nausea, gagged twice. I bent over and retched, again and again, sobbing as I did, furious and defeated, one hand out on a trunk supporting me, and then Henry was by my side, his hand cupping my forehead. I tried to pull away, but he held me firm, whispering, "It's okay, let it come, just let it come."

My knees buckled, and I sank to the ground on all fours. I cried long past the time I stopped throwing up. Henry kept his arms around me, and eventually I relaxed against him. The leaves fluttered above us, a million muted wind chimes. Every cell in my body felt like heavy cotton batting.

I pushed myself up, took the water bottle he offered, and rinsed and spit several times before drinking. The water felt good against the back of my throat. I sat down, lit a cigarette, and closed my eyes. I was conscious of the heat of his body next to mine. "Well, I feel like an idiot."

"Welcome to the human race." His tone was mild and gentle.

"Yeah."

"It's more than Luisa, isn't it?"

"It's enough," I said.

The trees fell silent. I could hear birds calling and answering, the shuffle of living things around us. I felt silly, suddenly, for bringing my gun. This man was not going to hurt me. I remembered the hesitation I'd felt the night I'd buried my police gear, the fear that made me hold one gun back, just in case. In case of what, I wondered now. That life was behind me, and I was going to have to find a way out of it. Into what, I had no idea. But it involved more than burying equipment and relics from a past life, that much I was beginning to grasp.

"That old man across the street from you," Henry said, "anyone ever told you about him?"

I opened my eyes, thrown by his question, still lost in my own thoughts. He was tracing a stick through the leaves. "Penny Face?" I shook my head, as much to shake away the memory of the glint of recognition in his watery blue eyes when I'd come back from the hospital.

He looked over at me briefly and smiled. "Good name for him. Lewis Jones. Do you like stories?"

I felt a rush of déjà vu and eyed him warily. "Depends."

"On what?"

"The point of the story."

He cocked his head slightly and expelled a short, soft breath. "Doesn't it exhaust you?"

"What?"

"Being so guarded all the time?"

Irritation and something deeper swept through me again, and then it was gone. "What is it you want from me, Henry?"

"I want you to understand."

"What?"

"We aren't alone."

The earnest look on his face made me laugh. "Jesus."

"What's so funny?"

"You. Sounding like a sci-fi movie: we are not alone. We're all alone, Henry. Luisa back there fighting for her life, Marisela and Jose frantic with worry and probably guilt, Doña Eva and her stupid stoicism, Isael seeing his sister like that, even Penny Face howling at whatever, and you with the need to feel better about yourself by taking care of others. Each one of us. Alone with our demons. And there's not a damn thing anyone else can do to help us."

"You're very wrong, Sarah."

I wanted to be angry, but there wasn't a patronizing tone to even one of his words. "Are you always so certain of everything?"

"Only the few things I know for sure."

I was tired, worn down; it seemed worthless to argue with him. I flicked my hand toward him and said, "So tell me Penny Face's story," and then stared at the leaves on the ground as he talked.

"He had three boys. Young, not a one over ten. He was gone a lot, some kind of sales job. His wife was one of Doña Eva's sisters. She wasn't real healthy, mentally fragile, a skittish girl from what I've been told. He came home one weekend and the boys were dead. She'd shot each of them in the head while they slept."

I winced, thought of Penny Face's eyes again, his absent self. They would never go away, those images; they'd always be with him. I'd run from them too, if I were him. "What happened to her?"

"State mental institution. She died not long after. That was nearly fifty years ago, and Lewis still blames himself, thinks he should have seen it coming, gotten her some help, gotten the boys away from her."

"Ah." I wondered again who Penny Face was really cursing with those wails—himself, his wife, fate? "That proves my point. No one can take his pain away. He's lost inside it. Alone."

"You're wrong. You've seen it. All of us out there with him. Why else could we quiet him?"

"But he still does it," I pointed out. "He sits like a statue when he isn't wailing. You haven't cured him."

"Cure is relative. It's a choice, isn't it, to fall into that hole or stay above it? There is some choice." He gave a half-laugh and folded his arms against his chest, his shoulder brushing mine. "And who's to say that his howling isn't a climb toward sanity? I'm sometimes tempted to join him myself."

There was an invitation in that last sentence, but I let the silence stretch out between us, my mind chattering, arguing. The sun had disappeared, and now the golden leaves appeared almost translucent in the dusk. "Luisa—" I stopped, briefly seeing her again in the ravine, feeling her draped across my body, sticky finger poking at my face. I took a deep breath. "Luisa mentioned something about a woman and baby dying."

His smile was tender and bitter at the same time; the upper lip curled halfway, but soft. The lines of his body softened too, and I realized he'd been waiting for this, that this was really the reason he'd brought me out here. It wasn't about me at all. Or Penny Face. It was about him. Everyone wants to tell their own story, eventually.

"Veronica. My wife. Marisela's cousin. She was pregnant with our first child." His fingertips moved restlessly across his legs. "I used to drink pretty heavily back in those days." Another long pause. "We were on our way back from dinner, out on Route 24. Another car was in the oncoming lane. He was drunk too. She was killed instantly, she and the baby. The other driver and I walked away."

Henry's story wasn't a new one. I'd seen variations on that story over the years. Usually someone walked away, and often that some-one was the person at fault. All the world's tragedies, I thought, big and small, were too much to grasp, to hold onto. They could dissolve me to boneless weeping if I dwelled on them too long, so I didn't. I didn't even go close. But an individual's tragedy was another matter, especially when it was staring you in the face. It didn't matter how inadequate it sounded or how inadequate I felt, but "I'm sorry," were the only words I knew to offer.

"I'm sorry," I said. I put a hand lightly on his knee. "I'm very sorry."

His hands moved slowly, restlessly, over his legs, like a living creature in motion simply because it was alive. "They couldn't determine who crossed the line first, who was at fault, him or me. We were both legally drunk. So we both went to jail. Four years. That house you live in? It was ours. When I got out of jail a couple of years ago, I moved back in. Doña Eva had left it just as it was." He took a deep breath. "But she told me I had to go, that I needed to find another place. One of the few times she's been cruel to me. It was hard, seeing them, Marisela and the rest of the family, knowing they must blame me. And then last year Doña Eva invited me to a family dinner. It was awkward at first. Always an edge there, of course. But, if anything, I've been closer to them than before, when Veronica was alive." He paused again, then said softly, "The hardest part was learning to forgive myself."

"And have you?" I asked very carefully.

There was that smile again, the one that filled his eyes. We looked at each other in the falling darkness, and I felt a slight tug inside.

"Have you?" His tone was kind and barely audible over the noise of the leaves.

I let the protest die on my lips and thought about Gwen and Doris Whitehead. I saw Jeannette's face again, Vince falling backward into the water, Roger's body on the ground. I felt the muscle memory of Luisa's body across my legs and sent a short, fervent prayer upward: *please spare her.* I thought about Penny Face and his howls and my police gear buried under the red dirt at the base of this mountain, and I knew that my own story was one I would tell only to myself, but over and over, for the rest of my life.

"No," I said softly.

"There you have it." He leaned over and kissed me very gently on the cheek.

We sat there for a long time in silence, our hands just touching, listening to the quaking leaves above our heads.